# INTRODUCTION

*Heart Full of Love* by Colleen Coble
Eden Walters is a nurturer. When she was eight, her brother and two sisters were ripped away after their mother died. Since she can't care for her own family, she takes in foster children to give them the love she never had. One in particular has her heart. She's adopted Katie, but if Katie's uncle Josh has his way, Katie will be ripped away from her as well.

*Ride the Clouds* by Carol Cox
Crista Richmond was only three when she started being shuffled from one temporary home to another. The foster family who left her feeling abandoned also gave her the message that Christianity was a farce. Can Brad Morgan help Crista find a sense of belonging in God's family?

*Don't Look Back* by Terry Fowler
With so much loss in her life, Angelina Collier's motto has become "don't look back." She is determined to do whatever it takes to keep her family together, never totally placing her faith in Jesus Christ. Wes Robbins has learned to give his worries to the Lord and is dedicated to enjoying life. He's determined to help Angelina do the same.

*To Keep Me Warm* by Gail Gaymer Martin
Tim Richmond, a widower, is left to raise his young disabled son. Separated from his three sisters and raised by an aunt, Tim longs to find his missing siblings and is determined to give his son a home filled with unconditional love. His purpose and fulfillment in life is to be needed. Though he is drawn to capable and independent Julie, he knows there is no hope for a relationship. She doesn't need him. Or does she?

# HOME FOR CHRISTMAS

*Love Reunites Four Orphaned*
*Siblings in Interwoven Novellas*

COLLEEN COBLE
CAROL COX
TERRY FOWLER
GAIL GAYMER MARTIN

BARBOUR
PUBLISHING

*Heart Full of Love* ©2001 by Colleen Coble
*Ride the Clouds* ©2001 by Carol Cox
*Don't Look Back* ©2001 by Terry Fowler
*To Keep Me Warm* ©2001 by Gail Gaymer Martin

Illustrations by Mari Goering

ISBN 1-59789-147-9

Published by Barbour Publishing, Inc., P.O. Box 719, Uhrichsville, Ohio 44683, www.barbourbooks.com

*Our mission is to publish and distribute inspirational products offering exceptional value and biblical encouragement to the masses.*

 Member of the
Evangelical Christian
Publishers Association

Printed in the United States of America.
5 4 3 2 1

# HOME FOR
# CHRISTMAS

# Heart Full of Love

by Colleen Coble

# Dedication

For all the young adults in our
Lifebuilders Sunday School Class.
You've brightened our lives and given us purpose.

# Chapter 1

I've come for my niece."

Eden Walters' smile faded, and she took a step back from the man's overwhelming presence in her doorway. Though she barely came to his broad shoulder, he would soon find he couldn't push her around.

"You—your niece?" Her thoughts ran through the children squealing in laughter behind her. The older children were playing Candyland while two-year-old Katie and infant Braden slept upstairs. Five children, three of them girls, but she had no idea which one this man wanted. She tilted her chin in the air, leery of handing any of her children over to this bulk of a man who oozed self-confidence that would put an emperor to shame. He was probably used to getting what he wanted with his size and dark good looks.

"Katie Leland. I'm Josh Leland." He thrust his hands in his pockets and stepped inside, shutting the door behind him.

"Now see here, Mr. Leland," Eden began.

"Isn't there somewhere quieter we can discuss this?"

Eden compressed her lips and reminded herself she

was a professional. "Very well, follow me." She led him to the library across the hall from the front parlor where the children played. Tugging on the pocket doors, she was panting by the time she managed to close them and turned to face Josh Leland.

His warm brown eyes took in the gap where they didn't quite close, then traveled around the room. Eden saw it afresh from his eyes. Stained and torn wallpaper that she wished she could afford to replace, old furniture she'd bought at Goodwill, and a threadbare carpet on the floor. She felt a bit like Jo in *Little Women* and suppressed a smile at the errant thought.

Those brown eyes were regarding her now, and she knew what he must think. A short young woman with flyaway blond hair, curves that were too generous, and clothes as shabby as her house. A warm flush started up her neck, and she forced her eyes up to meet his.

"I'm quite busy this morning, Mr. Leland. If you check in with Child Welfare Services, you will find you have no legal right to see Katie. Even if you really *are* her uncle."

He ran a broad hand through his thick brown hair. Eden always noticed hands. His were muscular with long fingers and neatly clipped nails. She pushed away the stir of attraction. His expression told all too clearly what he thought of her. Disapproval radiated from every pore of his immaculately clothed being.

"I don't want a visit, I mean to take her permanently. I've been to Child Welfare, and they tell me you have already filed adoption papers. Surely you can see it would be better for her to be raised by her uncle than by a stranger."

"I'm no stranger to Katie! I've cared for her—and loved her—since she was three months old. You, Mr. Leland, are the stranger. She is two years old. Where were you when her mother brought her to the welfare office and dumped her like an unwanted suitcase?" Eden clenched her hands to keep from slugging him. "You're the stranger, Mr. Leland."

Her barb struck home for he colored and lost a bit of his superiority. "I didn't know about Katie," he mumbled. "Last I heard, Mandy was in college and nearly finished with her degree in accounting. Then I was called and told she'd died." His face paled. "Drugs, they said. The college sent her stuff to me. That's when I discovered I had a niece. I chucked my job with Sutter Petroleum in Saudi Arabia and came straight here."

That explained the tan. Eden pushed a strand of hair out of her eyes and bit her lip. His bald recitation of the facts touched her more than she wanted to admit, but facts were facts.

"That's all very interesting, Mr. Leland, and I'm sorry for your loss, but I'm afraid you're too late. The adoption papers were signed yesterday."

"Yesterday?" He paled beneath his tan and sank onto the sofa. He breathed deeply, then raised his gaze to hers. "May I see her?"

Eden flinched at the thought of allowing this man to see her daughter. A surge of fear rushed up her spine. Katie was *hers*, in heart and legally. But would the welfare officials see it that way if he challenged the adoption?

"She's sleeping right now."

"I won't wake her. Please."

"I fail to see what good it would do."

"She *is* my niece, Miss Walters. Our parents are dead as well. Surely you can see I'd have some feelings for the child."

"And she's *my* daughter."

"I'm not leaving until I see that she's well cared for." He waved a hand around him. "You hardly seem old enough to be caring for a house full of children. And look at this place. It's practically falling down around your ears. I know foster care is hardly a decent living for you, let alone all the things a little girl needs. I could at least offer some financial assistance."

The fury Eden had been holding in check spilled over. "I don't need your money, Mr. Leland! This may be an old house and not up to Leland standards, but it's a house full of love and laughter. We have God to watch over us, and that's worth more than all the money you've made in the oil fields!"

A small hand rapped at the door. "Eden? Katie was crying so I brung her to you."

Eden nearly groaned but had no choice except to go to the door and shove it open. Ten-year-old Samantha, rail-thin with haunted gray eyes, held chubby Katie. Eden took the toddler and touched Samantha on the cheek. "Thanks, Sweetie, you're a good helper."

Samantha colored with pleasure, then cast a frightened glance toward Josh and scurried away. Eden turned slowly with Katie in her arms. The little one's chubby arms were around her neck, and Eden breathed in the sweet scent of her.

Josh stared at Katie with hungry eyes. "She looks a lot

like Mandy," he said. The muscles in his throat moved as he swallowed.

Was that a film of tears in the big man's eyes? Eden's tender heart smote her. She'd given no thought to how he must feel with his sister dead and his niece ripped from him before he even knew he had a niece. She could afford to be generous. God had given her Katie as a daughter.

Eden stepped closer to him. "Would you like to hold her?"

His eyes widened, and he nodded. He slipped his big hands around Katie and drew her to his chest the way he might hold a basket of eggs.

"She won't break."

"She's so little," he said. Katie regarded him solemnly, then reached up a chubby hand and pulled on his nose, released it, and peered inside one nostril.

Eden chuckled at the panicked expression on Josh's face. "She's fascinated with noses right now."

"I haven't been around many children," he said. "But she doesn't seem to be afraid of me. Is this normal?"

"It is for Katie. She's very secure and outgoing. She loves people."

He shuddered. "Makes me frightened for her in this world."

"Wabash is a nice town to raise a family in," Eden said. "I'll take very good care of her." She fought the words struggling against her lips, but they came out anyway. "You're welcome to stop in and visit her sometime. Just call first. Katie has plenty of love to share." She held out her hands for her daughter.

A muscle twitched in Josh's jaw, and his fingers

tightened around Katie. He took a step back. "I mean to raise her myself, Miss Walters. I give you fair warning."

Eden's olive branch was sliced in two, and the hair on her neck stood. If it was a fight he wanted, he'd get one. There was nothing he could do. The adoption papers were signed. "Give me my daughter," she said evenly.

With obvious reluctance, Josh handed Katie back to her. "I'll be back, Miss Walters."

"Look, Mr. Leland, I'm willing to let you see Katie. I think it's important for an adopted child to have as many roots of her heritage as possible. But Katie is happy here. Surely, you can see that. What's to be gained by disrupting her life now?"

Josh hesitated, then shook his head. "That's not enough, Miss Walters. She's all I have left of Mandy, and I mean to have her."

"You're not thinking of her, only of yourself."

He clenched his jaw. "I can give her much more than you can."

"Money isn't everything, Mr. Leland. You admitted yourself you were unused to children. What about caring for her when she's sick or fixing her hair and teaching her to bake cookies? I don't see a wedding ring, so I assume she won't have a mother. A girl needs a mother."

"And a father. I see no ring on your hand either. What do you propose to do about that?"

Eden felt the hot blush on her cheeks. "Neither situation is perfect," she admitted. "But you need to face the facts, Mr. Leland. Katie is my daughter now, and there's nothing you can do about it."

"We'll see." With that last parting shot, he brushed by

her and stalked to the front door. His brown eyes were haunted when he looked back. "I lost my sister, Miss Walters, I'm not going to lose my niece, too." He slammed the door behind him.

Her throat tight, Eden ran to the door and locked it. As if that could shut away the danger. "Don't worry, little one," she whispered. "I won't let him take you."

She still remembered the horror of being ripped from her brother and sisters. Eden was still tormented with nightmares about that time. She couldn't let that happen to her Katie.

# Chapter 2

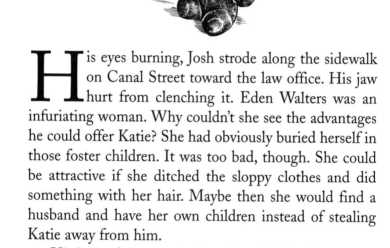

His eyes burning, Josh strode along the sidewalk on Canal Street toward the law office. His jaw hurt from clenching it. Eden Walters was an infuriating woman. Why couldn't she see the advantages he could offer Katie? She had obviously buried herself in those foster children. It was too bad, though. She could be attractive if she ditched the sloppy clothes and did something with her hair. Maybe then she would find a husband and have her own children instead of stealing Katie away from him.

His jaw softened at the thought of Katie. She was the most beautiful child he'd ever seen. Soft blond curls ringing cherubic cheeks he wanted to pinch. Looking into her blue eyes had been like seeing Mandy again. He couldn't lose her.

The bell on the door tinkled as he pushed into the waiting room of Grover Law Offices. The sound brought back memories of the old corner grocery with the jars of licorice and the old freezer full of Popsicles and fudge bars. And the Victorian storefronts along the street had set the mood well. Most hometowns didn't retain the flavor of

Wabash, Indiana. Too bad he wouldn't be staying long. It would have been a nice place for Katie to grow up.

An hour later he stalked those same streets back to his car. The attorney had not held out much hope that he could overturn the adoption. Preference was given to foster parents! After only six months? And Katie had been with Eden Walters almost two years now, since she was three months old.

His only hope was to get the woman to agree to give her up. He had to convince her it was best for Katie. After all, he could provide the best education and a stable home life where she was the adored only child—unlike growing up in a run-down foster home. He appreciated what Eden was trying to do, but let her take in some abandoned urchin without an uncle who wanted her.

He drove to his room at the Wabash Inn and planned his strategy. The first thing would be to run some paperwork to show her his assets. Maybe if she knew Katie would be his sole heir, she would relent. She didn't seem an unreasonable young woman.

He spent the evening jotting down reasons Katie would be better off with him and printing out financial information to show Eden. Eden. What kind of a name was that for a woman, anyway? But she looked the type to have an old-fashioned name. Maybe that was what drove her to take in all those kids.

The next morning he dressed in khaki chinos and a carefully pressed navy shirt. His shoes were buffed to a high shine and matched his belt. He wanted to make sure he looked the part of a conscientious father.

As he walked up the path to the front porch, he took

note of the house this time. An old Victorian Queen Anne, it was large enough to house an army, but sorely in need of a man's hand. The paint was peeling, and the porch railing had some missing spindles. He would point that out to Eden—in a reasonable way, of course.

He rapped on the door. Inside the house, he could hear screams and the clatter of something falling to the floor. When no one came right away, he debated about letting himself in and seeing if there was a problem. But before he could overcome his reluctance to barge in, the door opened, and a little boy of about five regarded him with sad green eyes.

"Hello," he said. "I'm Katie's 'Uncle Josh.' "

The little boy's eyes widened in alarm, and he started to shut the door.

Josh put a foot in it. "Is Miss Walters around?"

The little boy nodded. "She's in the kitchen." With an obvious show of reluctance, he opened the door wider and stepped aside. "You'd better come in. She can't come out here right now. Katie choked on a spider."

Choked? Alarm raced up Josh's spine, and he followed the little boy through the labyrinth of rooms to the kitchen. Eden crouched over his niece with her finger down Katie's throat. She paid no attention to him but probed and peered inside Katie's mouth. Katie wailed and thrashed, trying to escape the unwanted attention. Beside her were the soggy remains of a very large spider.

Josh shuddered. He hated spiders. His respect for Eden went up a notch that she could handle such an event with that competent air.

Katie saw him, and her wails increased in volume. She held out her arms to him, and he felt a stab of delight.

"What's going on here?" Josh scooped his niece away from Eden's attentions.

Dressed in a denim skirt and pink cotton sweater that had seen better days, Eden's fine blond hair was wadded on top of her head in a haphazard way that was very becoming. Wisps of hair trailed against her flushed cheeks, and she compressed her lips when she saw him.

"Mr. Leland, I expressly asked you to call before you came by. Right now is not a convenient time for callers."

His good intentions for peace blew away like a stray feather. "I can see that. My niece is being raised in a house overrun with giant spiders. If I hadn't stopped by unexpectedly, I never would have known how dangerous this place is." His arms tightened around Katie. "And there are spindles missing on the front porch where she could easily fall through. I don't think this is a safe house for children, Miss Walters."

Eden's green eyes flashed, and the color rose in her cheeks. "It was just a spider, Mr. Leland, not a monster. Katie is never on the front porch without me. I have the spindles, but I haven't had time to install them yet."

"You mean to install them yourself?"

"I am a woman, but I'm quite competent, I assure you."

He regretted his hasty criticisms. All he'd succeeded in doing was getting her back up. He wasn't going to get anywhere by taking this tone with her. He suspected the welfare authorities would fail to find a dead spider a reason to remove Katie from Eden's care.

He cleared his throat and softened his voice. "I'm sorry, Miss Walters. Please, can we start over? And call me Josh."

The angry sparkle in her eyes didn't dim. She looked

all too delectable to Josh, soft and round like a woman should be. Pressing his lips together at his flight of fancy, he shifted Katie to one arm and held out his other hand. "Truce?"

Eden hesitated, then nodded. Her handshake was firm, and her small hand had calluses on it. She was an enigma to Josh—so feminine, yet not afraid of hard work, and not easily cowed by a challenge. He didn't want to admire her. She was all that stood between him and Katie.

"Would you like a soda or a cup of tea, Mr. Leland?"

"Josh."

"Josh," she amended. "I have cola and iced tea as well as hot tea."

"Cola would be fine."

She poured the soda into a Mickey Mouse glass, then poured a glass of iced tea into a Cinderella glass. It didn't look to Josh like any of the glasses in the cupboard matched. She handed the soda to him and led the way to the parlor.

This room was in a little better shape than the library. The wallpaper was still intact, and a newer rug covered the oak floor. A Candyland game was on a table near the fireplace, and he nearly tripped over a small fire truck.

Eden had just sat down when a wail from upstairs echoed down the hall. She stared at Josh with appraising eyes. "May I have Katie, please? I need to see to the other baby."

Josh felt a stab of irritation. "I'm no baby thief, Eden. I want only what's best for Katie. Go see to the other baby. Katie and I will be right here when you get back."

She stared a moment longer. "Are you a Christian, Josh?"

At least she cared about such things. "Since I was ten." He held up his hand. "And an Eagle Scout. I promise you can trust me."

She nodded. "Excuse me a moment." She hurried from the room, and he heard her tennis shoes tread lightly on the stairs.

Josh stared at his niece. This place was like Grand Central Station. There was not a moment's peace. The sooner he got Katie to some quiet place, the better. Katie gave his nose one last pull, then slipped from his arms and went to play with the fire truck.

Josh watched her play until Eden came back down the stairs with an infant in her arms. The baby's tuft of hair stood straight up on end, and it was sucking its thumb.

"This is Braden," Eden said. "Could you hold him a minute while I fix lunch?" Without waiting for a reply, she plopped the baby in his arms and hurried from the room.

Josh stared into the baby's blue eyes. He started to pucker, and Josh hurriedly stood. "There now, don't cry. Er—your mama will be back in a minute." He jiggled him, and Braden gave him a shy smile. The triumph Josh felt was all out of proportion to the smile, and he shook his head at his own reaction.

Slipping a hand under the baby to adjust how he carried him, he felt a suspicious wetness. "Uh, oh," he said. He held him away from him. Dismay swept over him at the wet stain on his shirt. Now what was he supposed to do? Holding the baby away from him like a naughty puppy, he carried him to the kitchen.

"I think he needs changed," he told Eden.

"The diapers are in the changing table in the bathroom across the hall," she said.

"You expect *me* to change him?"

Eden stopped stirring the bowl of some kind of gluey-looking stuff, and he colored at the amusement in her green eyes. "Katie isn't potty trained yet. If you expect to spend any time with her, you'd better learn to change diapers."

"I've changed diapers before," he said stiffly. She didn't need to know it had been thirty years ago when Mandy was a baby and he was five.

"Good. There are wipes on the changing table as well." She went back to stirring that tasteless-looking concoction.

Josh stared at her, then shrugged and found his way to the bathroom. He laid the baby on the changing table and rolled up his sleeves. Surely it must be like riding a bike. He could do this. Gingerly, he unsnapped Braden's sleeper. Disposable diapers. That should be easy, at least he wouldn't have to worry about sticking the little guy with a pin.

He loosened the tabs and pulled the diaper down. The odor that met his nose made him cringe. Great. It was a dirty one. With one hand on the baby, he flipped open the box of wipes and pulled one out. Braden cooed as Josh swiped his bottom. Still keeping one hand on Braden, Josh bent to grab a clean diaper when it happened. A pale yellow arc of urine hit him squarely in the face.

Eden stood in the doorway with Katie in her arms. Her green eyes sparkled with amusement. "I can see you've done this often," she said.

# Chapter 3

Braden sucked contentedly on his bottle while Josh played on the floor with Katie. She had her dollies displayed for his admiration, and he had Katie's favorite, Bubbles, on his lap with a plastic bottle stuck in its mouth. Eden sneaked a peek and tried to hide her mirth.

Eden didn't know what to think about Josh. There was a gentleness about him in spite of his size. He seemed lonely to Eden, as though he searched for a place to call home. Of course, he'd been drifting all over the world for the past few years, so it was no wonder he seemed a bit lost.

Eden ventured another look. Katie looked a bit like him. It was in the shape of her mouth, that firm determination in her upper lip. Her eyes were shaped like his, though hers were blue. And Katie's hands had his long fingers and well-shaped nails. She didn't know what to do about him. He couldn't take Katie, but he was not the kind of man to give up easily.

The bottle plopped out of Braden's slack mouth, and Eden stood. "I'll just pop this little fellow into his bed and be right back down."

"I'd need to sleep too if you'd forced that concoction down my throat."

Eden chuckled, then glanced at Katie. "You want a nap, Katie?"

Katie's droopy eyes flew open. "No!" It was still her favorite word.

"Uncle Josh will read you a story." Josh stood and held out his arms for Katie.

Uncle Josh. Eden frowned. He had not even asked if he might identify himself to Katie as her uncle. She would have to talk with him about what role he would be allowed to play in her young life. Suppressing a sigh, she led the way up the wide staircase. She pointed out Katie's room to Josh then went farther down the hall and slipped Braden into his crib. He didn't stir, so she backed out of the room and pulled the door partway shut behind her.

When she entered Katie's room, she found Katie tucked into her bed with Josh sitting beside her. He was reading *Green Eggs and Ham*. Katie's thumb was corked in her mouth, and she had one arm around her Pooh bear. Her eyes closed and didn't open again.

" 'I do not like green eggs and ham. I do not like them, Sam I Am.' "

Eden chuckled, and Josh looked up. His eyes, as dark as a buck's, narrowed at her smile, but an answering one tugged at his own lips.

"She's asleep," Eden said.

He glanced down at his niece and nodded. Rising from the bed, he put the book on the bedside table, and they both tiptoed out of the room.

"Can we talk?" Josh asked when they reached the bottom of the stairs.

A prickle of unease ran up Eden's spine at the somber tone. She nodded. "You want something else to drink?"

"No, I'm fine."

His pacing made Eden's pulse race. He was a formidable opponent, but he would soon see he couldn't push her around. She crossed her arms over her chest and stared at him. "Sit down, you're giving me a headache."

He shot her a curious look, then dropped into the worn leather armchair by the fireplace. "How are we going to work this out?"

"There's nothing to work out. Katie is my daughter, legally and of the heart. I know this has been a shock to you. You thought you could waltz in here and take her with you, but that's never going to happen. I'm willing to allow you to see her, though. I think it's important for an adopted child to have access to her—her heritage." Her voice broke, and she looked away.

He cocked his head and stared at her curiously. "Why did you say it like that?"

Eden bit her lip. "I was a foster kid myself, Josh. Somewhere out there, I have two sisters and a brother that I'll probably never see again. I don't want Katie to have the pain of knowing she has blood relatives she's been ripped away from."

"Then surely you can see she would be better off with me," he began. He began to rummage in his briefcase. "Here, look at these financial figures."

She held up her hand. "I'm not interested, Josh. Katie is my daughter. I'm the one who nursed her through chicken pox and pneumonia. I'm the one she calls for in the night. She's just a link to your sister for you. I'm not saying that's bad—those links are important. But raising a little girl is not about remembering who her mother was; it's more about finding out who she is and helping her to realize she's special because God made her that way. It's about listening to her dreams, teaching her she's special in God's eyes. It's about seeing her go to school on that first day, then crying with her when her heart is broken by her first boyfriend."

His face grew more sober as she spoke. "Was your foster mother like that?"

Eden clenched her fists as the traitorous tears flooded her eyes. "I had a succession of foster parents. None of them replaced my mother. She taught me all I needed to know about mothering in the eight years before she died. The last foster parents adopted me, but they never took the place of my own parents. I know what it's like to be ripped away from the only life you've ever known, and I'll not subject Katie to that."

He stood to his feet. "Then I suppose there is no more to say. But I'm not giving up, Eden. Katie belongs with me. My sister and my parents would expect her to be with me. I'll be in touch."

Disappointment sharpened her tone. "Make sure you call first. I can't have you dropping by whenever you feel like it. Katie might begin to depend on you, and then you'll go flitting off to the Middle East or somewhere else. I don't want her hurt."

His jaw tightened, and he nodded curtly. "I'll call." He slammed the door behind him.

Eden sighed. That had not gone well. But everything she said was true. She knew what it was like to cry at night from missing her family. Katie couldn't be allowed to experience that heartache. Not while there was something Eden could do about it.

The next few days seemed particularly lonely to Eden for some reason. Twenty-four years since she'd seen her sisters and her brother. Where were they? The question never left her mind for long. With Mama sick so much, the children's care had fallen to Eden as the oldest.

Her arms still ached to hold Crista, the baby of the family. She yearned to braid Angelina's thick hair again, to see Timmy's face when he smelled the chocolate chip cookies she and Mama used to bake. Did they remember her at all? They were so young. Little Crista had been only three when they were separated.

How could anyone do that to children? To rip them apart from one another and send them to different homes, to change their names so they couldn't find each other. Not that she had tried very hard lately. The roadblocks bureaucracy had thrown in her way had left her feeling hopeless and alone. It wasn't fair. But God had never promised life would be fair. She had to remind herself of that all the time. He had gone with her through every trial, every heartache.

*But what if I never find them?* The question rang in her head, and she hunched her shoulders and reached for her Bible. She couldn't think thoughts like that. Someday she would find them. She knew this in her soul—if not here on this earth, in heaven. Their mother had prayed for them, and she had to believe her prayers had taken root. Those prayers had led her to Jesus, and she had to believe that Angelina, Timmy, and Crista had come to know Him as well. Without that hope, she couldn't go on.

The front door slammed, and the older children rushed in from school. Samantha had her book bag slung over her shoulder, her ribbon missing and her braid half undone. Cory immediately sat at Eden's feet. Amelia's shoelaces were untied, and her new blouse was stained with ink. Eden sighed.

"Eden, we seen Mr. Leland outside. I invited him for supper, is that okay?" Samantha dropped her book bag and stared at her with hopeful eyes.

Great. Just what she didn't want to have to deal with. And he hadn't called first, in spite of her admonition. Before she could answer Samantha, the doorbell rang. Eden's heart gave a funny hitch, and she frowned. She couldn't be attracted to the man, could she? He was the enemy. She would do well to keep that in mind.

She would act as though their harsh words had never happened, she decided. It was best for Katie if they could get along. Josh would eventually come to realize this was for the best. She pinned her smile in place and went to the door and opened it.

Josh looked good this evening. Too good. He was impeccably dressed, as usual, and she caught the faint whiff of his cologne, a spicy, masculine scent that reminded her of the woods. He carried a laptop computer and a briefcase, and she felt a stab of alarm. Was he serving her with papers or something? But that was silly, the sheriff would be the one to serve papers.

He smiled faintly when she raised an eyebrow and glanced to the briefcase. "I won't put you on the spot and demand supper. But I *was* invited."

Eden chuckled and stepped out of the way. "Come in.

If you like vegetable soup, there's plenty to share."

"With cabbage in it?"

"Lots of cabbage. It's cheap," she said, shutting the door behind him.

"I'll stay." He followed her to the parlor where Samantha sidled up to him and took his hand.

The little girl was quite smitten with him. Eden decided she might have to watch that. Samantha's feelings were easily bruised, and she'd been through a lot in the past six months.

Josh sniffed. "Smells good."

"Thanks." Eden didn't know what to say to him. Why had he come back, again without calling? And how long did he intend to hang around Wabash?

She went to the fireplace and lit her Yankee candle. She never had the money for such frivolous things, but her secret sister at church had bought it for her. The spicy aroma would soothe her frazzled nerves.

"Want me to make a fire?" he asked.

"You know how?" He didn't strike her as the outdoorsy type. Too urbane and sophisticated.

"You forget I'm an Eagle Scout. I live for my times in the woods."

He kept surprising her. "Be my guest."

He went to the fireplace and found the kindling. Within moments he had coaxed a flame and then piled three logs on the grate. He put the screen in front of the grate and went to the sofa. "I have some things to show you," he said.

Eden swallowed hard. She was afraid to see what he had in his briefcase. She had a feeling it might change her life.

# Chapter 4

J osh found it hard to think with Eden's green eyes on
him. They were darkened with trepidation as though
she didn't quite know how to take him. And how did
he know if his suggestion would be welcome or not? Maybe
she didn't want to know. Some people didn't. Possible rejection was hard to handle.

He cleared his throat and opened his computer.
"Where's a jack I can plug into?"

"Right beside you. The phone has a place in the back
of it."

He snapped the connector into place while the computer booted up, then clicked on the Internet icon. The
computer dialed up and took him to the site he'd looked at
earlier in the day. He thought Eden would be impressed.

He patted the space beside him on the sofa. "Sit here
so you can see."

Her eyes widened but she didn't object, just moved
from the rocker and sat beside him. She smelled sweet,
like vanilla maybe. Her gaze focused on the screen. He
heard her slight intake of breath but was almost afraid to
look at her. The last thing he wanted to do was offend

her. But his uncertainty vanished at the sight of her eyes widened in delight.

"I've heard of these adoption bulletin boards, but I've never been able to afford a computer to check them out. And with two babies, the library was out of the question." She moved closer and peered at the screen.

It was all Josh could do to drag his gaze from her animated face with that delightful dimple flashing in her cheek. "I would need to know all the information you have about your family. Do you know your family name?"

"Richmond. I was eight when Daddy left me at the preacher's so I remember quite a lot. My parents were John and Anna Richmond, and we lived in Covington, Kentucky."

"Kentucky, huh? You're not so far from your roots. Have you ever gone back there?" He tapped at the keys.

She shook her head. "There's never been the money for it. I called and talked to a woman at the state office, but she said my sisters and brother were sent out of state and wouldn't tell me more than that."

"Let's go to the Kentucky site first and see what their laws say." He selected the state and peered at the screen as the information scrolled up.

"This says siblings can petition the court to search for each other!" Eden grasped his arm in her excitement.

Josh glanced at her small hand on his arm and was shocked at his own desire to take it and hold it in his own. These inappropriate feelings toward his niece's care-taker had to stop. He cleared his throat. "As long as you're all over eighteen," he pointed out.

"We are. I'm the oldest, and Crista is the baby. She's five years younger than me, so that would make her about twenty-nine." Her voice grew dreamy. "Wouldn't it be wonderful if they were looking for me, too?"

Eden was thirty-four then. She had a freshness to her skin and eyes that had made him guess her to be still in her twenties. He dragged his gaze from the petal-softness of her cheeks and began to read the screen again.

He could sense Eden's excitement, and he felt a bit uneasy. What if he'd raised her hopes for nothing? His plan could backfire on him. If she failed to find her siblings, she might cling even tighter to Katie. He couldn't allow that; he had to find them.

"I'll call and request a form to begin the search," he said. "Now let's go to the bulletin board and post the information. Tell me everything you know."

"John and Anna Richmond. Four of us kids. Mama died of cancer." Eden's voice trembled, and she bit her lip. Tears shimmered in her eyes, but she blinked several times. "I loved my daddy, but he changed when Mama died. Then he lost his job and left us with Mama's preacher."

"How long were you with him?"

"A few months. Word came back that Daddy had died. I'm not sure what happened, I suppose I was too young to hear the full story. Anyway, his sister, our aunt Selma, came to see us. But she was a widow with no inclination to try to handle four kids who were still grieving for their parents. She kept Timmy and sent the rest of us to foster care."

Eden bit her lip and shivered. Josh had to fight to keep himself from putting his arm around her. She'd gone through so much, he could understand why family was so important to her.

"Crista was the first to go. When I heard that the state was allowing her to be adopted, I threw up, then cried for three days. Angelina was next. By then, I was numb. Too old to be appealing to childless couples, I was shunted from one foster home to another. But I never forgot my brother and sisters. And I never will. They're out there somewhere—I know it."

A lump formed in Josh's throat. There was a steadfast integrity about Eden that drew him. He cleared his throat and looked back to his computer screen. "Let's get this posted. Read this and see what you think."

*Seeking Richmond siblings.*
*Parents, John and Anna Richmond, died in 1975.*
*Eden, the eldest, seeks three younger siblings,*
*born in Covington, Kentucky.*
*Last known names: Timothy Richmond,*
*Angelina Richmond, and Crista Richmond.*

Eden touched the screen with a trembling hand. "Do you really think this might work, Josh? And why do you care? Why are you doing this?"

Josh tried to ignore the questions. "What's your address and phone number?" He typed in the information she gave him. When he looked up from the screen, Eden's green eyes were focused on him.

"Why are you doing this, Josh?"

How could he tell her his motives were so selfish when she gazed at him with such trust in her eyes? He felt dirty and longed to escape from the piercing light of goodness in Eden's face. Looking away, he shrugged. "At least they're still alive," he said.

Eden's face softened even more. "I understand," she said softly.

What a jerk he was! Leading her to believe he was doing this for altruistic motives. Josh had never felt so low. He would find her siblings and tell her the truth as soon as possible. He didn't feel good about misleading Eden; she was so innocent and had been hurt by so many. He cringed inside at how she would feel if she knew his true motives.

He clicked the Send button, then shut his computer down. "It will probably be a few days before we get any response."

Eden's eager smile faded. "If we get a response. They may not even remember or care."

"They would care about finding a sister like you." His gaze locked with Eden's. He almost felt as though their souls touched in that moment. Hastily dropping his gaze, he got to his feet. "Where's that vegetable soup with cabbage I was promised?"

Was that disappointment in Eden's eyes? Had she felt a special something that had stretched between them like a physical touch?

She stood and went toward the kitchen. "I'll put it on the table. Would you get Katie up from her nap?"

"You sure she won't be frightened?"

Eden put her hands on her hips and laughed. "Josh Leland, you can't tell me you haven't noticed how you've stolen the hearts of my children!" She shook her head. "She won't be frightened of her uncle Josh."

Uncle Josh. The sound gave him a warm fuzzy feeling. He grinned. "I'll get her."

"And change her diaper before you bring her down," Eden called.

Uh-oh, another diaper. But this was on a girl, and it was less dangerous. Josh took the steps two at a time and strode down the hall to Katie's room.

Lying on her back with her bare feet kicking the foot of her crib, she smiled when she saw him. She quickly scrambled to her feet and held up her arms for him to take her.

"Well, you are rather angelic, just as your mama said," he told her.

She corked her thumb in her mouth and regarded him soberly.

He felt her diaper. Rats! It was wet. But at least it was only wet. He laid her on the changing table and managed to change her without a hitch. Her diaper drooped slightly, but not so badly as Braden's had yesterday. He must be getting a handle on this diaper business.

He started down the hall, then heard noises from Braden's room. Josh peeked inside, and the baby began to bounce excitedly at the sight of Josh and Katie.

"I guess you're awake." How did he handle two of them at once? How did Eden do it? He put Katie on one hip, then scooped Braden up in the other arm and balanced him on the other hip. It seemed much more awkward than the way he'd seen Eden do it. And there was no way he was going to attempt to change Braden, too.

Biting his lip in concentration, he managed to get down the steps without a mishap. Katie gripped his ear with one chubby hand while Braden inspected Josh's teeth. There was more to this parenting business than he'd thought. But he would learn. He was not giving up Katie to anyone. Not even Eden.

Eden tried to tamp the rising excitement as she ladled the vegetable soup into bowls. There was no guarantee they would really find her brother and sisters. But this was the first time she'd really had hope in all these years. And she owed that hope to Josh. Her heart thawed toward him like the first glimpse of spring. Katie had a good uncle.

Josh came in carrying the two babies. Samantha's face brightened when she saw him, and she sidled up to him and gazed at him with adoring eyes. Cory backed away and hid behind Eden.

She touched Cory's head with a reassuring pat. He was still frightened of men, and no wonder. The bruises from his stepfather's blows still darkened his legs and buttocks. "It's okay, Cory," she said softly.

Josh raised one eyebrow and softened his voice. "You want to help me with these babies, big guy? They're a little more than I can handle by myself."

Cory regarded him with sober dark eyes, then hid his face against Eden's leg.

"He's had a rough time," Eden mouthed.

Josh nodded. "You want to take Braden for me, Sam?"

"She doesn't like to be called Sam," Eden said hastily. The last time someone had called the little girl "Sam" she'd thrown a vase and sulked in her room for two hours.

"He can call me Sam," Samantha said. She smiled hesitantly at Josh and took Braden from his arm. "I like it now."

Eden managed to hide her astonishment. Josh had quite a way with her kids, and she suspected it was innate. Kids just gravitated to him naturally. He'd make a wonderful father and a caring husband. Her face burned with mortification, and she turned away to finish supper. Where had that thought come from? She wasn't looking for a husband. Change was the last thing her children needed. Familiarity was key, and she'd see they got it. Any thought of romance was ridiculous.

Josh put Katie in her high chair. "Should I put this thing on her?" He held up Katie's Pooh bib.

"Please. She's a messy eater."

Eden managed not to laugh as he coaxed Katie to put her arms through the bib armholes. She hated her bib. He finally succeeded, then tied it in the back and sat in the chair next to Katie.

"I warned you, she's messy. If you sit beside her, you'll probably have to wash up afterward."

Josh's grin of nonchalance changed as Katie banged her spoon into the bowl of soup, and it splashed everywhere. He sprang to his feet and wiped a streak of soup from his cheek. Then to Eden's surprise, he sat back in the same chair.

"I've already been baptized. I might as well guard you

from the onslaught," he said with a grin. He made a credible job of containing Katie's mess through supper and kept the other children entertained as well.

"You should have a houseful of kids yourself," Eden said. As soon as she spoke, she wanted to retrieve the words.

Josh shrugged, and his gaze wandered to Katie's face splotched with vegetable soup. "I've never been in one place long enough to meet the right kind of woman. For the last five years I've been in Saudi Arabia, traveling from one city to the next. But I'm almost thirty-five; it's time I thought of a permanent home."

Eden's breath caught in her throat. For just an instant, she imagined what it would be like to have him come home from a hard day's work to her and Katie, to have Katie running to greet him and calling him "Daddy." Her face burned with humiliation. If he could read her thoughts, he would be out the door so fast an Olympic runner couldn't catch him.

She glanced up to find his dark gaze on her. Was that longing on his face? She was likely reading her own silly dreams in his expression. Glancing away, she rose. "I'll do the dishes. You want Mr. Leland to help with your homework, kids?"

"Yes!" Samantha and Amelia shouted. Cory's face whitened, and he shook his head without looking up.

Eden sighed. She didn't know what to do with poor Cory. He couldn't seem to get over his terror of men. Maybe having Josh around would be good. Cory would learn that all men weren't like his mother's new husband.

Before she could reassure Cory, Josh knelt beside the

little boy. "I'm not very good at spelling, Cory. Do you suppose you could help me?"

Cory bit his lip and shook his head. Huge tears hung on his lashes, and he cast a desperate glance toward Eden. "I'll dry the dishes."

Josh touched Cory's head, and the little boy flinched back. "I won't hurt you, Cory." Josh's voice was low and soothing. "I'd like us to be friends."

Cory slid out of his chair and ran to Eden. He buried his face in her lap. "Make him go away, Eden. Make him go away."

Eden ran her fingers through the little boy's rough curls. "Mr. Leland is Katie's uncle, Cory. He likes little boys, too."

"That's what Tom said." Cory's words were muffled in her lap. "But he didn't. He didn't."

The last words were a wail of despair, and Eden gathered Cory up into her arms. She looked to Josh and bit her lip. "Why don't you take the rest of the children in by the fire. Cory and I will do the dishes and join you later."

A muscle twitched in Josh's jaw. "Some man hurt him, right? What kind of person could hurt a little boy like that?" He stood and thrust his fists in his pocket.

"You'd be surprised what horrors adults inflict on children," Eden whispered. Cory was literally shaking with terror, and she hugged him closer.

"I'd better never meet the man who hurt Cory," Josh said. He took the washcloth and wiped Katie's hands and face, then lifted her out of the high chair. He set her on the floor, then cleaned Braden's face and picked him out of his chair and carried him toward the door to the living room. Samantha took Katie's hand, and they all paraded after Josh.

Eden sank onto her chair and rocked Cory for a few moments. This was not a new occurrence. Sometimes she despaired of repairing the damage Cory's stepfather had done. But with God's help and her love, she thought the tide might be turning. A few weeks ago, he wouldn't have even managed to stay in the same room with a man.

Josh was unusual, though; she had to give him that. She'd never met a man as good with children as he was. There was a loneliness in him that answered the yearning in her own heart. She was afraid to hope he found her as fascinating as she found him. Katie was the real draw. In her heart, Eden knew this. But it didn't stop her from being drawn to the man whose heart seemed to be as big as his physique.

By the time she and Cory finished the dishes, the girls were done with their homework and had coaxed Josh into a game of Fish. They all lay spread out on the rug in front of the fireplace, the lamps casting a glow over the picture that made Eden think of Norman Rockwell prints. She swallowed the lump in her throat and sank into the rocker by the fire.

"Go fish," Josh said with a cheeky grin to Samantha. She groaned and snatched a card from the pile. "These girls are smoking me," he told Eden. "They should be sent to bed right now so I can claim victory. It's the only way I can win."

Samantha's face clouded, and with the next hand she played recklessly. Josh gained some of the ground he had lost, and he cast an amused glance to Eden. It was obvious

Samantha was throwing the game to him.

By the time the game was over and the kids had been bathed, prayers heard, stories read, and tucked in bed, it was eight-thirty. Josh's hair stood on end where he had swiped a wet hand through it after bathing Braden. A warm glow enveloped Eden as she and Josh went back to the parlor. She could get used to evenings like this.

Josh sat on the sofa and patted the place beside him. "Let's fire up the computer and see if there happens to be an answer."

"So quickly?" She sank beside him and watched as he went to his E-mail.

"Probably not, but it couldn't hurt to check," he said.

A box appeared that said it was downloading five messages. Eden caught her breath. Maybe there was a response already.

Josh frowned as he scanned the list of downloaded messages. "Most of it is junk mail," he said. "But this looks promising." He clicked on the message with the subject RICHMOND FAMILY.

Eden's heart sped up, and she clenched her fists in her lap. Maybe this was the news she'd waited twenty-five years to hear.

# Chapter 6

Josh heard Eden catch her breath. Should he even have started her down this path? What if the search became fruitless? He would hate to be the cause of more pain in her life. She'd already had a lifetime's worth. But it was too late to turn back now. He'd opened this particular Pandora's box, and they would both have to live with the consequences.

He moved the cursor so they could read the message on the computer screen.

> *Pastor Markus Brittan once cared for a Richmond family after the mother died and the father disappeared. Could this be the family you mention? If so, I can give you Pastor Brittan's address and phone number.*

Eden's hand clamped on Josh's arm, and he nearly winced at the fierce grip. "I remember a preacher," she whispered. "I couldn't remember his name, but we went to church all the time. He had a cat named Spooky. It was all black with a white spot at its throat and used to leap on my legs when I went down the stairs."

Josh clicked Reply To Message and typed in a request for more information. "Let's see what the man has to say."

Eden groaned softly.

"What's wrong, Eden?"

He and Eden turned at Samantha's frightened voice.

Eden squeezed the little girl's hand and gave her a reassuring smile. "What are you doing up, Sweetie? Mr. Leland and I are just trying to find out some information about my family."

"Were you—adopted?" Samantha's face grew whiter at the dreaded word.

"Yes, Sweetie, but don't be frightened. Your daddy is working hard to get you back. You just saw him last week, remember?"

The terrified expression in Samantha's eyes faded, and she nodded. "He got a new job."

"That's right. You'll be with your daddy again soon. Now scoot back to bed."

What was the full story behind Samantha's removal from her home? He would have to ask Eden when the little girl wasn't around. Had her mother abandoned her or had she died? He glanced at Eden. There was one mother who would never leave her family. He'd never met anyone with a more nurturing soul. Her heart was so full of love for the children, he felt a little jealous. He watched her escort Samantha to the staircase.

Josh pulled his straying thoughts up short. Where had that come from? He'd best keep his mind on business. Eden had her life, and he had his. But she was so very appealing with her baby-fine blond hair curling around her face and those remarkable green eyes. If he were to hold her, that soft hair would barely reach his shoulder.

He dragged his gaze from her and turned back to the computer. The sooner he found her family and succeeded in retrieving Katie, the better. A new daughter would be enough of a change to his life; he wasn't ready for more than that.

Clicking the Send And Receive button, he leaned forward. "I'm bushed. I think I'll shove off."

"But what about the answer to the message you just sent? That lady might reply right away. It's only nine."

"And what is there to do tonight if she does? You can't go to Kentucky tonight."

"No, but you could call."

He caught the fact that she'd said *he* could call. She must be terrified. "I can stay awhile, I guess. But only if you fix some popcorn."

Relief lightened her face. "You've got a deal."

She hurried from the room, and Josh leaned back against the sofa. He was getting more and more entangled in the lives of this turbulent family on Hill Street. But he didn't remember any time he'd had more fun than he had tonight. Sitting around a family table with spills mixed with laughter, romping on the floor with a passel of children, watching the firelight spill red-gold over Eden's face had awakened a strange hunger in his heart. The feeling wasn't entirely pleasant, it was too new and filled with the trepidation of the unknown.

The aroma of popped corn wafted from the open kitchen door. The tinkle of ice in glasses followed, then

Eden walked back to the living room. She clutched a bowl of popcorn to her chest as she balanced two glasses of soda.

He leapt to his feet. "Let me help you."

"I've got it." She handed him the 101 Dalmatians glass and set her own Cinderella glass on the coffee table. She sat down, put the bowl of popcorn between them, and dug out a handful.

Josh scooped a handful of popcorn. For some reason, the fact that they ate from the same bowl touched him. He hadn't done that since he was a kid, and he and his sister shared popcorn with their parents.

Eden must have caught the nostalgia in his expression for she smiled. "We've talked about my past, but what about yours? What kind of upbringing did you and Mandy have?"

The pain that had subsided to a dull ache flared again at the mention of Mandy. *His fault.* "I don't want to talk about Mandy," he said.

"I think you need to. Katie is not your sister, you know. She may look like her, but she's her own little person. If you hope to find your sister again through her, you're making a big mistake. One that could hurt you and her terribly."

"I thought you were just a poorly paid foster mother. Since when did you get a psychology degree?"

Eden's face clouded, and he felt a shaft of shame. "I'm sorry, I had no right to say that," he said. He took a deep breath. "I suppose you're right. I should talk about it, but it just hurts."

Eden's green eyes softened. "You need a friend. I'm a pretty good listener."

She'd certainly been a good friend to his niece, a friend and a mother. Maybe he needed to talk about it. It couldn't be any worse than turning it over and over in his mind.

"I couldn't protect her," he said. "I tried when we were kids, but I was too little to stop him."

The color faded from Eden's cheeks. She looked older, filled with care and weariness. Josh knew she'd heard this same story many times in her profession. Shame tied his tongue, but he pressed on. "To the outside world, we looked the perfect family. Mom, Dad, nice house in the suburbs. Then *he* came to live with us."

Eden's eyes widened, and he knew she'd thought it was one of his parents who'd hurt Mandy. He rushed on, incapable of stopping now.

"Our uncle. He came back from Vietnam with bitterness that crouched on his shoulders like some vulture. He was always after Mandy to go places with him. At first she was happy to do it. She remembered the uncle John who'd gone away to war, the lighthearted, laughing uncle who brought us candy and presents."

He drew a breath and wished he could stop, wished he could erase the shameful knowledge of his own failure. Though Eden was silent, he could sense the waves of compassion flowing from her. He wanted to take her hand but was afraid he'd crush it as he told the rest of the story.

"I came home from school one day. The house was quiet. Mother and Dad were both at work. I called out, but no one answered. I poured a glass of milk and grabbed a handful of cookies, then went upstairs. I heard a noise, a cry maybe. I pushed open Mandy's door. Uncle John was there with Mandy. He had her by the arm. She was crying.

I shouted at him to leave her alone. He dragged her out the door past me. The whole time she was begging me to help her, to save her. I ran after them and tried to pull Mandy from his grasp, but I was only twelve, she was ten. Two little kids fighting some kind of demon that never let loose. He shoved her in the car and took off with the tires squealing. I ran back inside and called my mom. She came right home, but it was three days before we found Mandy. She called us after Uncle John took a bottle of pills and was dead. We drove to Missouri to get her, and she wasn't the same little girl who'd left. She was never the same again. And it was my fault."

A crushing weariness weighed him down. "And now she's dead. All I have left of her is Katie. Only Katie."

He started at the light touch of Eden's fingers on his. She took his hand and pressed it. He raised his eyes, and his gaze locked with hers.

"It's not your fault, Josh. You were a child, there's nothing you could have done."

"I should have saved her. Dad had a gun in his room. I could have gotten it or hit him with something." He raked a hand through his hair.

"Samantha's mom shoved her out of the bathroom, then slit her wrists and climbed in a tub of hot water and bled to death. Could she have stopped her?" She sighed, and the sound was filled with tender compassion. "Adults do terrible things sometimes, Josh. We don't know why God allows children to be hurt by their actions. It's one of the things I struggle with most. But I know this one thing. Though we suffer sometimes, God can use it to make us stronger."

"It didn't make Mandy stronger. She destroyed herself trying to erase the memories."

"But we have to let God make the difference. I could have wallowed in what happened to my family, but instead I chose to try to make some small difference in the lives of other children who suffer as I did. God made that difference. He could have made that difference in Mandy's life if she would have let Him."

"I wrote her once about trying to let go of the past, and she never answered."

"It's never easy. I went through a period of blaming God for my misfortune, too. But Mandy would have gotten back on her feet and forged through this. You have to believe that, Josh."

Exhaustion slowed his muscles, and he nodded. "In my heart, I do believe that." If only she'd lived. But all the regrets in the world wouldn't change what was finished.

"But God left Katie motherless."

"She's not motherless. She has me," Eden said. "And she always will."

Maybe he should tell her now he still intended to take Katie. He regretted the pain it would cause her, but he needed Katie. She would have to see that sooner or later. She was his lifeline.

# Chapter 7

E den glanced at Josh, and the veiled look of pain in his eyes made her want to take him in her arms and kiss away his hurts the way she might with Cory. The thought surprised her. He was an adult, but he still carried the scars of his childhood. The same way she carried them. No wonder he had wanted Katie so badly.

She could tell by the stiffness in his shoulders that he had erected his wall of defenses again, and she felt inadequate to scale it. She glanced at her watch. Nine-thirty. Such momentous revelations in only half an hour.

"Let's check the E-mail again, then I'll head back to my hotel." He took his laptop from the coffee table and clicked the Send And Receive button. Nothing.

Eden's keen sense of disappointment surprised her. This wouldn't happen overnight. And she'd waited this long to find them, what was a few more weeks or months? At least she was doing something about it now. Thanks to Josh.

He switched off the computer and stood. "Thanks for the great evening. Could I take you and the kids to dinner tomorrow? Just so you don't have to cook for me again?"

His teasing grin did funny things to her breathing. "Would you like to come to church with us in the morning?"

He grinned. "I was hoping you would invite me and I wouldn't have to invite myself."

Eden laughed. "You want to follow us or ride in the kid-mobile?"

He hesitated, and she laughed again. "Such a decision. Peace and solitude or sticky fingers and chattering voices."

He chuckled. "I'll take the sticky fingers and chattering voices. Peace and solitude sound boring. What time do we leave?"

"Nine-ten. Sunday school starts at nine-thirty, and our church is in the country about ten minutes away. It takes me a few minutes to get them all to their classes and Katie to the nursery."

"I'll bring donuts at eight and help you get them ready."

The shock of pleasure that went through her at his words brought her up short. Did he have any idea what a treat that would be for the children? There was rarely enough money for such an extravagance.

And she was enjoying his presence way too much. She needed to keep in mind that he would be leaving soon. He would soon tire of commotion and the small, daily trials of children. One day soon he would go back to his real life. She didn't want to be nursing a broken heart when he did. But, oh, how good it felt to have someone to share all this with, someone who thought of what the children needed besides her. She allowed herself to bask in the pleasure of it for a moment.

She shut the door behind him, took the remains of the popcorn and empty glasses to the kitchen, then turned off the lights and went to bed. Tomorrow she would try to remember this sharing of their lives was temporary, a chasing after the wind. Her life was here with these children who needed her so badly. His life was oil fields and the hectic world of business. Too different to ever meld.

In spite of her resolve, Eden saw her own flushed cheeks in the mirror the next morning and shook her head. The thought of spending the day with Josh had given her a glow anyone but an idiot would recognize. She took extra care with her makeup, then dressed in a grass green suit that slimmed her hips. Not that mere clothing would hide those extra pounds she couldn't seem to lose. She swept her hair on top of her head and let the curls fall in disarray.

Standing in front of the full-length mirror, she nearly groaned. She looked like a green sausage with a blond topknot. Josh could have his pick of glamorous women— real beauties who knew how to flirt and hold a man's interest. He would never be interested in a homebody like Eden who looked like she'd made too many cookies. But making them wasn't the problem, it was eating them.

The children were stirring. She turned from the mirror. Her appearance would just have to do. Josh wasn't interested in her anyway, so she could just quit obsessing. Eden changed Katie's and Braden's diapers, then got the older children dressed for church. Samantha brightened when she heard Josh was going with them, but Cory cowered. She wished she knew how to break through his fear of men.

The doorbell rang, and her heart jumped. She hustled down the stairs with Katie under one arm and Braden under the other and opened the door.

"We got another message!" Josh stepped inside with a white box of donuts in one hand and his computer in the other. He strode past her into the living room. Setting the box of donuts on the coffee table, he turned and enveloped her in a hug.

All thought left Eden's head at the feel of his strong arms around her. For the first time since she was a child, she felt safe and protected. She wanted to burrow against his chest and savor the sensation. But she felt him stiffen and realized what he would think. She pulled away hastily.

He dug in his pocket and pulled out a scrap of paper. "Here's the phone number and address. But rather than call, why don't we just go there?"

"To Kentucky? What if it's the wrong people?"

"They're the right ones, don't you feel it, Eden? When he sees you, he might recognize you. I have a feeling you haven't changed much since you were eight. You're not hardly bigger than a minute now."

Eden nearly choked, but she wasn't about to argue with him. Maybe he hadn't noticed her generous proportions, and she wasn't about to point them out. But Kentucky!

"I looked on the map; Covington is on the east side of Cincinnati. That's only three hours from here. We could leave after church, stop for lunch, then head to Covington. We could be there by four at the latest. I'll buy the gas."

"We may get back late. And I can't take my foster children out of state without permission."

"Can you get someone to watch them?"

She bit her lip and gazed into Josh's intent eyes. "Are you sure you want to go to the bother? What if he's not there?"

"He's a preacher. He'll be around on Sunday."

"All right, then, if you're sure. I'll see if Rick and Belinda can come. They've done it for me before."

"We can take Katie, right?"

She nodded. "Why are you doing this?" Eden asked Josh. "I really appreciate it, but it really isn't your concern."

He averted his eyes, and a flush stained his cheeks. Could he possibly be coming to care for her? She couldn't imagine any other reason for his reaction. She warned herself not to jump to conclusions, but it was hard to squelch the thrill of hope that lightened her heart.

"Take some clothes to change into for you and Katie. You pack, and I'll feed the kids their breakfast. It'll be a fun day." He took Katie and Braden from her arms and strode toward the kitchen.

Eden blew her bangs out of her eyes, then went to pack a change of clothes. Josh was a take-charge kind of guy. She supposed it was from being in command of others in his job. It was a nice change to let someone else have that role.

By the time she got downstairs with a satchel of clothing, Josh was washing faces and clearing away the breakfast things. Even Cory had eaten, though he watched Josh with a wary gaze as the man moved around the kitchen. Still, Eden thought he might be beginning to thaw.

"If you dress Braden, I'll dress Katie." Josh didn't wait for an answer but handed Braden to her and headed toward the stairs.

Eden followed with Braden in her arms and a frown

on her face. She was beginning to dislike the way he took control of Katie. The adoption was final, but maybe Josh was still unwilling to accept that. She shook her head. She was overreacting. He would naturally want to spend time with Katie; after all, she was his niece. And there was nothing he could do to change the situation.

She dressed Braden in a navy-and-red sailor suit and combed his hair. He kept snatching at strands of her hair that fell forward, and she knew she looked a mess by the time he was ready. She checked on the other children, but they were all ready.

Pushing open the door to Katie's room, she found Josh struggling to comb Katie's hair. She hated to have her hair combed and was trying to escape. The bow he'd managed to get in her blond curls was lopsided and barely hanging on.

Eden chuckled and handed Braden to him. Josh watched while she gave Katie a toy, then took out the bow and repositioned it.

"I'm new at this girl stuff," he said.

Though he laughed, Eden thought she detected a note of chagrin in his voice. "We'd better go," she told him.

He nodded, then scooped up Katie and carried both children to the entry. She and Josh popped the children into their jackets and went to the minivan. A twelve-year-old model, it was the best Eden could afford. Though the paint was faded and rust showed through in spots, the engine was sound, and it got her and the children safely where they needed to go. And the stains from their sticky fingers didn't matter so much on the worn upholstery.

At New Life Church she waved to her friend Tatiana,

then got the kids to class. Tatiana's husband, Gabe, took charge of Josh for her and led him off to the Life-builders class. She knew the class would make him welcome. Though Gabe and Tatiana Salinger were newlyweds, they were the ambassadors of the group. Tatiana had come from Russia to marry Gabe, and she was always conscious of making newcomers feel welcome.

Eden found Belinda in the nursery, and she readily agreed to come to the house to watch the foster children. Her daughter Andi was Amelia's age, and the girls were best friends. Eden was in such a flurry of excitement, she found it hard to concentrate on the lesson. Today she might find her brother and sisters. The thought made her giddy. She wanted to hug the knowledge close. She prayed all through church for God to give her the strength to face what she might find in Kentucky. Good or bad.

# Chapter 8

Y ou want to drive?" Eden asked Josh. She'd changed into jeans and a sweatshirt, then changed Katie's diaper and dressed her in pants as well. Josh had also changed into jeans. His hair was a bit rumpled, and his eyes sparkled with excitement and adventure.

"Sure." He took the keys from her outstretched hand. "Actually, I wondered if we ought to stop by and get my SUV. You think this old rattletrap will make the trip?"

"It hasn't failed me yet. What's the matter? You too good to be seen in this old tank?" She grinned to show she was joking, but his answer mattered more than she was willing to admit to herself.

"If you'd seen what I drove for five years, you wouldn't ask that. This is a rental. I drove a twenty-year-old Range Rover in Saudi Arabia with no bumpers and practically no paint. This is a luxury vehicle compared to it." He took Katie from her and buckled her into the seat belt.

Eden felt a rising sense of excitement. For too long she had followed the same schedule day after day, month after month, year after year. She was in a rut, and it felt good to break out, to smell the fresh air, to see something beyond the city limits of Wabash, Indiana. She clambered into the front passenger seat and fastened her seat belt.

Josh pulled into a fast-food drive-up lane and got them all a sandwich and fries. He glanced at Eden's face and grinned. "I'm too excited to eat here. I don't normally eat while I'm driving, but today I'll make an exception. It looks like you'd strangle me if I suggested a delay."

Eden's cheeks burned. "Does it show that much?"

"You just look like a kid on her birthday. And I have to admit I kind of feel like that myself. When is your birthday, anyway?"

"December fourth."

"Dare I ask how old you'll be?"

"A gentleman never asks a lady her age," she said primly.

"You look like you're about twelve with the way your eyes are shining." He pulled onto the highway and took a bite of his hamburger.

"My foster parents always forgot my birthday," she said. "I try to make birthdays special for my foster kids because of it. It's sad to think no one cares if you are alive or not. At least that's the way it always seemed to me." She looked down at her hands. "I want my foster kids to always know I consider them a special gift from God."

"You said you were eight when your mother died. Surely your parents celebrated your birthday. Do you remember much about them?"

"Oh, yes. Some things are fuzzy, but I remember one birthday I got a red wagon. I think Daddy might have found it in the junkyard, but he'd painted it and tightened all the wheels. I thought it was wonderful. A brand-new wagon wouldn't have meant as much as knowing the love that went into all his work. When he pulled me down the sidewalk in it, I felt like a princess. My daddy's princess." The remembered pain of her loss tightened her throat, and she struggled not to cry. "We didn't have much money, but we were happy. Mama was always smiling and cheerful, no matter what. We played games in the evenings, and she always read us a story before bed. I remember baking cookies and her teaching me how to crochet. Lots of memories." The sting of tears in the back of her throat stopped further speech.

Josh reached across the seat and squeezed her hand. "We'll find them again, Eden."

"I'm afraid to hope," she admitted. "After all these years, it seems almost impossible to track them down."

"I have a good feeling about today."

"I hope you're right." Eden leaned back against the seat and sighed. Josh's optimism was rubbing off on her. She needed to guard her heart in case of disappointment, but she was tired of doing that. She'd done that for years. It was time she let go and risked her heart. She'd never felt so reckless, so ready for adventure. She slanted a glance at Josh, and gratitude swelled in her heart. It was so kind of him to pursue this for her.

Before she knew it, they were merging into traffic around Cincinnati. She directed Josh where to turn, and they soon found the street. The houses were all small ranch homes from the forties with no garages or porches, just cracker-box houses that were all alike save for the occasional splash of color from an enterprising homeowner.

"There it is!" Eden's heart began a taut staccato beat

against her chest. She bit her lip and tried to slow her breathing. "What if it's the wrong pastor?"

"It isn't."

Josh's calm voice quieted her fears. She nodded. "This looks vaguely familiar. I can't put my finger on just why."

Josh put the car in park and turned it off. He glanced into the backseat. "Katie is asleep. Want me to stay in the car with her?"

At the thought of going to the door by herself, her throat grew tight. Josh must have seen the panic in her face, for he patted her shoulder. "Never mind. I'll carry Katie." He opened his door and got out. Slipping Katie from her seat, he cradled her against his chest where she hung in a dead weight like a rag doll.

Eden took a deep breath and opened her door. Her heart hammered against her ribs, and her blood pounded in her ears. Licking her lips, she shut her door and started up the walk behind Josh. He strode purposefully to the door and turned to make sure she was with him. The doorbell pealed inside.

Eden ceased to breathe. She swallowed hard and clenched her hands together. What if he didn't remember anymore?

Josh turned and gazed at her. "I just realized—there's no car in the drive or at the street."

A woman walking a small poodle with a pink bow on its head stopped in front of the house. "Are you looking for the Brittans?" the woman asked.

Eden turned to stare at her. The woman was about her age with bright red hair and a dusting of freckles across her friendly face. Eden felt a sense of recognition; a memory, faded but still full of warm feelings, came over her. A little girl with red hair and a smile that never dimmed. She couldn't tear her eyes from the woman's face.

"I'm Molly Larson. I live across the street. The Brittans are on vacation in Florida. They won't be home for a couple of weeks."

Eden barely heard the woman's words. The sense of familiarity grew. Molly. The name heightened the feeling that she should know this woman. A little girl's features began to overshadow the woman's. "Molly? Um, have you lived here long?"

Molly tilted her head and stared at Eden. "You look familiar to me."

"I'm Eden Walters. I lived with the Brittans for a few months. I used to be a Richmond."

Molly gasped. "Eden! I remember!" She rushed across the grass with her hands outstretched. "I thought of you just the other day. Let me look at you! Where did you go? You never answered any of my letters." She rushed on without waiting for an answer. "Remember the tree house we built in my backyard? It's still there, and my kids play on it."

Eden took her hand and squeezed it. The years fell away as if they had never passed, and she was eight years old again. "You were the best friend I ever had, Molly. I still have the diary you gave me when I went away."

Molly's smile was bright. "The Brittans aren't home, but I am. Let me get you a soda, and we can sit and get caught up on news."

Eden followed her across the street, barely conscious of Josh trailing behind with Katie. She should have introduced them, but she was just so shocked, she couldn't think.

The house was the same one Molly had lived in as a child. The carpet and kitchen had been updated, but when Eden asked to use the rest room, she found the same pink tile on the floor and walls. The sight brought the past back so vividly, Eden felt almost physical pain.

Katie was still sleeping in Josh's arms when she made her way to the kitchen. Molly was chattering to him as she dropped ice into glasses and poured soda out of a two-liter bottle. Eden sank into a chair and watched her old friend. She felt as though Molly might disappear and leave her bereft again.

Molly handed them each a glass and sat in the chair beside Eden. "Now tell me what you're doing here," she demanded. "And why didn't you answer any of my letters?"

"Letters? I never got any letters. I lost your address, and my foster mother said it was just as well, that it was best to break with the past."

"I sent you a letter every week for months." Molly frowned. "Do you suppose she kept them from you?"

"It's possible," Eden said slowly. "She was afraid to let me get close to anyone from school. I think she knew I wouldn't be there long. She taught me to iron and clean, and I was so busy I didn't have time to miss not having any friends. But I never forgot you, Molly."

"I even wrote your aunt once to see if she'd heard from you. She sent me back a very nice letter but said she hadn't heard a word and didn't expect to."

Excitement threatened to choke Eden. She gripped Molly's hand. "You have my aunt's address? I can't even remember her name. I only met her the one time."

"Oh, Eden, I don't remember either now!" Molly

slapped her forehead with the heel of her hand.

Eden's burgeoning hope faded, and she felt near tears.

Molly bit her lip. "Wait! I might still have the letter. My husband says I'm a hopeless pack rat, and I have a whole box of childhood mementos and letters. Let me look." She jumped to her feet and dashed down the hall.

Eden looked at Josh. "Hang in there," he whispered. "Don't give up hope yet."

She nodded, but her throat was too tight with unshed tears to speak. All this way for nothing. But no, not nothing. She'd found Molly. That was something.

A shriek echoed down the hall. "I found it!" Moments later, Molly came running down the hall. "Here it is, Eden! Her name is Selma Johnson, and she lives in Michigan." She held out a tattered envelope.

Eden reached out a trembling hand and closed her fingers on it. It was a link to her family. Her only link.

# Chapter 9

Josh watched the play of emotions across Eden's expressive face from the corner of his eye. The van hummed smoothly across the highway, trundling toward Wabash. Eden smoothed the letter from her aunt across her lap as though caressing a treasure. And he supposed to her it was. His own emotions were running high, so he could only imagine how Eden felt. They would be home soon, and then they could decide what their next step was.

Home. Already he was beginning to think of that dilapidated Victorian as home. Though shabby, its fading grandeur was enhanced by the warm presence of this woman beside him. Eden could make any house a home. She had a presence about her, a calming competence that set people at ease. He'd just seen her do it with Molly. People took to her right off, children and adults alike. Josh had never met anyone like her.

No wonder Katie adored her. He felt a stab of guilt at the thought of his plans to gain custody of his niece. Where was his trust, his faith in God? He'd been scheming and laying his own plans without even consulting God.

The problem was, he had a feeling God wouldn't slap a rubber stamp labeled APPROVED on his plan to take Katie. He knew Katie needed to be with family, but in his heart he admitted Eden was a better mother than Mandy would have been. It ached to admit it to himself, but it was true, nonetheless.

Eden's soft voice broke into his tortured thoughts. "You don't think we'll find them, do you? I thought you'd be glad we've gotten this much information."

"I am." He forced a note of cheerfulness into his voice. "I was just thinking about my future. Of course we'll find them. This is a great start. When we get home, I'll hop on the Internet and see what I can find out about your aunt."

"Your future?"

Was that alarm in her voice? He nodded. "I can't be unemployed forever. I have enough money to last a few months, but I need to be looking for a job."

"Where will you look?" She bit her lip and turned to look at the passing landscape. "I'd hoped you'd join us for Thanksgiving."

"I'm not talking about leaving this week. But once the holiday is over, I really should start sending out some résumés. I doubt there are any jobs around here for someone with my background. I'll probably have to go to Texas."

She barely nodded, and Josh's fingers tightened on the steering wheel. For a crazy moment he wanted to put his arms around her and tell her he'd never leave her and the children. What had gotten into him? His aching heart seemed to find solace and comfort in Eden's presence, and it had to stop. He answered to no one, and he liked it that way. This woman would tie him in one place, and he'd never see the world again.

*I've seen all the world I need to see.* He shrugged the thought away and concentrated on the road. He liked his life just fine the way it was. There was no reason to let a woman's green eyes tempt him from the life he'd chosen years ago. With just Katie, he could still pack up and move whenever he pleased. Eden would just complicate matters.

They stopped for supper at a truck stop near Indianapolis. The parking lot was full, so Josh knew the food must be good, though the place looked like it would have been right at home along Route 66 forty years ago.

Their table and every other one in the place had a small jukebox on it, back against the wall. The waitress, her jaw working as she popped her gum, took their order, then brought a high chair for Katie.

When their food was brought, Katie threw her green beans on the tile floor and refused to eat more than a few bites. Eden cleaned her up and shrugged. "She's not a good traveler. She likes her own bed and the other children."

"She'll learn to travel better," Josh said. He nearly winced when he realized what he'd said.

Eden looked at him strangely, a question in her eyes. "I don't travel much," she said. "She has no reason to get used to it."

"Do you want her to just see the four corners of Wabash? Don't you want her to experience the world and not spend her whole life in a little backwater town?"

"You're still planning to take her, aren't you?"

Eden's voice was soft, and Josh dared a glance at her. The steely glint in her eye was at odds with her gentle voice, and he knew she would never let Katie go without a fight. He didn't want to fight with her.

Josh's shoulders tightened. "Yes," he admitted. "I love her. She's all I have left of Mandy; she's the only family I have."

"I'm sorry, Josh." Eden laid a hand on his arm. "I'm sorry you lost your sister. But Katie belongs with me. I'll never give her up. Never."

The finality in her words struck Josh like a blow. He'd only been deceiving himself. There was no way to convince her to give Katie up without a fight. And he didn't want to fight with Eden. He was beginning to care way too much about her. His thoughts shied away from that direction again.

He forced a smile. "You've said your piece. Are you ready to head for home?"

Eden plucked Katie from the high chair. "Let me take her to the rest room and change her diaper first."

They were silent on the trip home. Josh mulled over his options. He could find a lawyer and take it to court. He thought he might have a good chance if the jury realized he had no family left except for Katie. But the thought of doing that to Eden hurt. No, his best bet was still to find her family. If she had her own kin, maybe she would realize just how important it was for Katie to be with him.

Light spilled from the windows of the house, and Josh felt a warm glow of homecoming. He stopped the van in the driveway and got out to lift Katie from her seat. Eden held the front door open for him, then shut it behind them.

Belinda was curled up on the sofa. The fire flickered in the fireplace, and the scent of the apple candle burning on the mantle added to the homey glow of the room.

Belinda put her book down and smiled at them. "There you are. Rick came and took Andi home with him, and the children are all asleep."

"I found my aunt's address!" Eden burst out. "She lives in Michigan. That's where Timmy is."

"What about your sisters?" Belinda stood and stretched.

"Molly heard Crista went to Arizona, but she has no idea where or who took her. She hadn't heard anything about Angelina."

"Well, at least it's a start." Belinda hugged Eden, then picked up her coat. "Maybe you'll find some of your family by Christmas. What a holiday that would be!"

Eden nodded. "I'm almost afraid to hope for that." She walked Belinda to the hall.

While Eden saw her friend out, Josh carried Katie to bed. She slept heavily, her thumb in her mouth. He pulled her shoes off and slipped her out of her coat. Trying to decide if he should put her in her pajamas and risk wakening her, he didn't hear Eden come up behind him.

She went to the bureau and pulled out a pink fleece sleeper. Josh lowered the side of the crib and laid Katie down. He watched while Eden deftly changed her without waking the sleeping toddler.

"You're good at that," he said. Again, doubts assailed him. Eden knew so much more than he did about raising a child. He'd had no experience. But he had a lot of love. He could learn.

She smiled. "Katie is a sound sleeper. You go on down and see what you can find on the Net. I'll be down as soon as I check on the other children."

Josh nodded and went down the hall to the stairs. He almost tripped over a fire truck on the stairs but caught the railing just in time. He picked up the toy to make sure Eden didn't stumble and carried it with him to the living room. Within minutes he was looking for Eden's aunt on the Internet.

Eden came in the room, yawning and stretching her back. "Any luck?"

He shook his head. "No trace of her."

"Could we go to Michigan and talk to some neighbors?"

Her eyes sparkled with determination, and he hoped he wasn't setting her up for a major disappointment. "I'm game if you are." Anything to keep that sparkle in her eyes. And as long as he felt needed, he wouldn't leave. The time of his departure could be pushed back once again. He wasn't ready to walk away from Eden. Josh shied away from examining just why that was true.

# Chapter 10

The aroma of roasting turkey filled the kitchen. The tart scent of cranberries mingled with that of pumpkin and cinnamon. Eden had tied balloons everywhere to add a festive touch. She loved Thanksgiving. This year she had something to be even more thankful for. Her heart filled with thankfulness to God for the gift of Katie. Her daughter. The thought sent chills of joy up her spine. This would be their first holiday as a real family.

And Josh would be here as well. Eden knew the camaraderie would soon be gone. One day he would decide it was time to move on, find a job, and settle down somewhere. The thought deflated the bubble of joy she'd been enveloped in, and she sighed. Picking up the wooden spoon, she began to beat the pumpkin mixture for pies.

The doorbell rang. "Samantha, would you get the door?" she called.

She heard Samantha's footsteps echo along the oak floors. A couple of minutes later Josh's broad shoulders filled the doorway. He wore black jeans with a garnet sweater. His hair was still a bit damp from his morning shower, and the spicy scent of his cologne added to his masculine presence. Eden forced her attention back to her pies.

He sniffed. "Smells great. I really appreciate your taking pity on me today. This will be the first real Thanksgiving dinner I've had in over ten years. Can I set the table or something?"

"Sure. But just set it for four."

He raised an eyebrow. "I thought the house seemed quiet. Where are the rest of the kids?"

"With their families for the day."

"Even Cory?"

She'd been trying not to think of that. "I tried to talk social services out of it. Cory's advocate said his mother had assured her the stepfather wouldn't be there today."

"And they believed her?" Josh's voice raised.

"They want to give her a chance. The goal is always to get the family back together."

"It shouldn't always be. When they hurt the child like that man hurt Cory, they lose the right." Josh scowled. "I'd like to get my hands on him."

So would Eden. She forced a smile. "They've been warned they'll go to jail if any harm comes to him. And that would be the least of their worries once you and I found out."

Josh's worried frown didn't dissipate. "We'd better pray for him today, the other kids too."

Eden had already done just that, but the fact that Josh felt comfortable enough with her to suggest they pray together touched her. She wiped her hands on her apron, then took both Josh's hands in hers and bowed her head.

The strength of his fingers calmed her heart. Josh cleared his throat. "Lord, we know You love these little ones even more than we do. We ask that You protect them today, give them a good day with their parents, and work in the lives of those families to help them come together again. In Jesus' name. Amen."

"Amen," Eden echoed. Josh didn't release her fingers, and she raised her head, catching his gaze with her own. His dark eyes seemed filled with an emotion Eden was afraid to name, even to herself.

"You have flour on your cheek," he said in a gentle voice. He let go of her left hand but kept a tight grip on her right. His fingers brushed her cheek, and he rubbed the smudge away with his thumb.

The moment drew out between them, and Eden was almost afraid to breathe. He pulled her into his arms and rested his chin on the top of her head. It felt right, as though she fit there, as though his arms were made for her. She breathed in the scent of his cologne and wrapped her arms around his waist without thinking. His heart thumped beneath her ear, a slow, steady beat that filled her with confidence. This was a man who wasn't afraid to be tender, who could laugh at himself yet knew when to be serious. A man who loved children and wasn't afraid to show it. Her man.

The thought shocked her, and she dropped her arms and would have stepped away, but Josh tipped her chin up, and his lips claimed hers. Eden closed her eyes again and tasted the sweetness of his kiss. Tentative but tender, his lips were firm yet soft. She cautioned herself not to read too much into it. Men kissed women all the time without promising anything. She had to guard her heart.

His gaze flickered over the strands of hair trailing around her face. "Eden, I—"

"I'm hungry!" Samantha stood in the middle of the kitchen, her hands on her hips in a belligerent pose.

She was jealous. Eden could see it in her resentful glance. She smiled at her foster child, but Samantha's stern gaze didn't falter. Her defiant gaze flickered from Eden to Josh, then she bit her lip and looked at the floor.

"It's almost ready." Eden stepped away from Josh. Trying not to wonder what he had been about to say, she turned and slid the pies in the oven, then set the timer.

"I'll get Katie," Josh said. "Want to come with me, Sam?"

The little girl's face brightened, and she shot Eden a triumphant glance before practically skipping out of the kitchen with Josh. Eden managed not to smile. Bless Josh for knowing just how to soothe the little girl. He had a knack with children that was unusual in a man. Maybe Katie *did* belong with him.

The thought was a stab of agony to her heart. She'd just told him it was important for families to be together if possible. That was the goal she worked for, the aim she always kept in mind for her foster children. Just because she wanted Katie didn't make it right. She pushed the knowledge away. Katie was hers, she couldn't give her up. But guilt gnawed at her. God couldn't want that of her, could He? She wouldn't believe it.

Her hands trembled as she carried the food to the table. Tears blurred her vision, and she took a deep, calming breath. She was just being emotional because of the holiday. They would enjoy the meal, play some games afterward, and she would forget all about this prick of guilt. It was nothing.

By the time Josh brought Katie down from upstairs, Eden had recovered her composure. She mustn't let him know she'd even thought about giving up Katie. He would be all over that idea like a duck on a June bug.

Katie snuggled against Josh's chest like it was made for her. Eden knew the feeling, and a smile curved her lips. She turned away before Josh could see it and ask why she was smiling. Heat bloomed in her cheeks at the thought of explaining herself.

The meal passed slowly and amicably. Katie even managed to keep most of her food on the tray of her high chair. Samantha chattered to Josh and seemed to have forgotten her earlier pique. When the buzzer on the oven went off, Eden took the pies out to cool. They would have dessert a little later in the afternoon.

Josh and Samantha pitched in to help wash dishes, and Eden couldn't help imagining what it would be like for them all to be a family. She had to stop that kind of thinking. Josh would be appalled if he knew where her imagination had taken her.

When the kitchen was clean, they all went to the living room. Eden flopped onto the sofa. "I'm pooped," she said.

"Oh, no, you don't," Josh said. "You know what was always traditional at our house on Thanksgiving afternoon?"

"Resting and playing games?" she asked hopefully.

He grabbed her hand and pulled her to her feet. "Nope. Putting up the Christmas tree."

She started shaking her head. "I always buy a live tree. There's nothing open today."

"Wrong again." He pulled her to the front door and opened it. A magnificent Christmas tree leaned beside the door. It was at least nine feet tall with full branches and no holes.

"Where did you get that?" Eden held her breath in awe.

"I bought it yesterday and brought it over when I came. You get the decorations out, and I'll bring it in." He lifted the tree and carried it through the door Samantha held open for him.

"He told me about it," Samantha said smugly.

"You kept the secret well." Eden squeezed her shoulder as she passed, and Samantha smiled, all traces of her earlier fit of temper gone.

Samantha kept an eye on Katie while Eden hurried up the stairs to the attic. The attic steps were steep, and she paid attention to her feet as she climbed them. She'd stumbled many times on them. Josh came up behind her.

He looked around. "I love these old attics. They don't build houses like this anymore."

"Sometimes I come up here and imagine these boxes are filled with things from my grandparents. Silly, isn't it?"

"No, it's not." He draped an arm around her. "Family is important. And you've made a family here, Eden. This is a great thing you're doing, something to be proud of."

Heat touched her cheeks, and a matching glow filled her. Sometimes she wondered if she should give up the fight, get a real job instead of working for the state with these children. She'd seen the way people looked at her when she said she was a foster parent. The abuses in the system were legion. But she cared too much about the children to abandon them.

She turned away and began loading his arms with boxes. "I have so many ornaments the children made. Samantha will be glad to see the one she made for me last year."

Josh carried a load downstairs, and Eden followed with her arms full of boxes too. Samantha was nearly bouncing in her excitement. Eden put her load down and held out her arms for Katie.

"You'll want to help Josh decorate," she said. "This little munchkin needs to be up and out of the way."

Katie came to her willingly. As she watched Josh and Samantha decorate the tree, she wished this could be the first of a lifetime of Christmases spent together. She nearly gasped at the realization. She loved him! When had that happened? She couldn't love him. He would leave her just like everyone else in her family had done. It wasn't safe to love him. But how did she kill love once it began? He had the ability to rip her heart out and take her daughter as well. But what would he say if she asked him to stay, to find a job here, and help her raise Katie?

# Chapter 11

J osh couldn't figure Eden out. Thanksgiving she had been so warm and sweet. Since then she'd kept him at arm's length. She avoided being alone with him, and her green eyes warned him to keep his distance.

He didn't want to keep his distance. Those minutes in the kitchen on Thanksgiving had awakened him to the fact that this emotion he felt when he looked at her was love. He was in love for the first time in his life. With a woman who smelled of baby powder and formula instead of expensive perfume and hair spray. A woman who thought watching a video with a roomful of kids more fun than going out to dinner. The realization astonished and delighted him. Eden was what he'd been looking for all his life. But how did he break through that wall she had around her?

Today might be a start. He glanced at Eden sitting beside him in the SUV. They had the whole day to themselves in their search for Selma Johnson. Belinda was holding down the fort, and it would be just he and Eden together today. They were nearly there, and Eden hadn't said two words to him.

She didn't look happy. Staring through the window, her profile was somber with no evidence of her dimples. Josh hadn't seen them since Thanksgiving. Had he gone too far with that kiss? Maybe she wasn't interested in him that way. His spirits sank at the thought.

"Penny for your thoughts," he said.

She turned and gave a halfhearted smile. "They're not worth that much. I wasn't really thinking, just staring out the window."

"Scared about your aunt?"

She shook her head. "I think I'll find my family eventually. I'm content with that."

"What's wrong between us, Eden? You've been acting strange since last week on Thanksgiving. I thought we had a nice time."

"I did, too," she said. She turned her head again. "Nothing's wrong. I've just been busy with making gifts for the children for Christmas. I'm sorry if I seem a little distant." She swiveled around to look at him. "Tell me, where are you planning to find a job?"

"Where did that come from?" No telling what thoughts were running through that pretty head.

"Do you plan to buy a house so you can have Katie stay occasionally?"

"I would like to find a large house like yours, one where she could feel at home. You might want some help with her once you find your siblings. You'll be busy catching up on old times."

She jerked her head up and stared at him through narrowed eyes. "Is that why you're helping me look for my brother and sisters?"

He felt his face burn, and he turned his attention back to the road. Guilt had to be written all over his face, for he heard her catch her breath.

"That's it, isn't it? That's why you've been spending so much time with us, why you're so determined to find my siblings. You think once I find them, I'll let you have Katie!"

"Look, Eden, maybe that was the reason at the beginning, but I soon learned to care about you and the kids. I really want to help you find your family." He needed to find a place to pull over. Driving down the road was no place to declare his love to a woman. It would have to wait.

"And I was feeling guilty for keeping Katie from you. I had even begun to think she belonged with you!" Eden's voice was choked with tears, and she bit her lip, then turned to stare stonily out the window.

How did he answer that? He swallowed and tried to think how to say he loved her. Did he just spit it out? Good grief, they were driving down the freeway! He wasn't going to propose in this kind of situation. He had it all planned, and this wasn't in the plan. He wanted them all to be together; he didn't want to take Katie from her.

"She's all I have left of my family," he said lamely. That would have to do until the right time.

She didn't answer him as he turned onto her aunt's street. It was lined with old oak and maple trees that hid modest, two-story homes. He gritted his teeth and pulled the SUV to the curb. Jumping out, he started to come around to open her door, but she hopped out before he could get there. He put his hand on her arm, but she jerked away.

"Don't touch me," she said. "You used me, Josh. You

used my need to find my family for your own purposes. I thought you cared about me." Her voice choked off, and she marched ahead of him to the house where her aunt used to live.

"Eden, please—"

"I don't want to talk to you right now, Josh. Let's stop while we're still civil." She rapped on the door, painted red with off-white trim.

Josh fell silent, and his own temper rose. Women! They wouldn't listen to reason.

❈

Eden masked her pain with anger. Josh's betrayal hurt more than she'd imagined. By the time she'd tried to protect her heart, it was already too late. He didn't deserve Katie. The sooner he was gone, the better. She could nurse her hurt and figure out a way to get over him. When they got back, she would tell him it was best if he left.

She felt him glowering at her back as she waited on the front stoop of the house. Straightening her shoulders, she rapped at the door again.

"I'm coming, hold your horses." Her gray hair scraped back in a bun, a short woman nearly as wide as she was tall opened the door and peered at them through thick glasses.

"Are you. . .Selma Johnson?" Eden heard her own voice quiver and bit her lip.

"Selma Johnson. Now there's a name I haven't heard in years." The woman took off her glasses and polished them on her stained apron. She perched the glasses back on her nose and opened the door wider. "Don't stand there looking like two possums in the porch light. Come in, and we'll jaw awhile."

Eden stared back uncertainly at Josh. Who was this woman? Obviously not her aunt. Josh gave Eden a slight nod, and she stepped through the door. The odor of sautéing onions hung in the air.

"Cooking liver and onions. I got plenty if you folks would care to join me for lunch."

"No, thanks," Josh said. "We won't be able to stay that long."

"You young folks, always rushing hither and yon," the woman grumbled. She pointed toward a chintz sofa, its once vivid reds and greens faded to a soft mixture of pastels.

Eden slipped off her coat and sank onto the sofa. "I'm Eden Walters, and this is Josh Leland. Selma Johnson is my aunt."

"Selma and I were neighbors for over fifty years. Maybe you heard her mention me. Gabby Summers."

Eden shook her head. "I'm sorry; I never knew my aunt. I only met her one time."

"Say, you must be one of them Richmond kids!"

Eden's heart sped up. "Yes, yes, that's right. I'm the oldest."

"It were a shame, splitting you young 'uns up like that. I told Selma it weren't right, but your aunt had a head as hard as a new walnut. It was hard enough for her to raise young Timmy, she said."

"Do you know where they are? Timmy and my aunt?" Eden put in eagerly. "I'm trying to find him and my sisters."

Gabby shook her head. "Selma's been gone near ten years," she said. "Timmy went off somewhere last I heard. I don't recall just where that was." Her voice trailed off in a mumble, and she stared vacantly toward the floor.

Eden shot a glance at Josh. He leaned forward and touched Gabby's arm. "Mrs. Summers?"

Her eyes focused again, and she shook her head. "It's gone, young Eden. Give me your number, though. If I happen to hear from Timmy or remember where he went, I'll call you."

Eden nearly gasped from the pain of disappointment. So close, and to come up empty-handed. It was almost more than she could bear.

Josh rose. "Thanks for your help, Mrs. Summers." He pulled a business card from his wallet. "I'm putting Eden's phone number here," he said, scribbling the number on the back.

"Sometimes things come to me in the night." Mrs. Summers took it, then turned away and tucked it into her purse.

Josh picked up Eden's coat, and she slipped her arms into it. All her bright hopes for the day lay in ashes. He squeezed her hand, and she choked back a sob. What was wrong with her? This lady might remember something. At least it was something to hope for.

Mrs. Summers led the way to the door. Eden paused in the doorway. "Was Timmy happy?" she asked softly.

"Oh my, yes. Such a lovely child. So well-mannered, good in school, very helpful. He used to rake my leaves in the fall and wouldn't take a penny for it."

Eden's eyes flooded with tears. "I don't suppose you have a picture of him?"

Mrs. Summers shook her head. "I'm sorry, little lady, I don't. But you keep your chin up. If I could just remember where he went off to, you might track him down through that."

"Thanks for your help." Josh laid a hand on Mrs. Summers's shoulder, then followed Eden through the door and pulled it shut behind him.

Eden stumbled toward the SUV. Gulping back her tears, she threw open the door and practically fell into her seat. Josh slid into the driver's seat. She felt his eyes on her face, and her lips trembled.

"Aw, Sweetie, don't cry."

Eden fished in her purse for a tissue. "I'm not crying," she quavered. "I never cry."

Josh touched the back of her head, and a sob escaped Eden. "She's dead. My aunt is dead and with her all hope of finding Timmy and my sisters."

He pulled her into his arms. "It's only a delay. We'll find them."

"You have to leave." With his arms around her and her nose buried in his chest, the tension in her shoulders began to ease.

"Not before your birthday tomorrow."

She pulled away and scrubbed at her face with the tissue. "How did you know December fourth is my birthday?"

"You told me, remember?" Regret twisted his lips, and his reluctance to let her go warmed her.

Eden sniffed. "I'd hoped to find them for my birthday." She laughed shakily. "Silly, isn't it? For some reason I thought my birthday would be the start of a new life for me."

"It's not silly. And you never know what tomorrow might bring." Josh turned the key, and the SUV roared to life. "Let's go home to our girl."

# Chapter 12

E den heard the children giggling with Josh in the kitchen. They had banished her to the living room while they prepared her birthday dinner. Josh had been acting strangely all day. She caught him staring at her several times with a bemused smile on his face.

He'd arrived this morning with his arms full of helium balloons. Katie had squealed with delight, and Eden was touched he remembered how much she liked balloons. Samantha had motioned him into the kitchen, and they'd scurried back and forth with their decorations.

Eden tried to occupy herself with wrapping Christmas presents. She'd been torn over whether or not to give Josh a gift. Then she had hit on the idea of making him up a scrapbook of Katie's life so far. Filled with pictures and cute captions, the scrapbook was almost too precious to give away. Josh would love it, though.

Smoke billowed from the kitchen. She jumped to her feet and ran through the kitchen door. "Where's the fire?" She grabbed the fire extinguisher by the back door.

Josh grinned sheepishly. "False alarm. I spilled some cake batter in the oven." The kids, including Katie, were busy decorating her cake. Katie had icing in her hair.

Eden wrinkled her nose, and he leaned over and kissed it. A rush of pleasure soared through her. What was with him today? She couldn't figure him out. He seemed carefree somehow.

"We're almost ready," he told her. "You go in the living room, and we'll bring the cake in there."

Eden laughed and went back to the living room. She didn't know when a birthday of hers had elicited such excitement. Usually there was no celebration other than a cake she baked for herself and the balloons she bought the kids. Now all these balloons were for her. The living room was full of them, bobbing from the ceiling, clustering around the Christmas tree, their ribbons hanging down like confetti.

She didn't have long to wonder. Josh came through the kitchen door carrying the cake. It canted to the left and drooped with runny icing. The candles flickered and sputtered wax over the top and left drips like wax petals. Eden bit her lip to keep from laughing.

Samantha and Amelia carried packages wrapped with more tape than paper. Katie's gift was clutched in her chubby hands, and the bow was now in her hair. The children placed them on the coffee table with a flourish.

"Sit down, Eden." Amelia clapped her hands in excitement.

Eden obeyed and sank onto the sofa.

"Mama," Katie said. Her dimples flashing, she offered her tattered package.

Eden took it. "Thank you, baby girl." Katie tried to help her open it, and Eden let her rip the wrapping paper. Inside was a candle. Katie sniffed. "It smells good, doesn't it?"

Katie nodded, then Cory sidled up to Eden and held out his package. "Uncle Josh helped me find it," he said.

*Uncle Josh?* Eden glanced at Josh and saw a smile of pleasure curve his lips. He'd worked so hard to get close to Cory. That was one of the reasons she loved him; he cared so much for others. His big heart had taken in all the children.

One by one she opened the packages from the children. There were bath salts, stationery, a lace throw for the piano, and a box of chocolates. Josh had gone to a lot of work with the children.

She sat back against the sofa and sighed with pleasure. It was the nicest birthday she could remember. Josh smiled and pulled the ribbon on a balloon in the corner of the room. He came toward her with a grin, but fear seemed to lurk behind his eyes.

He held out the balloon ribbon. "You'll have to break the balloon to get your gift from me."

"You didn't need to get me anything. You've already spent way too much money. We all know where the money came from for the gifts from the children."

"This is something special." He handed her a pin. "Give it a stab."

She laughed and took the pin. Poised over the balloon, she could see a stuffed bear inside. She held her breath and pricked the balloon with the pin. There was a loud *pop* then the bear dropped into her lap. Eden picked it up and hugged it.

"Mine!" Katie said. She tried to grab it, but Eden

held it away from her.

"No, Sweetie, it's Mommy's."

Josh was looking more uncertain. "What's wrong?" she asked him.

"Um, nothing's wrong. Did you see what the bear was holding?"

Eden glanced down at the bear in her hands. A small, velvet jewelry box was in the bear's hands. Her heart began to pound against her ribs, and she couldn't think.

Josh slid to his knees and took the box from the bear. Opening it, he held up a lovely marquis diamond ring.

Eden gasped, and tears filled her eyes. Her gaze sought Josh's, and the love she saw reflected on his face made it hard to catch her breath.

"I love you, Eden Walters, and I want to spend the rest of my life with you. Will you marry me? Before you answer, I want you to know I got a job here in Wabash so we won't be leaving our kids. I'm going to be working at Ford Meter Box in their export department. And I'm handy with a hammer. I can fix this old house up and make it a traffic stopper." He paused to catch a breath, and Eden laughed.

"All those things don't matter," Eden said softly. She cupped Josh's face in her hands. "I love you, Josh. And Katie loves you. The thought of your leaving has kept me awake nights. Yes, I'll marry you."

"Yippee!" Cory began to dance around the middle of the room, and Samantha and Amelia joined him. Katie tried to dance, too, but was only able to run to keep up with the older kids.

Josh leaned forward and kissed her. The love in his

kiss brought tears flooding to her eyes.

Josh pulled away and dug in his pocket. "There's one more thing," he said, pulling out a piece of paper. "I've got a lead on Crista. It looks like she might be in Arizona. How does Phoenix sound for a honeymoon? Warm sunshine, blue skies."

"You make the sun shine for me," she said, leaning forward to kiss him again. As he took her in his arms, she knew her haven in his arms was the home she'd longed for all her life. Wherever Josh and Katie were would be home.

## COLLEEN COBLE

Colleen and her husband, David, have been married thirty years this October. They have two great kids, David Jr. and Kara. Though Colleen is still waiting for grandchildren, she makes do with the nursery inhabitants at New Life Baptist Church. She is very active at her church where she sings and helps her husband with a young adult Sunday school class. She enjoys the various activities with the class, including horseback riding (she needs a stool to mount) and canoeing (she tips the canoe every time). A voracious reader herself, Colleen began pursuing her lifelong dream when a younger brother, Randy Rhoads, was killed by lightning when she was thirty-eight. *Heart Full of Love* is her fifth novella. Her seven novels may be ordered from Barbour Publishing.

# Ride the Clouds

by Carol Cox

"Sing to God, sing praise to his name,
extol him who rides on the clouds—
his name is the LORD—and rejoice before him.
A father to the fatherless,
a defender of widows,
is God in his holy dwelling."
PSALM 68:4–5

# Prologue

Crista McDaniel eased her foot off the accelerator and brought her car to a stop on the shoulder of Deer Valley Road. Ignoring the hum of traffic on the interstate behind her, she settled into a comfortable position and opened the lid of her mocha latte. Sipping the steaming drink, she turned her gaze toward the mountains to the east. Long shadows took form amidst the saguaros and sagebrush between her and the jagged peaks and gradually swelled into rounded outlines. Lights flared, and the shapes rose from the ground with stately majesty and hovered above the earth, glowing in the predawn dimness.

One by one, the hot air balloons lifted into the lightening sky, their brilliant hues in vivid contrast to the pink streaks of dawn. Crista stared, transfixed, her gaze never wavering from the floating giants until they all hung suspended above her. With a lingering glance, she turned the key in the ignition and swung her car around to the on-ramp, joining the early morning southbound traffic on I-17.

# Chapter 1

Remember, the three biggest time thieves you'll deal with are disorganization, indecision, and procrastination. See how they creep into your lives this week. Next class period we'll talk about how you can deal with them."

Crista straightened her stack of class notes with an efficient tap and looked across the lectern at her new students. When North Phoenix Community College first approached her about teaching short-term evening classes on time management, she'd refused abruptly. Providing training in a corporate setting was a far cry from teaching everyone from college students to harried housewives to retirees. The college's persistence and her eventual capitulation a year ago surprised her almost as much as her enjoyment of the class.

At the close of the opening class this second summer session, Crista felt gratified by the enthusiasm her students showed. She had seen lots of eye contact and plenty of note-taking, but not one sign of boredom.

"Please pick up a class syllabus on your way out." She set the papers on a small table near the door. "You'll find an outline of points I plan to cover in each session. Look them over and let me know if there's something you're interested in that isn't listed, or if you see a topic you'd like to explore in greater depth. I'll expect your input next time we meet."

She scooped up her teaching notes and filed them in her briefcase, smiling at each departing student. Quite a varied lot, she noted. Out of twenty pupils, only about half fit the profile she'd originally expected. Tonight's group included several business majors, at least two grandmothers, and several women who simply wanted help scheduling all the activities their busy families were involved in.

Funny how things worked out. As little as she'd wanted to begin teaching in the first place, the widely varied backgrounds of her students were what convinced her that a market for her services existed far beyond the traditional corporate setting. Without that seemingly unimportant step, she might never have broken away from her job to become a freelance efficiency consultant.

Crista snapped the locks on her briefcase and waited for the remaining student to leave so she could switch off the classroom lights. Instead, he paused in front of her. "I enjoyed the class," he said in a warm voice. "I can tell I'm going to learn a lot."

"Thanks." Crista found herself responding to the friendly light in his sky blue eyes. She tried to remember his name from the introductions earlier. "Brad Morgan, right?"

His smile broadened, forming creases in his cheeks. "Do you include memory-improvement techniques in the course, too?"

Crista matched his smile with one of her own. "Put that on your list of things you want to study. As I recall, you're here to learn ways to improve your business operations."

"Right again, and very impressive." His tone became more serious. "Actually, I need to learn more than just how to streamline things; I need to get a handle on the whole concept of being in charge."

Crista raised a quizzical eyebrow and reached for the light switch.

"Let me carry that for you." Brad picked up her briefcase and waited in the hallway while she locked the classroom door. "Would you mind answering a couple of questions on the way to the parking lot?"

Crista hesitated, then nodded agreement. They walked toward the exit while she waited for Brad to continue.

"I never intended to be a business owner," he explained, pushing open the outside door. A warm blanket of air enveloped them. "My uncle owned J&R Machining. He didn't have any kids, so when he passed away six months ago, he left the place to me."

"Had you worked for him for long?"

Brad grimaced. "I never worked for him at all." He laughed at Crista's startled expression. "Believe me, I felt the same way. The business was important to my uncle. He built it up from scratch. In a way, I think he nurtured it like he would have a child. He took great pride in it, and it's done well. His plan was to build it up further, retire in a few years, and let the income take care of his and my aunt's financial needs for the rest of their lives. The idea seemed to be working fine; he just didn't live long enough to reap the benefits."

Brad shook his head slowly. "Being asked to take over came as a total surprise to me, but he and I were always close. He knew I'd do anything I could to help him. He counted on me to see this through, and Aunt Rachel's depending on me. I just hope I can live up to their expectations."

Crista stopped beside her car and leaned against the driver's door. "You have quite a challenge ahead of you." She tilted her head and studied his face. "But you already know that. Being willing to admit you have a lot to learn is a big step in the right direction."

Brad grinned. "It looks like I've come to the right place to get started. Any suggestions on what I'll need to know in addition to the work you'll be assigning?"

"Good question. We'll cover a lot in class, but you'll need to learn much more. What's your background? Do you have managerial experience, or are you starting from square one?"

Brad raked his fingers through his dark brown hair and gave her a rueful smile. "Somewhere below square one, if you want the truth. You're looking at a rank beginner."

Crista couldn't keep her lips from twitching. "So we're talking about more than a slight deficiency here?"

"More like utter desperation. Do you take on special projects?"

Crista considered the prospect, then nodded. "I can loan you some books that will give you a start. We'll see where you want to go from there."

"Is there any way I can get them from you before the

next class? I don't think I have a minute to lose."

"Well. . ." She made it a policy not to socialize with her students, but his predicament touched her. "Where's your business located?"

"Twenty-first Avenue, just south of McDowell." He handed her a business card.

"That'll work. How about if I drop them off on my way to the airport Thursday morning?"

"I've run you out of town already?"

Crista laughed and unlocked her car door. "I do a lot of traveling. I have a seminar in Ohio this weekend."

His smile broadened. "That'll be great. See you Thursday."

❄

Crista strolled into J&R Machining, her nose wrinkling at the acrid smell of machine oil. The harried receptionist took a moment between calls to point out Brad's door at the end of the corridor. Crista took her time, noting the flurry of activity with both approval and concern. The business obviously had potential, but it needed a firm grip on the reins to keep it headed in the right direction.

She paused before knocking on the open door and took in the scene before her. Brad, shirtsleeves rolled up over muscular forearms, cradled the phone between his chin and shoulder and scrabbled frantically through the mound of papers scattered across his desk.

"Uh-huh, uh-huh." He tugged a paper from the bottom of a stack, then tossed it aside and renewed his search. "I'm sure we can beat that price. Just let me pull our spec sheet and get the particulars for you." His confident tone belied the increasingly desperate way he rummaged through the disorganized heap.

Crista leaned against the doorjamb, fascinated.

Brad's elbow dislodged a jumbled pile of papers, which slid to the floor despite his frenzied attempt to catch them. He vanished behind the desk for a moment, then reappeared holding a stapled packet aloft with an expression of triumph. "I have it right here," he announced in a matter-of-fact tone that made Crista bite her lip to keep from laughing out loud. "I'll fax it to you within the next few minutes."

He ended the call and glanced up, his eyes widening when he saw Crista. "How long have you been here?"

"Long enough to know you didn't sign up for my class a moment too soon." Crista handed him the books she carried.

Brad reached for them at the moment the phone rang. A haunted look crossed his face, and he walked past Crista to lean out of the doorway. "Bea!" he called to the receptionist. "Would you hold my calls for the next few minutes, please?"

He turned back to Crista and nodded at the books in his hand. "Thanks for taking the time to drop these off. Sorry about the interruptions. So what do these cover?"

"Some time management basics—setting goals and priorities, delegation. . ." Her gaze shifted to his desk. "Handling paperwork."

Brad followed her glance and winced. "My uncle Jess could lay his hands on anything he needed at a moment's notice, and the desk didn't look any better when he was here." He caught Crista's amused look. "Okay, a little better. But not much. I really am trying, but I just don't seem to be able to get a handle on everything the way he did."

His bleak look caught at Crista's heart. "There's hope," she promised. "And those books can point you in the right direction. At least you'll be making a start. Once you can put these things into practice—"

"Got a second, Brad? Oh, sorry." The stocky man who entered the office looked more irritated than remorseful.

"If you could give me just a few minutes, Nick." Brad's fingers raked a path through his hair.

"That's all right," Crista put in. "I'm just on my way out." She smiled and lifted her hand in a quick good-bye gesture, then started toward the exit. She had passed the receptionist's desk when Brad's voice echoed down the hall.

"Where do I start with these books?" he called. "Which one do I need the most?"

Crista glanced around. Bea spoke into the phone while two incoming lines rang insistently. Behind Brad, Nick drummed his fingers on the doorjamb. She gave Brad a gentle smile. "All of them."

❄

The airliner banked left over Lake Erie. The runways and terminal buildings of Cleveland Hopkins International Airport slid into the distance, and the city itself dwindled into a miniature landscape. Crista settled more comfortably into her seat with a satisfied sigh. The workshop had gone well, she thought, remembering the invitation she'd received to return for a more in-depth seminar in the spring.

Her gaze shifted out the window, and she leaned forward, watching the rolling farmland of Ohio pass by thousands of feet below. Ohio, the state of her birth. She stared intently, searching the depths of her being for some sense of connection or any spark of recognition. Nothing stirred within her.

She sighed, whether from regret or resignation, she wasn't sure. Somewhere down there lay Hillsboro, where she'd lived after becoming a part of the McDaniel family at age five, before their move to Arizona.

With practiced determination, Crista stifled the pang of longing that shot through her. No point in worrying about the dead past or birth parents who hadn't wanted her. The McDaniels had treated her arrival as their daughter as a highlight of their lives and had let her know every moment of the past twenty-four years how much they treasured her.

Fleeting questions danced through her mind, questions she thought she'd put to rest years before. What made her birth family give her up? Why hadn't she been good enough for them?

Pictures from her earliest days as Crista McDaniel showed a winsome child with long curls and huge hazel eyes. As often as she pored over the snapshots as a child, Crista couldn't see anything that would have made her parents not want her. The one remarkable thing about the photos had been the hint of sadness in those wide hazel eyes, and Crista was at a loss to pinpoint its source.

She turned away from the window, pulling a magazine from her briefcase. Better to leave such questions safely buried where they could cause her no heartache. She found immense satisfaction in her career and she loved her family with a fierce devotion. Life was good. Organized. Under control. No need to stir up doubts that would only lead to pain.

Thumbing through her magazine, she spotted an article titled "Twenty Ways to Streamline Your Work Space." Her thoughts flew to Brad Morgan, and she wondered how his weekend had gone. Crista leaned back against the headrest and closed her eyes, smiling at the memory of Brad's attempts to make light of the chaotic state of his office. She hoped he'd taken her seriously and had spent the past couple of days immersed in those books. If ever anyone needed to learn how to manage his time, Brad Morgan fit the bill.

Crista's smile broadened. What a challenge it would be to take him in hand and get him and his business organized! Her lips parted and her eyes flew open. Where had that thought come from? She had her seminars and her college class to keep her busy. Besides, she had a policy of keeping her relationship with her students confined to the classroom.

Then why had she broken that policy and gone out of her way to loan books to this particular student? The question accused her like a pointing finger. Because his was an extreme case, and his business was in danger of falling apart without immediate help, she told herself, bridling at the feeling that she had to be on the defensive. She had offered to drop off the books without a second thought, in the same way she would stop to render aid if she witnessed an accident.

Thus mollified, she reopened her magazine with a snap, determined to read every word between its covers on the way home.

# Chapter 2

Once again Crista watched her students file out the door. They chattered excitedly about the time wasters they'd identified this week, a sign they were putting classroom concepts into practice. She'd been able to meet her goal of matching all the names and faces by the second class of the session and had a better sense of which students had signed up for the class just for something to do and which would seriously pursue the strategies she would present over the course of the next few weeks.

Brad took his time putting away his notes and sidled up to her desk as the last students straggled out. "I brought these back." He held out her books. Crista suppressed a giggle when she saw the apple sitting atop the stack.

"Trying to bribe the teacher?" She raised one eyebrow in mock severity. Brad responded with a slow grin that sent a tingle up her spine. She took a quick count of the books and looked at him in surprise. "You've read them all already?"

"That's all I did this weekend except for going to church," he told her. "The more I read, the more I realized

I need all the help I can get." He shuffled his feet and cleared his throat. "Would it be totally inappropriate if I asked you out for coffee? There are a lot of things I read that I'd like to discuss, and it wouldn't be fair to the rest of the students to spend class time on my problems."

Crista hesitated, wondering whether she could take on this challenge and still maintain a professional distance between teacher and student. But it wouldn't be anything like a date, only the opportunity to give someone the extra help that might make all the difference between his failure and success.

❄

"I knew things weren't going as smoothly as they should," Brad confided, stirring cream into his coffee. "No surprises there. The books did help me get an idea of where I've been making some mistakes. I'm already spotting some of those time thieves you talked about, but I still don't know how to deal with them. Any suggestions?"

Crista sipped her latte and took a moment to think about her reply. "Let me give you a couple of examples based on what I saw last Thursday. No matter how hard you try, you're never going to accomplish anything if you don't make some significant changes, and soon. The telephone, for instance—does it ring incessantly?"

Brad propped his chin in his hand and nodded wearily. "Sometimes I think I spend more time answering that phone than doing anything else."

"You're probably right. But does anything productive come of it?"

"Not so you'd notice. Mostly it's clients wanting information on pricing, status of orders they've already placed, that kind of thing."

"So why are you answering those questions? Let your receptionist deal with that, or at least have her screen your calls and route things like that to someone else who can handle them. You're the boss, remember? You've got a company to run."

Brad flipped his notebook open and started scribbling.

"For the calls that do need to come to you, let your caller know right up front how much time you can give them. Don't let them ramble; get to the point, then get back to work. You can do that in a businesslike way and still be polite."

"Good," Brad muttered. "I don't want to run off customers."

"No, but you can't let them use you as a social outlet, either. And don't waste time looking for information while someone is holding on the phone." She grinned, remembering Brad's frantic search for the spec sheet. "If you can't lay your hands on whatever you're looking for instantly, let them know you'll get back with them later. Then follow through on that. You'll show them you value their time as well as your own, plus let them know you keep your word. Are you getting all this?"

"Just don't talk any faster." Brad shook his hand and flexed his fingers. "Sounds like I need to do some immediate restructuring."

"While you're at it," Crista continued, "do something about that desk. Set aside an evening or a day this weekend. I'll bet you could throw over half of those papers away. The rest need to be organized and filed by subject so you can find what you need when you need it. You'll be amazed at the difference it makes." Her mouth curved up in a playful grin. "And think what fun it'll be to find out what the surface of your desk looks like."

❄

Brad shot a quick glance at Crista then let his gaze linger on her face. Those enormous hazel eyes, usually so solemn, sparkled with mischief, and her impish smile revealed an unsuspected dimple at the corner of her mouth. His own lips curved upward in response.

"Thanks for the tips. I'll make some changes on handling the phone calls, and I promise I'll tackle that desk sometime this week."

❄

That fleeting glimpse of Crista's playful side stayed with Brad throughout the following week. When he cleared the last piece of paper from his desk after an all-day sorting marathon on Saturday, he could imagine her standing nearby, applauding his efforts.

He closed his eyes to picture her more clearly. With every approving nod, her shiny brown hair would sway across her shoulders in gentle rhythm, and the hint of a dimple would show at the corner of her mouth. Yes, he thought, shoving the last folder into its proper file, Crista would be proud of what he'd accomplished in only a few short days.

Why did that matter so much? The question stopped him cold. Brad hauled a trash bag full of papers to the Dumpster in the alley, deep in thought. Teacher or not, he realized he'd like to get to know Crista McDaniel on a more personal level.

He propped up the heavy Dumpster lid with one arm

and tipped in the bag with the other. "This is a real shock, Lord. Am I just being drawn to an attractive woman, or is this from You?"

He let the lid drop and trotted back to the building to lock up. Was Crista a believer? Their conversations so far had dealt with time management issues. Spiritual matters hadn't come up at all. He thought back to their last visit to the coffee shop. She hadn't let anything slip that would make him think she knew the Lord. But he hadn't said anything, either.

On the other hand, her actions spoke of kindness and concern for others. When they left their table to go to the register, a little girl had careened between the booths, barging right into Crista. Instead of snapping at her, Crista knelt beside the child to make sure she wasn't hurt. The little girl slipped plump arms around Crista's neck, and Crista gave her a quick squeeze in return. That seemed promising.

And when they paid their bills—separate checks at Crista's insistence—the cashier had given Crista an extra dollar in change. She hadn't noticed it until they were out in the parking lot and went straight back inside to square accounts. Would an unbeliever be that scrupulous?

He stretched his weary muscles and headed for his car. A hot shower and a session of prayer seemed in order.

❄

Droplets peppered the window, and Crista pulled back the curtains to enjoy the rain. With Phoenix getting only seven inches of rainfall a year, even a light sprinkle was an event she didn't want to miss. She settled back into her desk chair and slit open the next envelope in her stack of mail. Her face lit up with pleasure when she saw the confirmation for another seminar. The choice to set up her own Web page seemed to be paying off. This would be her tenth out-of-state seminar since last Christmas.

Double-checking the location and date, she jotted a brief note on her calendar and set up a file for the event, pleased that she'd be visiting North Carolina for the first time. When she stopped to think about it, she had as ideal a life as anyone could want—a loving family, an organized routine, and a job she loved. She'd worked hard to reach this point in her career and would have to work even harder to stay there, but the effort had been worth it.

She pulled her road atlas from her reference shelf and flipped it open to the page for North Carolina. Just exactly where was Wilmington? A quick search located its position not far from the coast on the Cape Fear River. A slow smile spread across her face. Maybe she'd schedule in an extra day for sightseeing and spend some time on the beach. Growing up in dry Arizona made the allure of so much water too tempting to pass up.

She chuckled at her mounting excitement. She ought to be able to find some wonderful gifts to bring back for the rest of her family, too. They teased her about her penchant for doing her Christmas shopping year-round, but they had to admit it paid off in the long run.

Speaking of family. . .Crista turned her attention to her planner. They'd be celebrating Lindsey's birthday on Sunday. A smug expression crossed her face. Her sister's present sat on the hall closet shelf, wrapped and ready. Her brother Rod probably wouldn't remember he needed to think about a present until Saturday evening.

Crista grinned, remembering Rod's panicked calls for last-minute advice in previous years. The family had been aware of her fondness for planning and efficiency long before she decided to make it her career. She knew it seemed strange to them when they first heard she planned to make a living out of being organized. It didn't fit the typical young-girl goals of being a teacher, nurse, or flight attendant, but it gave Crista a sense of fulfillment unlike any other she'd ever experienced.

Being organized meant being in charge of her life. It meant security and control. The McDaniel clan had eventually accepted her choice, although she suspected most of them shared her father's opinion when he pushed his glasses up on his balding forehead and told her, "I can't say I understand it, Honey, but if that's what you want, I'm behind you 100 percent." Only her mother seemed to understand her consuming need for structure, but the rest accepted her decision. Rather, they accepted her. That was enough.

Brad Morgan seemed to accept her, too. She closed her eyes, remembering his friendly smile and open manner. She found it easy to relax in his presence. It wouldn't be hard to get lost in those sky blue eyes.

Crista pulled her thoughts from Brad and checked her watch. Good, she could take a few more minutes before she had to get back to work. She leaned her elbows on her desk and propped her chin on her cupped hands, taking time to savor the sights and smells of a desert rain. Her sense of contentment grew.

"God sends rain on the just and the unjust," an elderly neighbor used to say. Crista didn't know that God spent much time considering how the weather He sent affected people, whether they were good or bad. But if He ever did spare a thought about Crista McDaniel, she'd suspect He'd worked overtime to give her a good life.

# Chapter 3

Brad loitered outside the classroom door. The more he'd prayed over the past few weeks, the more he felt God's urging to develop a deeper relationship with Crista.

It hadn't taken much persuasion. Tonight had been their last class meeting. If he missed this opportunity to move their relationship beyond the classroom level, he might not get another chance.

Two older ladies exited the classroom, talking a mile a minute. The one with tinted blue hair slowed her step and gave him a roguish wink. "Cliff had some questions she's trying to answer, but I'm sure she'll be out in a minute or two." Motioning to her companion to wait, she poked her head back inside the room and called, "Crista, you'd better get rid of that old geezer. There's someone out here who's a whole lot better-looking." Cackling gleefully, the two made their way to the exit.

White-haired Cliff appeared in the doorway and peered at Brad from beneath beetling brows. "You'd better be worth it, young fellow," he growled. With a playful poke in the ribs, he left Brad standing in the hallway.

Slowly, he reentered the classroom. Crista stacked her papers and packed her briefcase as efficiently as ever, but the spots of color high on her cheeks told him she hadn't been immune to the trio's needling.

"Are you up for coffee again?" he ventured, hoping their teasing hadn't scared her off.

He held his breath when she hesitated, then let it out in a whoosh of relief when she nodded assent and accompanied him to his SUV.

"How was your weekend?" he asked when they'd placed their orders, hoping a neutral question would break the uneasy silence.

She brightened. "Good. We celebrated my sister's birthday."

Finally, a topic that seemed safe. "Do you come from a big family?"

A faint shadow flitted across her face before she responded. "There are five of us. Mom, Dad, one son, and two girls. I'm in the middle."

Brad grinned. "As focused as you seem to be, I would have sworn you were a firstborn. So much for birth order." He took a bite of raspberry cheesecake and caught Crista's quick grimace. What was going on here? She obviously enjoyed spending time with her family. Why did talking about them make her so uncomfortable?

He tried another tactic. "Have you always lived in Phoenix?"

Crista blinked rapidly, then composed her features. "We moved here just before I started first grade. Before that, we lived in Ohio." She sipped her cappuccino and leaned against the booth's padded back, seeming more at ease. "My mom had problems with her health. Her asthma got so bad the doctor told my dad he needed to get her to a drier climate. You can't get much drier than Phoenix," she added with a grin.

Brad chuckled, relieved. Whatever had been bothering her, she seemed to have gotten past it. "That's the truth. My folks came from Oklahoma, but they moved here before I was born. My mom's taken up genealogy the past couple of years, and we've learned more about our ancestors than we ever really wanted to know. We tease her about it a lot, but I have to admit it's kind of nice to know about your roots." His smile faded at the dismal expression on Crista's face.

"What is it?" he asked, reaching out to cover her hand with his. "I feel like I said something wrong, but I don't know what it is."

Crista shook her head in a jerky movement. "It isn't you; it's me." She pulled her hand away and picked up her napkin, tearing tiny pieces from its edge. Without stopping her assault on the paper square, she looked up to meet his gaze. "The fact is, I'm adopted. I have no idea about biological ancestors, or roots, or anything like that."

A tiny smile played across her face. "I have the best family in the world, though, and I came to terms with the whole adoption thing a long time ago. I don't know what got into me just now. I'm sorry."

"You don't have any reason to apologize. I didn't mean to bring up a tender subject. Are your brother and sister adopted, too?"

"No, just me. They were born McDaniels. When I was four, I was placed in their home as a foster child.

They adopted me when I was five. Rod is two years older and Lindsey's three years younger, so I fit right in the middle. I really don't think about it much anymore. We're a family; how we got that way doesn't matter."

Brad felt a warm glow, surprised and pleased at her openness. "Do you know much about your birth family?"

The shuttered look returned. "No. I'm really not interested." Her fingers shredded more of the napkin into confetti. "So how are things going at your business?"

"I've made progress," he said, yielding to her obvious desire to change the subject. "I'm amazed at how much difference it's made just to have the responsibility for all those phone calls off my shoulders."

"Told you so." She patted the torn bits of paper into a neat pile. "What about your desk?" She raised a skeptical eyebrow.

"It's walnut."

Crista gasped delightedly. "You really did clear it off?"

"Of course. Didn't you expect your star pupil to follow orders?"

"No comment." Crista laughed and rose to accompany Brad to the register.

He laid his hand over hers when she started to open her purse. "This is my treat," he told her. "Tonight wasn't about business."

In the parking lot, he leaned against his fender, enjoying the balmy evening air. Crista joined him, only inches away. Brad wished he dared put his arm around her shoulder and pull her closer but refrained.

"Thanks for the coffee and the talk," she said. "I enjoyed it."

"Even if you had to listen to Cliff's heckling first?" he teased.

Crista laughed, a sound Brad decided he wanted to hear more often. "I guess it wasn't so bad." She twisted her fingers together. "And I really am sorry about getting so on edge about all that talk about my biological parents."

Brad frowned. "I wouldn't have brought any of that up if I'd known it would be a problem. I guess we all have issues that are sore spots."

Crista turned to face him. "You, too?"

Brad nodded, crossing his arms. "My dad is an alcoholic. He's a recovered alcoholic now, and these days we get along fine, but there were some times when I was growing up I'd just as soon forget."

Crista rested her hand on his arm. "That's a tough one. So how did you learn to handle it?"

"It wasn't easy. Nothing really worked. . .until I learned to turn the whole situation over to God." He studied her face, waiting for her reaction. When she stiffened and pulled away, he felt like he'd received a sledgehammer blow to the heart.

"I'm glad it helped you." Crista turned to open the passenger door.

Brad reached around to open it for her, trying to think of the right words to say. How could someone with such a sweet nature be so prickly about a mere mention of God?

❄

Crista stared out the window on the drive back to the campus, wishing the knot in her stomach would disappear. She'd hoped to get to know Brad better, and tonight things seemed to be progressing nicely. . .up until the point when he brought God into the conversation. The leaden weight of disappointment that settled in her chest unnerved her. What did his beliefs matter?

"I guess I said the wrong thing again." Brad's low-voiced comment brought her back to the present.

Crista sighed. "I believe in God. You can't look around and really think everything just happened by accident." She wet her lips. "But that's where it ends, as far as I can see. He started everything and put it into motion, but that's it. I don't see where He cares about any of us as individuals."

Brad didn't answer right away. "What about the people whose lives have changed because of Him?"

Crista pressed her lips together. "It's nice if they can pump themselves up and use that idea to help them through life, but I have my family. I don't need anything more."

"I see. You and your family seem really close." He paused, then added, "Did you ever go to church together?"

Crista relaxed, and a smile spread across her face. "At Christmas," she said. "Christmas is absolutely the best time of the year. All the giving, the sharing, spending time together. The tree and the lights." She sighed, lost in happy memories. "We used to go to the Christmas Eve service every year to watch the kids' program and hear the Christmas story."

Brad turned into the college parking lot and pulled to a stop beside Crista's car. "I don't get it." He swiveled in his seat to face her. "How could you enjoy the story of Christmas so much and still miss the idea that God cares about each one of us?"

Crista shook her head wearily. "Look, you spend Sundays going to church, right?"

He nodded, looking puzzled.

"You enjoy spending time with the people there?"

"Sure. Fellowship is a special part of it."

Crista smiled in triumph. "Well, that's what I do with my Sundays, too. I have fellowship—with my family—but I don't have to go to a church to do it."

Brad rested his arm on the steering wheel and leaned toward her. "There's more to it than just fellowship. I'm talking about a relationship with God."

The knot in Crista's stomach tightened. "And the people who know God are the ones you find in church, right?"

Brad hesitated, looking like he'd walked into a minefield and didn't know where to step next. "Right," he said, drawing the word out slowly.

"Then I'm not interested." She opened the door and got into her car before Brad could get out to help her.

She turned the key in the ignition and drove away, giving Brad only a brief wave of her fingers. By the time she reached her driveway, she was already rebuking herself for her rudeness.

"What is wrong with you?" she scolded, crunching across the buff gravel of her yard to her front door. "You blew a chance to make a good impression on him."

She let herself in and sank onto the couch. Brad seemed like a wonderful person and she felt a definite chemistry between them. Or did until she threw her temper tantrum, she reminded herself. But was it all her fault? Why did he have to bring God into their budding relationship?

If she hadn't been edgy about the adoption discussion, she probably wouldn't have overreacted like that. She needed to apologize. If the subject came up again, she'd have to hold her tongue. But maybe it wouldn't. Surely something like that couldn't dominate Brad's life.

❄

Brad stared at the ceiling, the twisted sheets attesting to his inability to sleep. "I guess that answered my question, didn't it, Lord?"

He punched his pillow and tried to find a comfortable position. He'd been so sure Crista believed. Her gentle spirit, her willingness to help. . .everything pointed that way. But her reaction tonight had set him straight. Now what?

There went the dating relationship he'd halfway mapped out. He'd seen too many friends ignore the biblical injunction against being unequally yoked and fall into the trap of dating an unbeliever. They'd been hurt or, worse, compromised their faith in situations that should never have been allowed to start. He'd consciously avoided entanglements like that and had been relieved at the trouble it had saved him.

But now. . .the sharpness of his disappointment surprised him. He'd only known Crista a brief time; surely it shouldn't be hard to forget her and move on.

"Then why can't I sleep?" He sat up and leaned against the headboard, wrapping his arms around his knees. Try as he might, he couldn't shake the feeling that God had brought Crista into his life for a purpose. Could it be possible that God intended him to know her strictly as a friend, as someone placed in her life to help lead her to Christ?

Brad sighed and dropped his head onto his arms. "If that's what You want me to do, Lord, I'm willing. But You'll have to help me dial down my feelings and be ready to just be her friend."

# Chapter 4

Crista pushed open the door to J&R Machining and strode down the hallway to Brad's office, hoping her cool professional demeanor would hide her nervousness. How would he react to an unannounced visit after her behavior the other night?

She paused beyond Brad's range of vision outside his open door and surveyed the office. He really had cleared his desk, she noted with delight. More than that, he'd managed to keep it clean, a positive sign.

She raised her hand to knock, then dropped it back to her side, overcome by unaccustomed shyness. Would he think her unbearably pushy to show up this way? She knew she hadn't acted well during their last visit, but she'd felt so defensive with all his talk about religion. Now that she knew he had strong feelings in that area, she could steer the conversation away from that dangerous ground.

Unless he was some kind of fanatic, he wouldn't bring God into every discussion. Her attraction to Brad was undeniable, and she wanted to pursue their relationship. She knew that looking for perfection in anyone was unrealistic.

Everyone had some irritating flaw. If Brad tended to be overly interested in religious things, it didn't need to color their whole friendship. She could overlook it.

Lifting her hand before she could change her mind, she rapped on the doorjamb. Brad looked up, his face creasing in a smile when he saw her. Crista's heart lightened, then fell when his expression changed to a more formal one.

"I just thought I'd stop by and see how things were going," she told him, keeping her voice neutral. She nodded at his desk. "Looks like you've really made progress here. How's the situation with the phone calls?"

The ring of the telephone interrupted Brad's answer. He gave Crista a sheepish glance and picked up the receiver. After a quick exchange of words, he transferred the call back to Bea. "Delegated without a twinge of guilt," he announced. "How was that?"

She couldn't help but mirror his triumphant grin. "Not bad. Now what about—"

"Brad, we need to—" The stocky man she had seen on her previous visit burst through the doorway, stopping just before he barreled into her. He looked at Crista, then at Brad, and sighed. "Will you be long?"

Crista bristled at his tone. She could be a new customer for all the man knew. Brad's business wouldn't be helped if every visitor to his office met the same surly attitude.

"I'll call you just as soon as I'm through here, Nick." Brad looked at Crista apologetically when they were alone again.

"Nick's been the mainstay here since I can remember.

He knows more about running this place than anyone except Uncle Jess. Every time I wonder what on earth I'm doing here, I know that Nick is wondering twice as much."

Crista bit her tongue to keep from reminding Brad who was in charge.

"I can't fire him." Brad's comment paralleled her thoughts so closely she jumped. "I'll admit his attitude is irritating, but his whole focus is on how to make the business better. He's the biggest asset Uncle Jess left me."

"Even so," Crista said, "you have to protect yourself from interruptions like that. If Nick has ideas on improving the business, fine. But you need to establish a set time for doing that. Maybe you could discuss his ideas just before closing time every afternoon. If he knows you'll be here and ready to listen, he can save up all his suggestions for then."

"Good idea." Brad glanced at his watch. "I'm running late for lunch today. Have you eaten?" When Crista shook her head, he motioned her toward the visitor's chair. "If you'll wait here while I let Nick know we can talk later this afternoon, I'd like to take you to lunch." He gave her a friendly grin. "Call it payback for all the free advice I've been getting."

Crista settled into the chair, her heart pounding in relief. Brad hadn't held a grudge. Maybe they could get things back on track.

❄

Brad pulled into the parking lot at Garcia's. "I hope you like Mexican food," he said, escorting Crista inside. He hadn't believed it when he looked up and saw her standing in his doorway. He hoped he'd covered up his joy quickly enough that he hadn't looked like a lovesick schoolboy. His focus was on friendship now.

They followed the hostess to their table. Crista had a point. He was the boss. He didn't have to clock in and out of the office. Today he was going to take a long lunch and not worry about what Bea or Nick or anyone else thought about it.

He ate at Garcia's often enough to know he'd order one of their incredible chimichangas, so he contented himself with studying Crista's profile while she looked at the menu. A stray strand of hair wisped across her forehead, and he stopped himself from tucking it back into place.

*Friends,* he reminded himself. *Just friends.* Crista's spiritual status had to be the important thing here. Resolutely, he determined to squelch his feelings and keep things on a platonic level. Nothing had ever been said or done to imply otherwise. They could go on just as they had begun. Crista didn't ever have to know he once intended to pursue something deeper.

❄

Crista watched Brad bow his head briefly when the waitress brought their meals, and her brows tightened in a quick frown. He hadn't made a big production of it, though, hadn't prayed out loud, or asked her to join him. Her forehead smoothed again. If he didn't try to drag her into praying with him, she could ignore it.

His gaze locked with hers as soon as he raised his head. Crista lost herself in the depths of his eyes, marveling at how much he could stir her feelings after such a brief acquaintance.

Already a special connection seemed to exist between them. A connection Crista realized she'd be happy to see grow and flourish. She couldn't name one negative quality Brad had, unless she counted his preoccupation with God and church. But surely she could wean him away from that.

A thought struck her. He spent his Sundays at church because he enjoyed being around people he felt comfortable with. Why not get him involved with the most special group of people she knew? She realized Brad was talking and focused her attention on him.

"I'm curious," he said, eyes twinkling. "What's the schedule of an efficiency expert like? I know you have your evening classes and do some seminars out of state, but what do you do the rest of the time?"

Crista smiled, enjoying his interest in her. "I do a lot of workshops and corporate training sessions here in the valley. In fact," she added, trying not to sound boastful, "I'm pretty well booked for the next six months. That's really exciting to me because I've only been working freelance for the past year. When I started, I figured I could use my savings to help me get through the dry spells until I got established, but it hasn't been necessary."

Brad's eyebrows raised admiringly. "Pretty impressive. So how do you manage to fit it all in?"

"It isn't hard. Really," she insisted, laughing when Brad rolled his eyes. "Just a matter of organization. I schedule my local work during the first part of the week to leave weekends free for trips out of state. When I'm not traveling, I read trade journals, study, or plan upcoming seminars. It's simple."

Brad gave her a quizzical look. "What about evenings. . . on the nights you aren't teaching, that is?"

"That's when I take care of household details—paying bills, shopping, things like that."

"No time for yourself?"

She shrugged. "I love my work. I'm very happy doing things exactly this way."

"But what about fun? Don't you ever schedule in some time to relax?"

What an opening! Crista couldn't have set it up better if she'd tried. "As a matter of fact, I do. Want to see for yourself?"

Brad grinned. "A chance to watch scheduled relaxation? I wouldn't miss it."

"You're on. I'll be in Wisconsin this weekend, but how about dinner at my parents' the Sunday after that?"

Brad raised one eyebrow. "That's your big day out?"

"Trust me. You'll see how much fun it can be. Straight up noon, all right?"

Brad shifted uncomfortably. "Church doesn't let out until twelve or a little after."

Crista tensed. Couldn't he let go of church for one day? "I'll talk to Mom and see if we can put it back a little. Say between twelve-thirty and one?"

Brad smiled. "That'll be fine." He glanced down at his plate, then back at Crista. "Why don't you come to church with me? That way you can keep me organized and make sure I get to your parents' house on time."

Crista didn't miss the challenging glint in his eyes. She tensed, then relented. Fair was fair. If she showed a willingness to meet Brad halfway, maybe he'd be more inclined to see things from her point of view. What harm could one church service do? "Okay," she said, squaring her shoulders. *But don't get used to it,* she added to herself.

❄

Crista took her time dressing for church, trying on three different dresses before she settled on one she hoped would be suitable. She smoothed the flaring skirt over her slim hips and checked its lines in the full-length mirror. Why had she let herself in for this? "Because you're looking at the long-term goal instead of one day's discomfort," she told her reflection.

She placed clothes to wear after church—jeans, a polo shirt, and sneakers—in a canvas bag and waited for Brad to pick her up. Remembering the undeniable flicker of interest her parents had shown when she informed them she would be bringing a male guest along, she hoped she wasn't sending out the wrong signals to her family.

Surely not. Her family had always kept an open house to her acquaintances. She and Rod and Lindsey had invited plenty of friends over before. And Brad was quickly becoming a close friend.

Her thoughts turned back to their lunch together. After the way things had gone so well, she'd half expected him to kiss her good-bye when they returned to his office, but he'd only squeezed her hand and promised to pick her up for church today.

Crista had to admit their relationship confused her. She sensed Brad felt as attracted to her as she did to him. He lit up when they were together and seemed to enjoy her company. Why, then, did he pull away emotionally at times?

She picked up her brush and ran it through her shoulder-length hair for the fourth time, making sure the ends curved under in smooth lines. Her reflection showed an oval face framed by soft brown waves. A face with the regulation two eyes, one nose, one mouth, all in their proper places.

Maybe she wasn't anything exceptional, but she couldn't see anything drastically wrong. Yet her birth parents had found something so unacceptable they didn't want to keep her. The knowledge gnawed at her. Did Brad see the same thing? Did that explain his emotional distance?

She heard his SUV pull into the driveway and sighed. Time for church.

# Chapter 5

Brad watched Crista fidget in the pew beside him. He knew she didn't have much church background, but he'd never expected her to be this edgy. She tried hard not to show her uneasiness, but the constant tiny motions she made with her feet and the whiteness of her tightly laced fingers gave her away. It couldn't be more evident that she wished she could be anywhere but here.

He frowned. What kind of unbelieving nonsense had her family instilled to make her so antagonistic toward the things of God? And what kind of afternoon did he have to look forward to with people like that?

Not for the first time, he wondered how wise he'd been to accept Crista's invitation. At first it seemed like a way to get to know Crista better and open further opportunities to share the gospel. But would it come across to her family as having more than a friendly interest in her?

They stood for the last hymn. Brad tried to forget his misgivings about their afternoon together and pour his heart into the song of praise. Beside him, Crista barely moved her lips. Her stoic expression tore at his heart. If she could only get past whatever hurdles her family had placed in her way to discover the freedom found in knowing Christ.

Brad had envisioned a lively discussion of the morning's sermon on the way to her parents' house, but they made the drive in near silence. Crista spoke only to direct him and to point out the house when they arrived. When he pulled to a stop in their driveway, she grabbed her bag and bolted from the vehicle.

Brad followed slowly, trying to prepare himself for whatever lay ahead. He surveyed the house and yard. In contrast to Crista's easy-care desert landscaping, this lawn flourished green in spite of the late summer heat and showed the results of meticulous grooming. The stucco house looked equally well kept.

"Hi, Hon. Come on in," called a voice in response to Crista's knock on the screen door. "We're back in the family room."

Crista led him through an airy living room done in earth tones and into a large informal area. Three people rose from the massive trestle table to greet them. "We missed you last week, Sweetie." The older woman enveloped Crista in a warm hug, then turned to smile at him. "You must be Brad," she said, squeezing his hands. "We're so glad you could come."

"Thanks." Brad had barely responded to her welcoming smile when a meaty hand enveloped his own.

"Good to have you here, Son." The stocky, balding man clapped him on the shoulder with a force that knocked his breath from him.

Crista chuckled. "We aren't much for formal introductions, Brad. You've just met my parents. And over here," she nodded at the athletic-looking brunette watching the scene with unconcealed interest, "is my sister, Lindsey."

"Nice to meet you." Lindsey stepped forward and shook Brad's hand, then pointed out the large windows overlooking the backyard. "That's our brother, Rod, out there, trying to keep up with his munchkins." She indicated a slender, dark-haired man chasing a Frisbee with three little girls. Lindsey turned to Crista. "Mary's out of town visiting her mom, so Rod gets to baby-sit today."

"It'll do him good." Crista laughed. "He doesn't look any too upset about it."

"Nope. Rod's a terrific dad. Just like Steve's going to be someday."

"Where is Steve, anyway?" Crista asked her sister.

Lindsey grimaced. "He had to work this weekend. Kind of like someone else I know," she said, slanting a playful look at Crista. "Steve's my fiancé," she informed Brad, "and Mary is Rod's wife. So today you're getting the full effect of the McDaniel clan without any of their softening influence." Her sparkling eyes made it clear that she didn't mean her words to be taken seriously.

Crista went off to change before lunch and came back looking much more relaxed in her casual clothes. Mrs. McDaniel seated Brad between herself and Crista and kept his plate filled with pork chops and mashed potatoes until he had to beg her to stop.

Rod's three daughters kept up a lively conversation all through the meal. Afterward, Mrs. McDaniel insisted on cleaning up while the rest went to the park across the street to "work some more of the steam out of those youngsters," as Mr. McDaniel good-naturedly put it. He settled himself in a leather recliner and disappeared behind the Sunday paper.

Crista and Rod tossed the Frisbee to the kids and each other, leaving Brad and Lindsey to seek out the only shade available under the spindly branches of a paloverde tree. They settled themselves on the sparse, sun-bleached grass. "So what do you think of our family?" Lindsey asked, leaning back against the paloverde's pale green trunk.

"I think you're all pretty wonderful." Brad's answer to her direct question came without conscious thought, surprising him with its truth. What happened to the dysfunctional clan of his imagination who had turned Crista against church and the things of God with their ungodly ways? He'd never felt so at home with a group of strangers in such a short time.

"Have you and Crista been seeing each other long?" Lindsey's casual tone didn't match the quick look she shot at him from beneath lowered lashes.

"We haven't. . .we aren't exactly 'seeing each other,' " Brad said. "Not in a dating sense, anyway. We met in one of the night classes she teaches, and we've become good friends." He wasn't prepared for the pang of disappointment this reminder brought.

"Oh." Lindsey sounded as deflated as he felt. "Crista said the same thing when she told us you'd be coming, but I'd kind of hoped. . .well, never mind." She grinned at him, sweeping her long dark hair back with both hands and twisting it into a knot. "I'm glad she has you as a friend. I just thought it would be nice if she'd finally let herself get interested in someone."

"What do you mean, 'let herself'?" Brad asked, ignoring the twinge his conscience gave him at his nosiness. Lindsey seemed to have no compunctions about discussing her reserved sister. If he wanted to understand Crista better, this might be a good way to get the information he needed.

Lindsey shrugged, seeming to search for the right words. "Don't get me wrong. Crista's a great sister and a wonderful person. It's just that she holds on so tight to her feelings. We've shared everything since we were kids, but even with me, there are areas of her life that she keeps to herself. I think maybe she's afraid of getting hurt." She turned a concerned gaze on her sister, romping with their nieces, then looked back at Brad with a rueful smile. "I guess making a good friend is a start."

Brad shifted, crossing his legs and leaning his elbows on his knees. He hated probing like this, but if Lindsey was in a sharing mood, maybe he'd find out as much as he could while he had the opportunity. "You said something about getting hurt. Did she have a bad experience with a boyfriend?"

"Nothing like that." Lindsey shook her head in a decisive gesture. "Crista's always kept a bit of a wall around her, but she's built up a higher wall over the years. She loves spending time with the family, but she doesn't have much of a personal life besides that, have you noticed?"

Brad murmured assent. Lindsey's revelation echoed his own observations. He drew a deep breath, wondering if he was venturing out on forbidden territory. "Do you think it has anything to do with her being adopted?"

"She told you about that? Good." Lindsey gave him a relieved smile. "I think that may have a lot to do with it," she said slowly. "But not in the sense you might think. She's a part of this family just as much as Rod and I are, and she knows that. But it bothers her that her birth family gave her away. I think it bothers her a lot. Sort of like she feels secure with us because we're the ones who love her, but if her original parents didn't want her, she's afraid to open herself up to that kind of rejection from anyone else. Does that make sense?"

Brad nodded, sorting this new information out in his mind. "I think it does. Does she know anything about her birth family? Anything that would let her know why she was placed for adoption?"

Lindsey paused before answering. "I think she knows some of the story, but not all of it. Maybe I'm wrong, but I have this feeling that if she could locate them and find out the truth, it might be the key to letting her relax and enjoy life." She plucked a blade of grass from the hard-packed ground. "I worry sometimes about the long-term effect this will have on her. She needs to deal with the past and forgive them and go on with her life, you know?"

The Frisbee clipped Brad on the shoulder and landed between them, followed by three squealing little girls. Brad filed Lindsey's comments in his memory, wishing their conversation hadn't been interrupted.

❄

"So what did you think about my family?" Crista leaned back in the seat, looking more relaxed than he'd ever seen her. She looked younger, he thought. More open, more vulnerable.

"They're great. I don't know when I've enjoyed an afternoon more." Brad stopped for a red light, then turned onto I-10.

"Even a Sunday afternoon?" She smirked and shot him a glance from the corner of her eye. "Okay, that wasn't fair. I admit it. But can you see now why I don't feel the need for church people to fill some so-called void in my life?"

*Walk cautiously*, Brad warned himself. "So Sunday's always been your family's day together?"

"Mm-hm. Ever since I can remember. When I was little, we'd go to the zoo, or spend the day at North Mountain Park, or pack a picnic lunch and eat it out by some petroglyphs Dad knew about. We always had something special going on." She sighed and leaned her head back against the seat. "You seemed to get along well with him."

Brad grinned. "Your dad? He's quite a guy. I really enjoyed talking to him. We seemed to be on the same wavelength about nearly everything."

"See?" Crista leveled her gaze at him. "People can be nice without being churchy."

Brad racked his brain and sent up a quick prayer for the right answer while he maneuvered his vehicle into Crista's driveway. "You're absolutely right. They can be nice. The trouble is. . . ," he paused, hunting for the words he wanted, "being nice just isn't enough when it comes to eternity."

Crista's brow wrinkled in consternation. "What do you mean?"

"You can be the nicest, most moral person on earth, but without Jesus as your Savior—"

Crista sat upright, her relaxed posture disappearing. "Come on, Brad. Are you trying to tell me just going to church makes it all okay? Be honest. Haven't you ever known one of those oh-so-pious churchgoers who was a real stinker at heart?"

Brad winced, able to think of several who would fit that description. "I won't argue that one," he conceded. "But you see, just going to church doesn't do it either."

"But you said—"

"I said that without Jesus in your heart, you're lost. . . for all eternity. Jesus—having a relationship with Him—is the key to the whole thing."

Crista pressed her lips together and seemed inclined to drop the subject. Brad decided to let it go for the time being. She'd probably had enough to think about for one day. He circled around to let her out, then walked her to her front door, searching for a neutral topic.

Her dangling earrings caught his attention. He reached out and tapped one with his finger, making the tiny bauble dance in the sunlight. "A hot air balloon? I don't think I've seen earrings like that before."

Crista touched her earlobe self-consciously. "I've always had a thing about them. Balloons, that is."

"Really?" Brad warmed to the topic. Here was something they could discuss safely. "I'm partial to them myself."

Crista studied his face. "Why don't you come in?" she invited, swinging the door wide open.

Brad stopped just inside the doorway, lips pursed in a silent whistle. "That's some collection." He eyed the room with interest. Dainty china balloons appeared ready to lift off from an oak coffee table. A three-dimensional needlepoint balloon complete with gondola and tiny passengers hung suspended from the center of the ceiling fan. Every available surface, from the lamp stand to the knickknack shelves held something relating to the hot air balloon theme.

Crista shoved her hands in her pockets. "People collect all kinds of things: owls, or horses, maybe even frogs. I collect hot air balloons." She shrugged and gave him a sheepish grin. "I don't show these to many people. Even my family thinks I'm a little crazy to love them like I do." She smiled and waved him to a seat on the couch. "Thanks for not laughing."

Brad returned her smile. "No way. I'm a little crazy about them myself. How many times have you been up?"

Crista blinked. "Excuse me?"

"How many times have you gone up in a balloon?"

"Gone up? Um. . .never."

Brad's eyebrows shot up toward his hairline. "Never?"

Crista folded her arms across her stomach and stared at the floor. "I. . .have a problem with heights."

Brad started to chuckle, then tried to cover it by clearing his throat when he realized she wasn't joking. "I don't get it. You fly all over the country. That isn't high?"

"It's a whole different thing. A plane is enclosed. It's almost like being in a building. I went to the top of the Sears Tower once, and it didn't bother me at all. But the idea of standing in a little basket hundreds of feet in the air with nothing between me and the ground. . .uh-uh. No way."

Brad held his hands palms up. "Then why the fascination with them?"

Crista raised one shoulder, a tiny smile tilting her lips.

"It's a puzzle to me, too, but I've loved them ever since I was a little girl. Something about them touches a place deep inside me. They make me feel peaceful and happy. Loved." Her cheeks grew pink. "Sounds pretty silly, doesn't it?"

"All that from a balloon?" Brad did chuckle this time, then touched her chin with his fingers, tipping her face upward. "No. It doesn't sound silly at all." The warmth of her skin sent an electric tingle through his fingers, warning him that he'd better get out of there if he intended to keep things on a friendship level.

"I had a good time," he told her, rising to leave. "Thanks for inviting me." He tapped his index finger on the tip of her nose. "Have a safe trip to North Carolina."

He drove home, mulling over the events of the day. Had he shared enough? Too much?

*If she could find out the truth.* Lindsey's words kept running through his mind. Why wouldn't Crista make the effort to find out more about her birth parents?

"The truth will set you free." The familiar verse took on a new slant. Could finding her parents set Crista free in more ways than one? The thought sent a surge of excitement through him as speculation became certainty. Learning the truth might be painful, but confronting it was the only way Crista could free herself from the past. If only he could convince her of that.

A new thought burst into his mind: Could he find Crista's parents for her?

135

# Chapter 6

Wilmington was even lovelier than she'd expected. Glad she had given in to her urge to schedule an extra day for relaxation, Crista strolled along savoring the gentle breeze.

The cooler weather made a nice change, with Wilmington's 80 degrees in stark contrast to the searing Phoenix heat. At home, temperatures remained well above the century mark, despite the calendar's insistence that fall loomed just around the corner.

She slowed her steps, not certain what to do with her unaccustomed free time. She had wandered for several hours already. What else should she do with a day off? Maybe Brad had a point about her needing more time away from work.

Brad. Maybe she should spend some of her time trying to figure out where their relationship seemed to be heading.

Thoughts of him hadn't been far from her mind, even while presenting her seminar, and she couldn't decide whether that irritated or pleased her. He seemed interested only in being friends, and that was fine with her on one level. Another, deeper part of her longed for more. But she wasn't about to make the first move.

Crista stopped at the entrance of a red brick church. An unfamiliar urge to enter swept over her, and she pushed tentatively on one of the tall wooden doors. It swung wide at her touch, and she stepped into the tranquil interior. In that moment, a sense of peace washed over her. She spent a quarter of an hour examining the ornate pews and stained glass windows before she resumed her stroll. How sad, she thought, that she couldn't carry that peace along with her when she left.

A nearby strip mall caught her attention, and she strolled over to investigate. She hadn't yet purchased any gifts to take home, and this looked like a good place to remedy the oversight. In a shop that catered to the tourist trade, she found a book beautifully illustrated with photos of many of the city's historical buildings. Her mother would love it, she decided, carrying it to the register.

Several stores farther down, she spied a number of stained glass pieces. Intrigued, Crista went inside. The man behind the counter looked up. "Browse all you want," he called. "Let me know if you have any questions."

Crista smiled in reply and moved through strategically lit display units, resisting the urge to stroke the delicate pieces with her fingers. Their deep colors and unique designs took her breath away. She admired the variety of patterns, everything from bouquets of flowers to biblical scenes. Scanning the items arranged near the far wall, one captured her attention, and she caught her breath in a little gasp.

A hot air balloon in bright reds and yellows floated in a sapphire sky above rolling fields. Crista stepped closer, unable to tear her gaze away. Even inside the shop, the colors shimmered. With sunlight streaming through it, the effect would be gorgeous. She reached up to turn over the price tag and swallowed hard. The figure there wasn't as much as she'd feared, but more than she'd normally spend on an impulse purchase.

"You like balloons?" The voice came from so close behind her, she jumped.

"I do," she admitted, turning to face the beaming proprietor.

His smile widened a notch and he stared at Crista, then a tiny frown furrowed his forehead.

"Is everything all right?" she asked hesitantly.

He started, an embarrassed grin spreading across his face. "Sorry about that. You just made me think of someone I know." Crista smiled and the man's eyes widened. "You even have a dimple like hers. I can't believe how much you look alike! Do you mind if I call her? She works right next door."

Crista's smile froze in place, and she tried to keep from rolling her eyes. "Sure, I guess." She turned back to study the balloon piece while he went to the phone. Should she buy it? The more she tried to talk herself out of spending that much money, the more she wanted it.

She examined a collection of sun catchers hanging nearby. Several smaller hot air balloons dangled there, their vibrant colors sending prisms of light dancing across the walls. Maybe she should buy one of those instead. No, she decided, she would get one of the sun catchers for Brad. It would make a nice souvenir for him, symbolizing their common interest. And for herself. . .

Behind her, she heard the door open and the man speak excitedly. With a sigh of resignation, she turned to meet her "double." Her lips twitched when she saw the other woman, a petite, green-eyed blond wearing a white pharmacy smock. Just as she'd expected, the only resemblance was in the man's mind, despite his repeated protests. Her supposed twin evidently felt the same way, but graciously made an effort to gloss over the uncomfortable situation.

Crista mentioned the large balloon piece as a diversion, then realized that in her heart she'd already decided to take it home. She pulled out her credit card and made arrangements for shipping it after the other woman left.

She chatted with the salesman a few moments, then strolled out of the shop, Brad's tissue-wrapped sun catcher nestled safely in her shoulder bag. Funny, she mused, how many people looked alike in some way. As a young girl, she had looked for those similarities, fantasizing that someday she'd find someone related to her by blood. Even in her early teen years, spotting a person with similar features would cause her heart to race. Not long after that, though, she'd stopped looking. Similarities didn't make another person family. Love did, and the McDaniels had given her plenty of that.

She headed to her hotel to pack for the next day's flight back home.

❄

Brad stared at his computer monitor through bleary eyes, wondering how many on-line hours he'd put in tonight. Typing in a request for Internet sites dealing with adoption searches yielded far more sources than he'd imagined. First he tried to peruse all the information on every site, but quickly realized he'd have to skim and hope he was reading the items that mattered.

Brad rubbed his weary eyelids and turned the computer off for the night. He wasn't quite ready to start his search for Crista's parents, but at least he knew what he needed to get started. That would be the tricky part. He couldn't very well come out and ask Crista for that information, but Lindsey might be willing to help. He'd call her in the morning.

❄

Crista put the finishing touches on her upcoming presentation and returned the folder to her file cabinet. Turning at the ring of the phone, she lifted the receiver and smiled when she recognized Brad's voice.

"Are you all rested up from your trip last week?"

"So much that I've actually gotten ahead of schedule." Crista basked in the feeling of accomplishment.

"Great. That means you can pencil me into that calendar of yours for Saturday. All day Saturday."

"All day? Doing what?"

"Something productive. Like finding out how to be unstructured for a change."

"And what's wrong with structure?" she demanded.

Brad laughed. "Not a thing, as long as you keep it in perspective. Learning those organizational skills from you has made my life easier in a lot of ways, and don't think for a moment I'm not grateful." He paused. "But you can't live your whole life by a planner."

Crista bristled. "I don't agree. I'm a lot more comfortable knowing what I'm doing ahead of time."

"Think how much you enjoyed taking that extra day in North Carolina just to look around."

"It's not the same at all. I knew I was going sightseeing. I didn't know exactly where I'd end up, but I had a basic plan."

Brad's voice softened. "Just give it a try, Crista. I think you'll be glad you did."

His pleading worked where persuasion had not. "You win. But you've got to give me some idea of what to expect."

She could tell Brad was smiling, even over the phone. "I'll tell you this much. Dress like you would for one of your family picnics and bring a jacket. I'll pick you up at seven."

# Chapter 7

He appeared at Crista's door right on schedule and hustled her out to his SUV. "This should tide us over until breakfast," he told her, indicating the thermos and bakery sack between the seats. "I picked up coffee and croissants. I hope that's okay?"

Crista poured the steaming coffee into foam cups and handed Brad one of the flaky croissants. "Looks like you thought of everything. Now where are we going?"

He threw back his head and laughed. "Nope. I told you—this is the day you learn the joys of spontaneity. Just sit back, relax, and let the day happen."

He turned down Northern and took the northbound on-ramp for I-17. Crista munched her croissant. When they passed Deer Valley Road, she instinctively craned her neck to see if any balloons were being launched that morning. Not spotting any, she settled back into the seat and watched the scenery roll by.

She waited for Brad to take one of the exits at the north end of the city, but he didn't slacken his pace. Instead of city sprawl, they now drove through rolling hills thick with scrub brush and saguaros.

"It's easy to forget just how close we are to the wide-open spaces, isn't it?" she mused aloud.

Brad murmured agreement, then fell silent again.

Crista became so involved in watching the play of light on the stark mountains that nearly an hour passed before she remembered to ask where they were going. She had just opened her mouth to do so when Brad took the exit to Highway 69.

"Another thirty minutes and we'll be there." Brad glanced from the road ahead to Crista and gave her a warm smile. "With all the Sunday outings your family took, you must have come up this way before."

Crista shook her head. "We went south to Tucson a few times. Once we went to Tombstone and did the whole tourist bit at the OK Corral, but we seldom went north of Phoenix at all. I've only been to Flagstaff and the Grand Canyon once," she admitted.

Brad let out a slow whistle. "Then this should be even more fun for you than I thought."

He guided the four-wheel-drive vehicle around the sweeping curves. Crista noted the signs marking each community they passed through: Mayer, Dewey, Prescott Valley. She looked at Brad, puzzled. "We drove this far just to get breakfast?"

"Not just breakfast, a change of pace and some fresh air." Almost as soon as he spoke, the heavy fragrance of pines filled the vehicle.

Crista closed her eyes and inhaled the pungent scent. She opened them again to find turn-of-the century buildings rolling by, interspersed with more modern structures.

"Welcome to Prescott," Brad told her. He pulled into

a parking place in front of the Courthouse Plaza.

"It's beautiful," Crista said, eyeing the historic store-fronts with delight.

"I'm glad you like it. It's one of my favorite places." Brad tucked her hand into the crook of his arm and led her across the street to the old hotel on the corner where they ordered a hearty breakfast.

Afterward, they wandered up one street and down another, with Brad sharing from his extensive fund of stories about the town. The small shops and gingerbread-laden Victorian homes charmed Crista, and she stopped to read every interpretive marker in front of the well-preserved buildings.

"I can see why you like it," she said, catching Brad's enthusiasm for the place. "It's really lovely."

He nodded contentedly. "I always thought I'd like to live here someday. Now that I'm running Uncle Jess's business, that isn't in the picture anymore, but at least I can come up on weekends."

He laced his fingers through hers in a companionable way on their walk back to the SUV. She paused in front of the Bashford Building, imprinting the tranquil scene on her mind. "Thank you for bringing me here," she said softly.

"Wait till you see what comes next," Brad said, helping her into her seat. "We haven't even gotten started yet."

Crista's stomach rumbled and she clasped her hands across it, embarrassed. "I hope there's some food in the offing. This mountain air is giving me an appetite."

He pointed the SUV north on the highway, turning at Ash Fork to head east on I-40 for a few miles, then taking off on a bumpy Forest Service road.

"Don't tell me there's a restaurant up here where we're stopping for lunch," Crista said between gritted teeth, bracing her feet to keep from being bounced against the door.

Brad smiled. "You don't expect me to tell you and ruin the surprise, do you? Just hold on and see what happens."

"I'm trying to hold on," she retorted, clutching the armrest.

They turned onto an even more primitive road before Brad stopped and turned off the ignition. "We're here," he announced.

Crista surveyed her surroundings, seeing only trees and grass. "Where's 'here'?"

Brad chuckled at her bewildered tone. "Fine dining in the outdoors." He opened the back hatch and pulled out an enormous picnic basket.

Crista closed her eyes and rubbed her temples. "Brad, what exactly are we supposed to *do* here?"

He spread an old quilt on the ground and opened the basket with a flourish. "Relax. It's time you learned how."

They took their time over their late lunch. Crista repacked the basket, assuming it was time to leave, but Brad went to the SUV and pulled out a canvas bag.

Crista lifted an eyebrow. "Another surprise?"

Without speaking, Brad took her arm and led her down the rutted road at an easy pace, pointing out the various types of trees and vegetation they passed. He stopped by what looked like a small pond.

"We're going fishing?" Crista eyed his bag skeptically. "Isn't that awfully small for a tackle box?"

Brad merely smiled. "Come on." He guided her to a large pine and scooped up needles to make a cushioned seat. He took two cameras from the bag and handed one to Crista. "You wanted something specific to do," he said in a low voice. "Okay, here it is. We're going to sit here and wait for wildlife to come in to this tank for water. You can just watch or take photos. Your choice."

Crista stared at him, dumbfounded. "We just sit? For how long?"

Brad glanced at his watch. "Shouldn't be more than an hour or two before we see something." She opened her mouth to voice a protest, but he placed his fingers gently over her lips. "Shh. You have to be quiet, or you'll scare them away." He settled against the tree trunk. "In the meantime, we get to practice one of my favorite Bible verses." He gave her a wink. " 'Be still, and know that I am God.' "

Crista sat rigid with disbelief. He wanted to sit and do nothing? For two hours? What a ridiculous waste of time! She started to speak, but Brad held up a cautioning hand and she subsided into a frustrated silence.

Made drowsy by the afternoon sun's warm rays, Crista's taut muscles relaxed in spite of herself. Little by little, the peace of the sylvan setting penetrated her soul. An hour passed. She saw Brad tense and followed the direction of his gaze. Two cow elk appeared from the island of trees across the meadow.

Crista watched, entranced by their calm grace. When they had crossed half the distance to the tank, Brad pressed his shoulder against hers and nodded toward the trees. A huge bull elk stepped forward and sniffed the air, his enormous antlers glinting in the late afternoon sun. Crista gasped and stared in wonder until the three stately animals had drunk their fill and left.

"That was amazing," she told Brad when they had loaded up and started for home. "I can't believe they came that close to us."

"Shows you the value of being still, doesn't it?" His teasing grin made her laugh.

"Except I was so fascinated by them I forgot to take any pictures."

"That's okay, I took plenty. I'll share." He reached over and gave her hand a gentle squeeze. "I'm glad you enjoyed it. At one time, I'd given serious thought to taking up wildlife photography professionally. There's nothing quite like experiencing them up close."

Crista's lips parted in surprise. "You're that good?"

"I've sold a number of photos to some of the better-paying magazines. But now I have a business to run." His voice trailed away.

Stars blossomed in the gathering darkness. Despite her best efforts to stay awake, Crista nodded, then dozed.

❄

Brad pulled into her driveway and turned off the ignition. He watched Crista for a moment, enjoying the sight of her delicate lashes fanning across her cheeks. He touched her shoulder and she blinked sleepily. She shook herself fully awake and stretched. "I can't believe how relaxed I feel. You may just have something there about taking a day off now and then."

Brad smiled in response, hoping her receptive mood would continue. He reached over the back of his seat and drew out a plastic bag, then opened it to reveal a gaily wrapped package. He placed it in Crista's lap.

"What's this?" She eyed the bright holiday wrapping uncertainly.

"Call it an early Christmas present." Brad chuckled at her suspicious expression. "You're not the only one who can shop ahead, okay?"

She pulled the paper loose, looking at Brad quizzically when she saw what lay within. "A Bible?"

"I can't think of a more appropriate gift for Christmas." He watched her trace the imprint of her name on the cover. "You said it was your favorite holiday. You need to get to know more about it than just the lights and tinsel."

Crista shot him a wary look but didn't hand the book back. Feeling encouraged, Brad went on. "I marked one of the verses." He flipped on the dome light and opened the Bible to a page marked by a navy ribbon. "Read it and see if that doesn't seem to be written just for you."

Crista scanned the words Brad had underlined. " 'Sing to God, sing praise to his name,' " she read in a whisper. " 'Extol him who rides on the clouds—his name is the LORD—and rejoice before him. A father to the fatherless, a defender of widows, is God in his holy dwelling.' " She turned to Brad, searching his face.

"That's what God wants to be for you," Brad said gently. "A Father. One who'll never leave you."

# Chapter 8

B rad walked up to the stucco house, wondering if he was crazy for doing this. As far as the McDaniels were concerned, he barely knew their daughter. What gave him the right to pry into their family's affairs?

The door swung open before he reached the front step. "Come in, Brad. It's nice to see you." Mrs. McDaniel's warm greeting allayed some of his nervousness. She led him through the house to the patio, where a tray with frosty glasses of lemonade awaited them.

"Lindsey told me about your talk," she said, indicating a chair to Brad and settling in another. "If it will put your mind at ease, I want you to know that I think you're doing a wonderful thing."

Brad sipped his lemonade to give himself time to frame his reply. "Frankly, I wasn't sure how you'd take this. I know how close your family is, and I didn't want you to think I was intruding."

Crista's mother shook her head and smiled. "When you adopt a child, knowing they'll someday be curious about their birth family is something you have to accept as part of the package. I've tried to prepare myself for it

149

from the moment she became ours."

She moved the bottom of her glass in circles on the table, studying the swirls the condensation left behind. A tiny crease appeared between her eyebrows. "This is something Crista should have dealt with long ago. She needs to resolve her bitterness toward her birth parents about being placed for adoption."

She looked up at Brad with an unflinching gaze. "It's something I can't help her with. That's why I'm glad you're willing to take on this project. I'm not completely happy about doing it behind Crista's back, but I doubt she'll give you any cooperation."

Brad straightened and leaned forward. Now that the door was open, he was eager to learn all he could. "Has she ever talked to you about her biological parents?"

"Once. A number of years ago." She stared at the trees beyond the back fence. "It was the year Rod graduated from high school, so that would have made Crista about fifteen. She sat down with me after supper one night and told me she wanted to know about them." A faint smile crossed her face. "She was so careful to try to phrase it so she wouldn't hurt my feelings and make me think she didn't love me and her dad."

"Did you have any information to give her?" Brad prompted.

Mrs. McDaniel's face darkened, and she caught her lower lip between her teeth. "I told her all I knew, but it wasn't what she wanted to hear. We had taken Crista in as a foster child when she was four, but it wasn't long before we knew we'd like to make her a permanent part of our family. She seemed like one of us right from the start." Her eyes grew misty with remembrance.

"In those days, very little information was given out to adoptive parents. All we knew was that she had been abandoned, and there were no problems getting her birth mother and father to relinquish their parental rights.

"I didn't tell Crista about that," she went on, "but she pieced it together from what came next. She asked me if I knew whether her parents were alive, and all I could tell her was what I'd seen on some notes in her file when we visited the agency in Cincinnati." She closed her eyes, as if to see the scene more clearly.

"The caseworker left the room for a few minutes. I didn't dare pull the folder over to me or get up and go around the desk, so I had to try to read upside down. In the brief time I had, I could see a last name: Williams. The first name looked like Melvin or maybe Martin. There were also several brothers and sisters listed, but I couldn't make out individual names.

"The only other thing I saw before the caseworker came back into the room," she said, looking at Brad again, "was a notation under the parents' names. Something about them being active in a local church. That's all I could tell her."

Brad suppressed a groan. No wonder Crista didn't hold churchgoers in high regard. "So her parents are still living?"

Mrs. McDaniel nodded slowly. "And they had other children. Children they apparently kept." She pressed her fingers to her lips and drew a shaky breath. "At that point, Crista told me she wasn't interested in finding them anymore, and that was the last she ever said to me on the subject.

"She's always been reserved, Brad, but after that she just seemed to put up a wall around herself with everyone but the family. Until you came along, anyway." She smiled and stood. "I wish you luck. I hope you can help her."

❄

The whine of the engines grew increasingly louder. Crista dutifully fastened her seat belt and waited for the 727 to take its place in line for takeoff, watching the runway lights glow against the growing dusk.

She relaxed against the seat back but shook herself awake before her eyes closed. The flight home from Dallas/Fort Worth International Airport only lasted a little over two hours. Tired as she felt after a grueling round of back-to-back seminars, napping now would mean she'd be too wide awake to get back to sleep at a decent hour. Instead, she opened her planner, pulled out a pen, and forced herself to focus on her schedule for the next month.

Halfway into the flight, her eyelids drooped despite her best efforts. Her fingers loosened their grip on the pen, and she drifted into a peaceful slumber.

Brad waited for her across a meadow, arms outstretched, the warm light in his eyes shining like a beacon guiding her home. Without hesitation, Crista flung herself toward him, wanting nothing more than to be wrapped in his embrace and know she belonged there. Twenty paces from him she stumbled, then stumbled again. What was getting in her way? No rocks marred the smoothness of the grassy expanse, but still she tripped. Brad seemed farther away than ever. Then the ground fell away under Crista's feet.

She sat bolt upright, straining against the taut seat belt.

Her momentary relief at knowing she'd been dreaming vanished with the realization that the ground was still falling away. Disoriented, she looked around wildly, but what she saw only frightened her further. Bodies sprawled across the seats and in the aisles. Panicked screams echoed her own sense of terror.

"We're going to die!" shrieked a woman across the aisle.

Crista believed her. She had no idea how long they had been falling or how fast, only that the plane was plummeting through the darkness and showed no signs of stopping. The time had come for her to face eternity. . .and she was unprepared.

"Dear God, please help us! I'm not ready to die!" Her involuntary cry mingled with the anguished wails of the other passengers.

With a lurch, the plane bounced, then settled. Crista wondered if they had hit the ground and rebounded, then realized they were still airborne. A moment later, she heard the pilot's voice over the intercom.

"That was quite a ride, wasn't it?" came the soothing Texas drawl. "You folks probably didn't expect a rodeo on this flight." His voice changed, becoming more clipped and professional. "Ladies and gentlemen, we've just experienced some unexpected turbulence. We seem to be past it now, but for your safety and comfort, I suggest you keep your seat belts fastened for the remainder of the flight."

A flight attendant pulled herself to her feet just behind Crista's row and attempted to reestablish her practiced smile. "Is everyone all right?" she inquired, giving each row a quick but thorough scrutiny.

Slowly the cabin resumed a semblance of normalcy.

Crista tuned out the nervous laughter and the solicitous tones of the flight attendants and stared out the window, reliving that moment she was sure would be her last.

Fear, pure and simple, had consumed her. She laced her fingers together, trying to keep her hands from trembling. Just how close had she come to facing eternity? And why had the plane's violent pitching stopped so suddenly? Could it be a result of her loud plea for divine intervention, or was there another explanation for their abrupt deliverance?

Crista couldn't even feel embarrassment about her uncharacteristic outburst. The cry had been torn from deep within her, responding to the deepest longing of her soul. All the things she had told herself about self-sufficiency and control vanished in that one moment of complete clarity. What did it matter if she had every moment of her life in perfect order if in the end she didn't have her accounts settled with God? She didn't see how she could dare go on another day of her life without Him. Or Brad.

That realization rocked her almost as much as the first. Had the near crash destroyed her reason? Brad wanted only to be friends; he'd telegraphed that message in a hundred different ways. The contentment she felt when they were together, that ache to hold him close and be held in his arms—Brad didn't share those feelings. If she wanted to maintain their friendship, she must put aside her yearning for something more and settle for what he did offer.

❄️

"Thanks. Sorry to have bothered you." Brad hung up the phone and penciled a line through the name on the notepad before him. Another dead end.

He pinched the bridge of his nose between his fingers. Some investigator he'd turned out to be. His Internet search had turned up a number of Melvin and Martin Williamses in Cincinnati, but none of them admitted to knowing Crista. Widening his search, he'd typed in the names of Cincinnati suburbs, this time including any first name beginning with *M.* He'd contacted them all, except for the last name on his list, Milton R. Williams.

Before making the call, he paused, assailed by Crista's own doubts. How could a family give away one of their children? Were these the kind of people he ought to bring back into Crista's life?

He punched in the numbers, conflicting thoughts flashing through his mind. Did he have the right to do this, not knowing what kind of Pandora's box he might be opening? *Lord, if I've misjudged Your direction in this, please don't let this call go through,* he prayed, counting the rings. One. . .two. . .

"Hello?"

Startled by the quick answer, Brad took a moment to respond to the soft voice on the other end of the line.

"Is this the Williams residence?"

"Yes." The voice took on a guarded tone, and Brad realized he'd better clarify his purpose for calling.

"Please don't hang up. I'm looking for the Williams family who lived near Cincinnati twenty-five years ago." He took a deep breath. "I'm calling about Crista." He waited, hardly daring to breathe.

The woman turned from the phone and called, "Honey, come quick! Somebody's calling about Crista!" She spoke to Brad again. "It's been so many years, I just can't believe this. Nothing's wrong, is it?" she asked, her excitement changing to concern.

"No, not at all." Brad's mind reeled. How could she sound so happy after two and a half decades with no efforts to contact her daughter? Of all the possible scenarios he had imagined, none of them had been close to this. "I'm looking for information about her adoption."

Mrs. Williams sighed. "It was the hardest thing we've ever done, letting that little mite go. She'd become like one of our own. We've never quit praying for her, even after all these years."

Brad blinked. "One of. . . Mrs. Williams, are you telling me Crista isn't your child?"

Her astonished silence confirmed his guess even before she spoke. "Well, of course not. What made you think she was?"

Brad scrubbed his forehead with the heel of one hand. "Something isn't adding up here. Let me start from square one. My name is Brad Morgan. I'm a friend of Crista's, and I'm trying to help locate her biological family. The only information her adoptive mother could give me was that they adopted Crista from an agency in Cincinnati and that her family's name was Williams."

Mrs. Williams clucked in dismay. "No, we only went to church with Crista's family. So sad when that poor woman died and left her husband with all those little ones. The pastor kept them all for awhile, but when their daddy didn't come back, he couldn't keep on doing it indefinitely.

"I taught Crista's class in Sunday school and knew what a sweet little thing she was. We wanted to help, so we took her. I'm afraid I don't know where the rest of them went," she added apologetically.

"How many children were in the family?" Brad asked, his excitement mounting.

"Three or four, near as I can remember."

"And none of the others went with you?"

"Goodness, no. We had four of our own. It was just that I knew Crista from my class, and the thought of that poor little thing being thrown in with strangers was more than I could stand. Although. . ." Her voice faltered. "I wonder now if they might all have been better off if they'd been kept together instead of being parceled out like that." She paused. "You say you're a friend of Crista's. How is she? What's become of her?"

"She's fine. She was adopted by a wonderful family, and she's done very well for herself. Has her own business, as a matter of fact."

"Well, if that don't beat all! Hard to believe she once lived with a family of factory workers, isn't it?" Her voice softened. "I feel better, hearing that. I'd always hoped we did the right thing in giving her up, but it was hard to know for sure. It looks like the Lord's hand was in it after all."

Brad spoke hesitantly. "You obviously cared for Crista a great deal. Do you mind me asking why she couldn't stay with you?"

A sigh echoed through the phone line. "Milt worked in the factory from the time he was fifteen, but loyalty didn't matter when they started laying people off. When he lost his job, we barely had a nickel to our name." She sighed again, then went on. "Having to watch those five little ones get by on one meal a day nearly tore our hearts out. We held on to Crista as long as we could, but as young as she was, we didn't think we had any right to take chances with her health that way."

Mrs. Williams paused. "I'm glad to hear she did all right. So very glad." Her voice grew brisk. "Now let's get back to the reason you called. You say Crista's trying to find her family?"

"Not exactly," Brad hedged. "Actually, I'm doing this on my own. She doesn't know a thing about it."

"Why are you doing it on your own?" Her voice held curiosity rather than censure.

Brad hesitated. Why indeed? "The only thing I can say is that I feel God wants me to."

Mrs. Williams gave a low chuckle. "Well, Honey, that's the very best reason there is. Is there anything I can do to help?"

"Yours was the only family name her adoptive mother saw. Do you know what Crista's last name was?"

"Well, of course. It was Richmond." She spelled it for him.

"Richmond." Brad jotted it on his notepad. "A Richmond family from Ohio. Thanks a lot; that will really help."

"Not Ohio, Hon, Kentucky."

"Kentucky?"

"Sure. That's where we all lived at the time. Just across the river in Covington. We didn't move to Ohio until Milt was laid off and we went looking for any work he could find."

"Kentucky," Brad repeated dully. "Thank you, Mrs. Williams. You've helped more than you know."

He hung up, then stared at his scribbled notes. Crista's mother was dead and her father had disappeared, but she had siblings. Siblings named Richmond.

Brad booted up his computer with renewed optimism and logged on to one of the adoption search message boards. He had a name and a state. The right ones, this time.

❄

Crista sat on the edge of her bed, staring at the open Bible in her lap. Her gift from Brad contained a wealth of study notes, and she had spent hours since her arrival home looking up passages pertaining to knowing God. She smiled in astonishment when she read that a person could be adopted into God's family. It all connected with her conviction that families were built on a foundation of love. The McDaniels had brought her into their family; God wanted to bring her into His. It was a concept so simple, yet so profound that she could barely take it in.

She returned to the notes in the back and reread the section on salvation. That was what she needed. Hadn't she cried out for that very thing when she thought the plane was going down? She slipped from the bed to her knees and lifted up a heartfelt prayer. "Oh, Lord, I want You to be my Father. . . ."

# Chapter 9

Brad had gotten so used to scanning the entries without success that he almost skimmed past it. "Searching for siblings born Covington, Kentucky," it began. He read it again more slowly, then went over it a third time. "Parents John and Anna Richmond." The right name, the right area. His mouth went dry. Could it be?

This entry contained a link to a Web site. He clicked on the link and waited for the site to open. It told the story of Eden Richmond, her separation from her siblings and attempts to locate them, and her hope to reunite them all. Brad stared at the last paragraph. "One sister may have moved west, possibly to Arizona."

He noted the woman's E-mail address and began to compose a message:

> *My name is Brad Morgan. I'm helping a friend in Arizona look for her family. Her birth name was Crista Richmond, and she was born in Kentucky. If this sounds like anyone you're looking for, please give me a call.*

He added his phone number, then pressed the Send button.

❄

The minister moved into the final point of his sermon on deepening one's walk with Christ. Brad leaned back in the pew and glanced at Crista, seated beside him. He'd hardly believed it when she called and asked if she could accompany him to church this morning. As if he'd say no! Watching her, he marveled at the difference between her last visit and today. Gone was the fidgety behavior. She leaned forward slightly as though she didn't want to miss a single word.

Was God softening her heart and drawing her toward Himself? If only he could believe that.

When the last song had ended and the congregation began filing out, Brad remained seated and turned to Crista. The gladness shimmering in her eyes made him wonder if his prayers had already been answered. He hoped so, but he had to be sure.

"Something's happened, hasn't it?" he asked.

She nodded happily, tears glistening on her lashes. "I'm part of God's family now."

Her arms circled his shoulders in a joyful hug. Brad wrapped his arms around her for the first time, rejoicing with Crista and wondering if God was opening the door to answer yet another prayer.

"You were right," she whispered close to his ear. "I can feel the difference. This changes everything."

*More than you know,* Brad thought.

❄

Brad checked his hair in the mirror. It appeared as

well groomed as the last time he'd looked. And the time before that. He glanced at his watch. Crista should arrive any minute. Thank goodness she hadn't minded driving to his house. When negotiations over a major new contract ran later than he'd expected, he knew he'd never be able to get ready, pick up Crista, and still make it in time for their dinner reservations.

He patted his jacket pocket to reassure himself the tiny jeweler's box still nestled there. Crista's news had removed all but one obstacle to letting her know his feelings. He had to let her know about his search for her family, and he had to do it tonight, before he asked the question that could change their futures.

Tires crunched on the driveway. Brad hurried to the door and smiled at the sight of Crista in a teal silk dress. He could get used to seeing a sight like that every day of his life.

Crista looked around his living room, brightening when she spotted the sun catcher she'd given him. The smile faded and she turned to Brad, a solemn expression on her face. "Are we in a hurry? There's something I'd like to tell you."

Brad nodded and motioned to the couch. He sat beside her, close enough to take her in his arms. How he'd like to do that and have the waiting over with! He tried to pull his attention back to what she was saying.

"I've decided you were right," she stated. "If God has forgiven me, I have to forgive, too. I've decided it's time to start looking for my birth family."

Brad stared at her. He'd hoped for an opportunity but hadn't planned on leaping into it quite this quickly. "I have something to say to you, too." Taking her hands in his, he gazed into her eyes, steeling himself for her reaction. "The fact is, I've already started searching for them." He felt Crista stiffen and try to pull away, but he tightened his hold on her hands and went on. "I know it must seem like a terrible intrusion, but I felt like God was telling me to do this." Would she believe him?

Slowly she relaxed, although her expression remained troubled. She studied Brad's face. "So what have you found out about the former Crista Williams?" Her tone was light, but Brad could hear the pain beneath the surface and sense her fear of reopening the old wound.

He stroked the backs of her hands with his thumbs. *This isn't going to be easy, is it, Lord?* "Well, for starters, your name wasn't Williams." He watched her eyes dilate and waited a moment for the news to register. "You were born Crista Richmond, and your mother died when you were just a little girl. Your father left you in the care of his pastor, but I don't know what happened to him after that. I do know that a church family named Williams took you in later on. They loved you very much, but had some serious financial problems and weren't able to provide for you. Just after that, your mom and dad became your foster parents, and you know what happened from then on."

"You have been busy, haven't you?" Brad could feel her fingers tremble. He gave them a gentle squeeze. At least she was still talking to him. He might as well tell her the rest.

"There's more," he said, plunging ahead before he lost his nerve. "I may have found your sister."

The trembling spread through her whole body. "I

have a sister? Besides Lindsey, I mean?"

Brad smiled. "At least one, maybe more. There's no guarantee the woman I found is related to you, but I wanted you to know about the possibility."

Crista nodded, apparently at a loss for words. And who could blame her? Surely he could have dropped this on her more gently. He slid his arm around her and pulled her to him, cradling her head on his shoulder.

"Is there anything else?" she asked in a shaky voice.

Brad chuckled and stroked her hair. "That's it. Only one bombshell per day." *Unless you count a proposal.* Could he spring that on her now? Maybe he'd wait until after dinner and give her time to collect her thoughts.

"Do you still feel like going out to eat, or would you rather order in?"

Crista shook her head and pressed her hands to her cheeks. "Going out is fine. I just need a little time to assimilate all this."

"I don't blame you a bit. And you aren't angry with me?"

She shook her head again, a small smile lighting her lips. "Surprisingly, no." The smile widened into a grin.

Brad's shoulders slumped in relief. The evening hadn't been ruined. A sense of elation welled up inside him. There was still hope.

"In that case, what do you say we head for Mario's?"

Crista smiled assent and reached for her wrap. Brad held it for her and was just draping it over her shoulders when the phone rang. He looked at Crista apologetically. "Do you mind if I get it?" he asked. "It might be about that new contract."

"Go ahead." She smiled. "It'll give me a minute to catch my breath."

Brad hurried across the room and picked up the phone, expecting to hear Nick's voice. "Hello?"

"Mr. Morgan? This is Eden Richmond Leland."

Brad started. He shot a frantic glance at Crista, then turned his attention back to the phone. "Yes," he said cautiously. "This is Brad Morgan."

"I'm sorry I haven't called sooner, but I've been out of town and just got your message." She drew a deep breath, clearly audible over the wire. "I think your friend may be my sister. I'm the oldest, and Crista is the baby. She was born in Covington, Kentucky, and she'd be twenty-nine years old now. Does that sound like we're talking about the same person?"

Did her voice sound anything like Crista's? Brad couldn't tell. He risked another glance at Crista, hoping his expression wouldn't give him away. She was looking at the sun catcher, turning it to catch light from the lamp. Brad breathed again and turned his attention back to the phone.

"I think we might be," he ventured. "How can we find out for sure?"

Eden gave a nervous laugh. "I haven't the faintest idea. After getting this far, I have no idea what to do next. She was only three years old when our mother died. I don't know if she'd even remember me, so we can't go over shared memories."

Brad's fingers tightened on the phone. Everything checked out so far, but how could he be certain? He couldn't bear the thought of sending Crista's hopes soaring only to chance having them plummet again. "That does present a problem," he said. He shifted position so his back was toward Crista and lowered his voice. "Do you remember anything about what happened after your mother died?"

"It's all just bits and pieces, I'm afraid. Losing our parents and then being shuffled around like that was such an upheaval. I do remember that we stayed with our pastor for awhile, but then we all went with different families and our world fell apart all over again."

It had to be the right woman. There couldn't be more than one situation like that in the same place at the same time. "That checks out with what I've learned."

Eden yelped with joy. "I can hardly believe it! How can I get in touch with her? Do you think she's ready to talk to me?"

"Hold on a minute." Brad looked across the room at the woman he loved. The evening he'd planned so carefully had just crumbled into dust, but who was he to complain about God's timing?

"Crista," he called softly. "Your sister's on the phone. Her name is Eden. Would you like to talk with her?"

Eyes wide in disbelief, Crista moved across the room like a sleepwalker. Brad nodded with more confidence than he felt, then pressed the receiver into her hand. He stepped away, as much to get a grip on his own feelings as to give Crista privacy, and watched as she spoke to her sister for the first time in twenty-six years.

❅

Thirty minutes later, Crista hung up and turned a radiant face to Brad. "God has been so good to me!" she exulted. She pulled another tissue from the box he'd handed her earlier and dabbed at her cheeks. "Can you believe it? Eden has been looking for me for ten months, and once I turned my life over to God, He worked it all out."

Brad crossed the room and wrapped her in a bear hug. She buried her face in his shirt and returned his embrace.

"I'm so happy," she said, looking up at him through a film of tears. "First I find God, then my birth sister. I feel whole for the first time, and it's all because of you. You're such a wonderful friend."

Brad's elation deflated like a leaky balloon. He'd been so sure Crista's feelings matched his own, but now he wondered. Had guiding her toward Christ and helping her locate her family been the only reason God placed him in her life? And if it was, could he accept that?

He'd struggle with that answer later. At this point, he only knew one thing: There would be no proposal this evening. He glanced at his watch. They'd missed their reservations at Mario's, but they still needed to eat.

He picked up her wrap from where she'd dropped it on the couch. "Let's go get dinner."

# Chapter 10

"How would you like to go cut your own Christmas tree this year?" Brad stretched one arm across the back of Crista's couch and cradled a mug of cocoa in the other hand.

Crista carried her own mug to the couch and settled next to him. "Could we? Where?" She'd heard stories of her parents cutting trees in snowy Ohio, but growing up in Phoenix didn't give one opportunities for treks in the woods.

"Up north, not far from where we saw the elk. I already have the permit," he told her with his slow grin.

"Not bad." She laughed. "You mean I finally have you planning ahead?" It felt good to hear that teasing note in his voice. In the three days since Eden's call, he'd seemed a bit subdued, although she'd been sure he shared her happiness.

"Yep. See what a good influence you are?" He wrapped his arm around her shoulders and hugged her close. "What are you doing the Saturday after Thanksgiving?"

Crista pulled away so she could stare into his face. "Thanksgiving? I always put my tree up a week before Christmas."

Brad's mouth dropped open. "You're kidding. You're missing out on an early start to the season."

"And having needles all over the carpet for weeks on end."

Brad pulled her back to his side and rubbed his chin against her hair. "Needles on the carpet are a traditional part of Christmas," he murmured, stroking her cheek with his thumb.

"A tradition you just created?" Crista snuggled closer, reveling in his nearness.

"Mm-hm," he admitted with a low chuckle.

Well, why not get an early start on her favorite holiday? This Christmas would be the best ever. She'd found her family, she had Brad in her life, and most importantly, she finally knew the Reason for the celebration. "Okay. The Saturday after Thanksgiving."

She sipped her cocoa, then rubbed her cheek against Brad's sweater. "Planned any resolutions for the new year yet, Mr. Organization?"

Brad straightened and placed his mug on the coffee table. "As a matter of fact, I have." He leaned back, lacing his fingers around one bent knee. "I've learned a lot about what makes a business work these past few months, not to mention a lot about myself. I've decided the best thing I can do for J&R Machining is to turn it over to Nick."

"What?" Crista couldn't hide her astonishment.

Brad nodded decisively. "He loves the company. He's been with it since the beginning, and he knows it better than anyone. Being able to have the final say in what happens without having to run everything past me will be the best thing that ever happened to him." He held her gaze with his own. "And getting out from under a job I was never suited for in the first place will give me the chance to see if I can make one of my dreams come true."

Crista cupped her hands around her mug and tried not to show how much his announcement had shaken her.

Brad's faced creased in a boyish grin. "Now that J&R is back on track, I'm going to use my new business skills to start a freelance photography venture. In Prescott."

"You're moving?" Crista's voice came out in a hoarse croak.

He nodded. "Right after Christmas. I want to enjoy life, not just get through it, and I need to slow down to do that. Not that I won't stay organized." He chuckled and gave her a hand a light squeeze. "I just want to go at an easier pace."

"I see." Crista drained her mug and stared into its depths.

❆

Brad didn't allow his expression to change, but inside he felt like punching his fist in the air with a victory shout. More than her words, Crista's crestfallen reaction to his announcement told him what he needed to know.

❆

Thanksgiving dinner with her family always brought more temptation than Crista could resist, but she'd outdone herself yesterday. She stepped out of her jeans and exchanged them for a pair of sweatpants with an elastic waist. Maybe having Brad there had boosted her appetite. She walked out to check her mailbox, smiling at the memory.

Bills, more bills, and some Christmas sale flyers. Crista

wrinkled her nose in annoyance. She always did her Christmas shopping way in advance, but here it was the day after Thanksgiving and she still needed gifts for everyone but her mother.

An envelope slipped from the stack, and she bent to retrieve it, frowning at the unfamiliar return address. Inside she found a Christmas card with a discount coupon from the stained glass shop in Wilmington. She tossed the rest of the mail on her counter and tapped the coupon thoughtfully, eyeing the shop's Web address at the bottom. She typed the string of characters into her computer and watched a dazzling array of photos appear on screen.

He'd added even more to his inventory. She made note of several items that would be perfect for her family and started to send an E-mail, then stopped. A phone call would be better this close to Christmas. If some of her choices were out of stock, she could ask him to recommend alternatives. The line was busy, so she propped the card next to her phone as a reminder. She had errands to run today, but she could call again tomorrow.

No, next week. Tomorrow would be spent with Brad, selecting the perfect Christmas tree. She wrapped her arms around herself, looking forward to another day with him, then sobered at the thought it might be one of the last times they had together.

She laid out clothes for the next morning. Brad planned to pick her up before sunup. When she protested the early hour, he'd alluded to some mysterious errand he had to take care of before they went in search of the tree. "It's just off the interstate, not out of our way at all," he assured her.

❄

"This is your errand?" Crista stared doubtfully at the long shape on the ground as it swelled gradually in the predawn light, taking on a more rounded appearance. Flames shot from the propane burners, and the balloon slowly lifted off the ground.

She pulled her jacket more snugly around her and reached for Brad's hand. "I'm not so sure about this."

"You'll be fine." He smiled, giving her fingers a reassuring squeeze. "Trust me."

Crista looked into his eyes. She did trust him. That was one miracle. She glanced at the gaily colored balloon hovering overhead. If God would help her overcome her aversion to heights, that would make two.

The pilot jogged over to them. "Ready?"

Brad turned to Crista, one eyebrow raised questioningly. She drew a deep breath and nodded. "Ready."

Stepping into the wicker gondola wasn't so bad. She rested her arms on the leather-padded rim. As long as it sat on the ground, she could be quite comfortable. She could hear the whoosh of the burners behind her and swallowed, knowing that the increase in heat would produce the added lift needed for them to take off. She let her gaze travel up the steel cables to the load tapes, then on to the vivid hues of the balloon itself, hoping the ripstop nylon envelope was really as strong as Brad had told her it was.

Brad turned from conferring with the pilot and put his arm around her, pulling her close. "It's going to be okay," he promised. Crista closed her eyes and breathed a quick prayer. When she opened them again, she realized they were off the ground.

Brad laughed at her startled expression. "Not as bad as you expected?"

Crista shook her head in wonder. "I can't believe how smooth it is. I don't even feel the breeze."

"You won't," the pilot told her. "We're moving with the wind, so there's no sensation of it blowing. You won't even get any turbulence, the way you would in an airplane."

"Good," Crista said under her breath, the memory of her near disaster all too recent.

The gondola hung steady beneath the balloon. Crista leaned against Brad, finally prepared to relax and enjoy their flight.

"Beautiful, isn't it?" she murmured, watching the scene beneath them unroll in a living panorama.

"Absolutely breathtaking," Brad agreed.

She turned her head to find him watching her instead of the landscape. Their gazes locked. Brad cupped her face in one hand, stroking her cheek with his thumb. "I'm glad you came today," he said, his voice a husky whisper. "I'd like you to always soar above the challenges of life." He brushed his lips across her forehead, then tilted her chin up to receive his kiss.

"Crista," he said, clasping both of her hands in his, "I'd like to meet those challenges with you." Reaching into his pocket, he pulled out a small, square box and flipped open the lid to reveal a delicate ring set with a glittering diamond. "Will you marry me?"

Crista melted into his arms and sealed her acceptance with her kiss.

Behind them, the pilot cleared his throat. "Hard to

tell about people sometimes. They pay good money to ride in a balloon, then they don't even look at the scenery. Go figure."

Crista caught Brad's amused look, and they laughed together. Held in the warm circle of Brad's arms, she rested her head against his chest, feeling the steady beat of his heart keeping time with her own. They hung suspended between the heavens and the earth, the splendor of creation spread out before them.

" 'Sing to God,' " she said in a voice barely above a whisper. " 'Sing praise to his name.' "

Brad's voice joined hers. " 'Extol him who rides the clouds,' " they finished together. " 'His name is the Lord.' "

"Looks like we're starting our descent," Brad murmured in her ear.

Filled with unspeakable joy, Crista could only nod. Today she had ridden the clouds, both in the balloon and in her spirit. Even after they landed, she knew her heart would still soar.

## CAROL COX

In addition to writing, Carol's time is devoted to being a pastor's wife, home-school mom to her teenage son and young daughter, church pianist, youth worker, and 4-H leader. The Arizona native loves any activity she can share with her family in addition to her own pursuits in gardening, crafts, and local history. She has had three historical novels published in the **Heartsong Presents** line as well as five other novellas from Barbour Publishing. Carol and her family make their home in northern Arizona.

# Don't Look Back

by Terry Fowler

# Dedication

To my brothers and sisters in Christ—
how glorious to be a member of the family of God.

# Chapter 1

W e need to talk."

Rattled by the man's demanding tone, Angelina Collier lost count of the pills in the tray. "What can I do for you, Sir?" she asked, a hint of irritation in her tone.

"I want you to fire my daughter."

Fire his daughter? Angelina supposed that in the course of employing people to work in her store, his daughter might be in her employ. Still, she was curious why she should do as he requested. "Who's your daughter?"

"Melody Robbins."

Angelina gasped. Of all the possibilities, Melody was the one she most hated to think of losing. Back in mid-June, she'd taken the college student in, offering room and board and a small salary in exchange for a few hours of babysitting each week. The arrangement worked well for everyone.

In a short time, Angelina and her children had come to love Melody so much. She was more like the children's older sister than a stranger in their home. Angelina's parents had even adopted the young woman into their extended family.

Angelina took a moment to study Melody's dad. For the life of her she couldn't recall his first name. She'd been curious about him since seeing the photo of her parents on Melody's nightstand. Based solely on his daughter's age, she'd guess him to be in his early forties. Just under six feet, he appeared to be fairly health conscious, weighing in around 175 pounds. In keeping with the pleasant summer temperatures, he wore a golf shirt and shorts with worn sandals on his feet.

His thick, salt-and-pepper hair was combed straight back, neatly blow-dried and styled. The chiseled face contained strength to match penetrating brown eyes that had the luster of expensive mink fur.

"And exactly why should I fire her? She's the best employee I've ever had."

He beamed a bit at her words of praise, obviously proud of his daughter but intent on his purpose. "You're making her old before her time. She's too young for the responsibility you've placed on her shoulders."

"Responsibility?" Granted, Melody was spending longer days with the children over the summer, but they had already discussed the plans for when classes started. Based on her calculations, Melody would have the children on her own for around three or four hours a day in the afternoon.

"You always respond with a question?"

"Do you?"

"Look, Mrs. Collier, this is getting us nowhere fast."

"I agree, Mr. Robbins." From what Melody had told her, she knew her mother had died a couple of years before and her father lived in Atlanta. What was he doing here now? "Are you visiting Melody?"

"Call me Wes. Actually, I'm relocating to Wilmington. I don't like being so far away from my only child."

"Have you seen her yet?"

"I wanted to surprise her."

*You'll do that,* Angelina thought. She glanced at the two women approaching the pharmacy. "Excuse me. Your prescriptions are almost ready, ladies. Just one more minute."

❄

Wes stepped back from the counter and waited. He half listened as she directed the women on the use of the medication, thinking she had the perfect voice for her work. The soft tones would certainly soothe the sick.

Glancing around, Wes noted her stock included the standard drug store stuff. A display of summer items ran through the middle aisle—plastic rafts and beach toys inexpensive enough to be left behind after vacation and picnic supplies for those who cared to commune with nature. A couple of beige plastic bucket-shaped chairs sat nearby, momentary respite for those too sick to stand while they waited.

He took a moment to look over the display of suntan lotions, some with SPFs so high that even this woman's milky white complexion wouldn't burn. Wes considered making a purchase. He'd forgotten to pack his.

To say Angelina Collier was a bit of a surprise would truly be an understatement. Melody raved about the woman, her children, and even her parents. Studying her from the corner of his eye, Wes felt certain most men found her attractive. Far from the superwoman image his daughter had instilled in his head, he decided diminutive was the only word to describe the petite woman who probably weighed in at little more than one hundred pounds.

A true blond, she wore her shoulder-length hair pulled back in a clasp. Her facial features were perfect with the exception of a slightly tip-tilted nose that gave added cuteness and a dimple that winked when she smiled.

Maybe it was a bit of insecurity at seeing himself replaced as family that forced him to come here and confront the woman. Could it be that he was so afraid of losing his daughter's love that he wanted to break up the happy environment she'd created for herself the moment she moved out on her own?

No, that had nothing to do with the situation. He was definitely right about the level of responsibility Angelina Collier had put on his Melody's shoulders. She shouldn't be worrying about someone's children. She should be concentrating on earning her degree, enjoying her college years, and making friends.

"Mr. Robbins?"

He jerked out of his reverie at her calling his name. The line to the pharmacy had lengthened, and Wes realized he would have to talk with her after business hours.

"I'm going to be tied up here awhile. Perhaps we can continue this conversation later?"

"Tonight?"

"I have a church meeting. Tomorrow?"

"Fine. Here's the number at my hotel. I'm staying there until I finalize my moving plans."

"I'll be in touch."

❄

A weary Angelina closed the etched glass front door and

locked it for the night. As if the marathon day at the store hadn't been enough, she'd spent the last two hours planning an upcoming church homecoming. Easing her aching feet from her shoes, she padded across the slate tile to the family room to find Melody on the sofa, the television playing low in the background.

Now that she'd met the father, Angelina could definitely see the resemblance between the two. The young woman wore her dark hair long, midway down her back. When standing, she towered over Angelina, at least as tall as her dad. The lines of her face were much softer, but her eyes were the same beautiful shade of brown.

"Everything go okay?" she asked, dropping into the green leather recliner that had once been her husband's. For the moment, the room was toy free, everything neat and clean. She knew Melody had enforced their nightly cleanup rule.

"They tried the usual delay attempts," Melody said, grinning broadly, "but I hung in there and only read them one story before lights-out."

"Good for you. They'd have you reading all night if they got their way."

"Your mom called. Said to tell you she can't go shopping with you tomorrow. The baby's sick."

Disappointed, Angelina asked, "Did she take him to the doctor?" She'd been looking forward to spending a few hours with her mother.

"She said he's cutting teeth and has been a real bear."

"Poor little guy."

"She claims there's no sense in taking him for the doctor to tell her what she already knows."

"It's not like she doesn't have a world of experience," Angelina agreed. Her mother had helped more than her share of infants through teething. "What did you do today?"

"We went to the beach. I slathered the kids with sunscreen, and Bee didn't burn this time.

Melody had learned about the fair-haired child's tendency to burn easily the hard way. She'd been right by Angelina's side, doing everything possible to comfort and cool Bee's heated skin, promising she'd never make that mistake again.

"What did you have for dinner?"

"We feasted on sloppy joes. There are leftovers in the fridge if you're hungry."

Angelina shook her head. She'd grabbed a grilled chicken sandwich on her way to church.

"Good movie?"

"I don't have a clue. After I read my E-mail, I turned the television on and fell asleep. The sun takes a lot out of you."

"Not to mention the kids. Do you ever feel it's too much?"

The young woman looked up, a curious expression touching her face. "What do you mean?"

"Everything. The kids. The chores. Do you ever feel I've placed too heavy a burden on you?"

Melody shook her head. "I love living here with you and the kids, Angelina. I knew immediately that I couldn't live with my friends, and truthfully, I don't much care for the idea of sharing a dorm room or an apartment with a stranger."

"But we were strangers," she pointed out.

"Not really. It's hard to explain, but from the minute we met, I felt like one of the family."

"You should be enjoying your summer. Hanging out with your friends."

Melody shrugged. "I do those things."

"And you play mom to two rowdy children."

"Is something wrong?"

Angelina sighed, worrying that she'd already said too much. "No, not at all. I suppose I should tell you that your dad came by the pharmacy today."

"He went to the store?"

"I take it you've heard from him already?"

"He called tonight. Wants to have breakfast to discuss his plans. What did he say to you?"

"He's concerned that I've placed too much responsibility on you for your age. I don't want to believe that's the case. You would tell me if it got to be too much, wouldn't you?"

Melody pushed her feet to the floor and sat up. "What is he trying to do? Dad knows how much I love my job here. Why would he make statements like that?"

Angelina reclined the chair, dropping her head against the cushioned back. "Probably because he's worried. He's entitled, you know. I suppose I'd feel the same way if someone told me my daughter had taken on two children in her spare time."

"Compared to the jobs some of my friends have, taking care of Rob and Bee is a walk in the park."

Angelina chuckled at the young woman's analogy. "Well, it is that, but it's also a constant battle of wills with a four and three year old."

"I'll talk to Dad. Make him understand how I feel about him interfering."

Fear welled up inside Angelina. She didn't want to be the cause of an argument between father and daughter. "Don't be too hard on him, Melody. He loves you and only has your best interests at heart."

"I'm a grown-up, Angelina. He needs to let me decide what's in my best interests. You don't know Dad like I do. When I was a child, he was never there. Now he wants to make up for lost time. But I'm not his baby anymore. He has to let me grow up."

Empathy for Wes Robbins's plight touched Angelina. "I suppose it's something you won't understand until you have children of your own, but parents can never totally relinquish their leadership role. He's doing what he thinks is in your best interests."

"How can he know what's in my best interests? He hasn't bothered to ask what I want."

She wanted to warn the young woman, tell her what was about to happen, but Angelina knew it wasn't her place. The two of them would have to deal with the situation, and she would have to do her best to remain an impartial bystander. *Yeah, like that would happen.* She loved Melody, and no matter what her father thought, she was fairly certain Melody loved them and her job.

"I'm sure you two will work it out. Just promise to let me know if things get to be too much."

"I love this job so much that if I didn't need the money, I'd do it for free."

Angelina knew the young woman was telling the truth. From the beginning, she'd been struck by Melody's generosity and honesty. Her parents had done a wonderful job with her. "You don't need to convince me. I know how good you are with the kids. I think you'll make a wonderful teacher."

The conversation drifted between them until she could hardly keep her eyes open. "I'm going to turn in. I still have to take the kids shopping tomorrow. Both of them are outgrowing their clothes faster than I can buy them."

"I heard there's a new gently used children's clothes store off College Road. Might be something you want to look into."

"Gently used?" Angelina repeated unbelievingly. "When have you ever seen Robbie and Bee being gentle with their clothes?"

"Well, their Sunday things are in pretty good shape."

"Robbie is growing like a weed. I can't believe he starts kindergarten next year. Where has the time gone?"

"Go to bed, Angelina, before you start fixating on your kids like my dad does."

Apprehension touched deep down inside. "Melody, I don't want to be the cause of trouble between you and your dad."

"You aren't. Dad's more than capable of stirring up things on his own."

Recalling his abrupt entry at the store, Angelina agreed Wes Robbins was that. "Enjoy your breakfast. If you want to spend more time with your dad, I'll be here with the kids."

"Kelly wants me to go with her to visit her grandmother, so I'll probably meet her after I see Dad."

"Have fun and be safe. Night."

Upstairs, Angelina checked on the children and then prepared for bed. Settling in the queen-sized bed, her thoughts drifted for a moment to Wes Robbins. Did the man really intend to attempt to force Melody to give up her job? The parent in her understood his concern, but she also felt Melody resented her dad's interference.

"Father, please help them," she whispered softly. "Guide Wes Robbins's actions so that he doesn't alienate his daughter, and guide Melody's so she doesn't hurt him. Help them to understand just how precious their relationship is—how lucky they are to have each other to love."

The prayer drifted into praise for all the blessings in her life, and soon Angelina's eyes closed in sleep.

# Chapter 2

When the doorbell rang late the following morning, Angelina thought maybe her mother had changed her mind about the shopping trip. Instead, she was surprised to find Wes at the door.

"Hi. You've caught me at a bad time."

"When is a good time for you?"

She detected the note of sarcasm in his voice. "If you'd called, we could have set a time." Angelina knew he had the number. He'd called Melody on her direct line for weeks now.

"I won't take long. I just wanted to thank you for making my daughter angry with me."

"I didn't—"

"Save it," Wes interrupted. "Melody and I had breakfast. From the things she said to me, I'm fairly certain you shared our conversation with her."

"Not really. I did ask if she felt I'd placed too much responsibility on her."

"And now she's pretty upset with me."

"I'm sorry. I was addressing your concerns. I didn't see any other way to handle it than to ask outright."

"You think she's going to admit the job is too much for her?"

Perhaps Melody was right. Her father didn't seem to realize how capable she was. "I think Melody is a mature young woman with a good head on her shoulders. And yes, I do believe she was honest with me."

"I don't understand any of this," Wes declared, shoving his hair back with spread-eagled fingers. "All I heard for weeks were Melody's pleas to let her come to the beach and get an apartment with her friends over the summer. Next thing I know, she's moved into your house and taken a job as a part-time nanny. It doesn't make sense."

"Maybe she decided it was better to live free of charge and get paid, too."

Angelina didn't add her suspicions that Melody didn't care for the living arrangement with her friends. The young woman's comment about going a bit far in testing their wings led her to believe Melody's friends' lifestyle had been more than she expected.

"Perhaps," Wes agreed, shrugging his shoulders.

A loud crash came from the distant parts of the house. "Fereby?" Angelina yelled, racing in the direction of the sound.

Her daughter sat between an overturned coffee table and a jumble of sofa cushions.

"Mommy," the little girl called, holding out her arms. She touched one hand to her head. "Boo-boo."

"What have I told you, Bee? You're going to break your neck if you don't stop climbing on everything." She quickly checked her head, sighing relief when there were no cuts or abrasions.

"Who that?"

Angelina followed her daughter's finger to Wes. Swinging Fereby into her arms, she said, "It's not polite to point, Bee. This is Melody's father, Mr. Robbins."

"Mr. Wobbins?" the child repeated.

Wes walked across the room and touched the child's cheek. "Yes, Cutie. And who are you?"

"Fairbee," she announced.

"This is my daughter, Fereby."

"How old are you?"

Angelina smiled when the child worked her fingers until she held up three. She was just beginning to master the new age.

"I really do have to go. I have to pick up my son from day school and take them clothes shopping." She thought for a minute. "Tonight's pizza night. You're welcome to join us."

Wes's serious gaze rested on her face. "I think I will."

"See you around six o'clock then. We eat early because of the kids."

❋

Wes watched the white SUV pull out of the driveway before starting his own car. Was there ever a time when Angelina Collier wasn't rushing around? He'd truly like to know.

The little girl was definitely a cutie complete with her mother's hair, eyes, and dimpled smile. No wonder Melody was so attracted to the child. It would be interesting to see how she interacted with this family. Perhaps being a member of a larger group was what appealed to his daughter.

Maybe by tonight, Angelina Collier would be able to

settle down long enough for them to complete a conversation. Meanwhile, he had lots of details to work out.

Wes honestly felt God had directed his path to this new city. He had prayed and asked how he could strengthen his relationship with Melody, and this had been God's answer. He would miss Atlanta, but in truth, he missed his child more and wanted to be where she was.

❄

"Daddy? What are you doing here?"

He kissed Melody's cheek. "Mrs. Collier invited me."

She looked puzzled. "Why would she do that?"

"I stopped by earlier today when she was rushing off, and she suggested I come back tonight."

Melody eyed him suspiciously. "You didn't say anything else?"

Wes thought maybe it was wiser that he keep his earlier accusations to himself. "I'm not happy about this, Melody."

The struggle between parent and adult child was evident in their stubborn expressions. "And I told you I want to keep this job."

"Melody? Is it the pizza delivery?"

Wes recognized Angelina's voice.

"It's my dad."

Angelina stepped into the foyer. "Wes. Come in. Can we get you something to drink?"

"Whatever everyone else is having will be fine."

"Iced tea it is. Unless you'd prefer milk?"

He grimaced at the suggestion. He hadn't drunk milk with his meals since he was a child. "Tea is fine."

After serving him, they all settled in the family room.

Melody sat in the corner of the sofa with the little boy curled up at her side while the girl chose her mother's lap.

"These your new sneaks?" Melody asked the sturdy little boy, rubbing her fingers over his freshly trimmed hair.

*He must resemble his dad with that reddish blond hair and hazel eyes,* Wes thought as the child launched into a description of how the new shoes lit up when he walked.

"Mel never had shoes like that," Wes said.

The child giggled and repeated the name.

"You didn't have to call me that."

"It's my pet name for you."

"I want a pet," Robbie announced.

"No, Robbie. A pet name is like when we call you Rob or Robbie. Dad, this is Robert Collier, Jr. Robbie, this is my dad, Wes Robbins. I think you've already met Bee."

"Nice to meet you, Robert."

"Robbie's my pet name," he said. "Robert's my daddy. He's in heaven."

"I'm sorry to hear that. I know you must miss him a great deal."

"Robert died last year following an extended bout with cancer," Angelina explained.

Wes knew all about the insidious disease that showed no respect for family as it ripped loved ones from their homes. "My wife died of cancer two years ago."

Angelina offered him a sympathetic smile. "Melody told me. It's a tragic loss."

Wes nodded, offering his daughter a small smile when she touched his hand.

The chiming of the doorbell alerted them to the arrival of dinner.

"First one to the door gets the cheese pizza," Melody called, jumping from the sofa. The two children raced after her.

"She always lets them win. I think she's on to something with her game. They eat better when they think they're winners."

"The things parents do to get food into their kids. Mel was quite a picky eater."

They returned to the room, Melody carrying the pizza boxes. "I don't think Angelina wants to hear about my pea-throwing skills."

Angelina laughed and moved to settle the two children at the coffee table. "Not in the presence of these two. Robbie, it's your night to say grace."

Wes was both surprised and entertained by the little boy's version of grace. Robbie didn't recite a standard prayer. Instead, he thanked the Lord for food and then shoes and a variety of things until his mother called his name softly. He hurriedly added his mother, sister, and Melody, and said amen.

Wes found himself enjoying being in the midst of a family again. The pizza was consumed amidst much laughter and talking. Melody was as quick as Angelina in meeting the needs of the kids, wiping hands and encouraging them to try one more bite, acting more like an older sister than a caregiver. Afterward, she set up the VCR for them and returned to the sofa.

"What did you do this afternoon?" Melody asked him.

"Looked at a house. One of those old places downtown. It has a private apartment if you're interested."

His daughter rolled her eyes. "You don't give up, do you?"

"Bee, Robbie, time for your baths," Angelina said, apparently attempting to give them privacy to discuss the matter.

He appreciated her sensitivity to the situation. Melody quickly foiled the plan.

"I'll take care of them, Angelina."

"Visit with your dad."

"We'll only argue. You should stick around and referee."

"Melody!" he blurted.

"Well, it's true. I like my life the way it is. What else did you do today? I bet you looked at stores, too."

He had rented the unit next door to the pharmacy. The shopping center seemed pretty active with a good mixture of businesses, and the unit was large enough for him to offer classes to small groups.

"I knew it. Don't you ever take time to reconsider an action?"

"Not after the Lord answers my prayers."

He noted the way Angelina's head popped up at that. "The unit next door to yours caught my eye when I was there the other day."

Melody flashed him an angry look. "Angelina was thinking of expanding into that unit."

"Sorry. I called, and it was a good deal so I snapped it up."

Angelina shrugged. "That's what being indecisive will do for you. What's your business?"

"Stained glass. I create and sell pieces and stock supplies. I plan to offer classes in small groups after I get open."

"I'll have to check out your work. I love stained glass."

"Maybe you should take a class and create some of your own."

"I work far too many hours to take on anything else."

"Daddy, about the house-hunting, a condo or town-house is all you need," Melody pointed out.

"I'm supposed to look at some places at the beach tomorrow."

"Now you're talking."

Wes grinned and directed his next words to Angelina, "Tell me I don't know my child. The beach is exactly why she chose to go to college here."

"Along with most of the other students," Angelina agreed. "UNC-W by the Sea is quite popular." The phone rang, and Angelina picked up the cordless from the end table.

"Hi, Mom. Sitting around talking. Melody's dad's here." From the way Angelina lowered her voice, Wes could tell the woman was asking questions. "Yes, he's right here. How's the baby?"

"Baby?" Wes repeated, thinking it strange that Angelina's mother would have a small child.

"The Atkinses have two foster children, Jeremy and Eddie," Melody explained. "The baby was running a temp last night. He's cutting a tooth."

"They live here in town?" Melody nodded. "Why don't the kids stay with their grandparents?"

"They do."

"No, I mean, why does she pay you to baby-sit when their grandparents are here?"

"Angelina doesn't feel right about asking them to take on her responsibility."

"But it's okay to ask you?" he inquired, lowering his voice.

"It's a job, Daddy. We've got the schedule worked out."

"And what about when classes start?"

"Robbie will be in half-day school, and his grandfather will pick him up afterward. Bee will stay with her grandmother. I pick them up when I get out of school and keep them until Angelina gets home around 6:30. Then we fix dinner and share the chores."

"Sounds pretty complicated."

"But it's not," she insisted stubbornly.

"You want to go house-hunting with me tomorrow?"

"Sorry, can't. I have the kids."

"When do you have another day off?"

"Sunday, but I usually go to church with Angelina and the kids."

"Mind if I tag along?"

"Not at all."

"Are you okay with my move?"

"Daddy, you know I love you. And I've missed you. I just want you to understand this is important to me."

Angelina replaced the receiver and moved to get the kids in motion for bedtime preparation.

Melody jumped to her feet and kissed her father's cheek. "Night, Daddy. I'll take care of their baths."

"I suppose I've been dismissed," Wes said when his daughter shepherded the kids from the room. "Thanks for your hospitality."

"You're welcome. I'm glad you could come."

"Melody seems to really love it here, but she's right about one thing. I don't give up. I'm going to encourage her to come live with me."

Angelina nodded. "If Melody tells me that's what she

wants, I won't stand in her way."

✻

After closing the door behind Wes Robbins, Angelina found herself thinking how nice it was to hear a man's voice in her home again. She missed Robert dreadfully. Even though they'd married in college, their time together had been much too short. Robert had been the type of husband women dreamed of having, always encouraging her to reach for her goals and never letting their family stand in the way of her accomplishments.

Not only had his loss left her lonely, it had left a hole in her security net. All her life Angelina had struggled with security, never able to fully trust anyone for fear she would be let down again. She had been a child the first time it happened, and the second time had been just as difficult. The feeling that she had to depend wholly on herself never left her.

She understood Wes's feelings about his child. Her struggle to combat the fear of providing for her children and herself made her accept that he would probably be victorious in his quest. But what Wes failed to see was that she loved Melody as well and only wanted the best for her.

# Chapter 3

W hile working two weeks later, Angelina considered Wes Robbins's invasion of their lives. No matter where she went, he was there. He often popped into the pharmacy during the day after checking the renovation progress in his store and, under the guise of seeing his daughter, had slipped into the habit of spending time with the family.

That first Sunday Wes attended church with them, her mother invited him to dinner. He fit right in, cuddling the kids, teasing her mom, bonding with her dad, and turning them into his extended family.

Her plan to distance herself from the situation as much as possible was shot to pieces in the first few days after determining father and daughter required a mediator. In one sense, Angelina didn't feel it was her place, but then her mothering instincts kicked in, and she felt she had to be the voice of reason.

Though Melody didn't say so, Angelina knew he still encouraged her to give up the job and come live with him in the two-bedroom condo he'd found at the beach.

The phone rang and she answered, not the least

surprised to find Wes on the other end.

"Hi, Angelina. You busy?"

"Hello, Wes. What can I do for you?"

"Melody and the kids are helping unpack boxes."

She knew that. Melody had called to ask if it was okay to take the kids with her to her dad's.

He certainly didn't allow anything to slow him down. He'd flown to Georgia to pack up and put his house on the market and returned the night before driving a truck filled with his possessions.

"I'm not sure how much help Robbie and Bee are," she pointed out. Her two little ones were probably more of a hindrance than anything else. She should have suggested Melody check with her parents.

"We've got the kitchen and living room in passable condition and thought maybe you'd like to come over for dinner."

"You're too busy settling in," she argued. "I'll pick up the kids after work, and Melody can stay and help. You'll be finished in a fraction of the time."

"It's spaghetti. My mom's recipe. The sauce cooks for hours. You'll think you've gone to heaven," he promised. "Besides, you have to eat. I'm making garlic bread. Mel said the kids love spaghetti, and they sort of know what we're having for dinner."

Wes wasn't playing fair. Telling her children he was preparing their favorite food and making garlic bread, which was her weakness, seemed like calculated temptation to Angelina. Besides, after her long day, the idea of going down to the beach wasn't necessarily appealing, but then again, the thought of not having to cook more than made up for the drive. "Okay. How do I get there? And it'll probably be close to seven before I arrive."

"Perfect."

"How's the store coming along?" she asked, not sure why she felt the need to extend the conversation.

"Great. They promised to have the renovations completed by next week. I hope so. I've already got an order in for stock."

The old adage about time being money sprang to mind. When it came to business, every day the store was closed cost the owner. "I can probably loan you a corner if it arrives before they finish."

"I don't think that'll be necessary, but I appreciate the offer. Oops, better get back to my spaghetti. See you soon."

❄

"Why did you give me that second helping?" Angelina moaned as she laid her napkin on the table.

A knowing grin covered his face as Wes countered, "I don't recall forcing it on you."

She grimaced, resting one hand against her well-filled stomach. "I'm not sure I'm going to be able to move."

Melody picked up her plate and reached for Robbie's. "Sounds like you need a walk. Why don't you join Dad on his nightly constitutional? He has doctor's orders to walk every day."

"Doctor's orders?" Angelina repeated.

"I had a heart attack a few years back."

The news rocked Angelina to her core. He appeared to be in the best of health. There was no outward indication that he was less than robust. "That must have been frightening."

"I was lucky. It didn't do much damage. Of course, I had to change my lifestyle."

"Why don't we all go?" she suggested.

"No, you two go," Melody insisted. "I need to do the dishes, and the kids are tired. They've had an exciting afternoon."

"You're spoiling me, you know."

The two women shared a smile. "I know. I figure I'll hit you up for a favor soon."

"Hey, I cooked," Wes reminded. "Do I get a favor, too?"

"I'm walking with you, aren't I?" Angelina teased.

It was a beautiful evening. The warm night was only a hint of the hotter ones to come. Now and again the scent of Wes's aftershave tantalized her nostrils, and Angelina found she liked the manly scent.

They dodged an incoming wave. "I've been meaning to tell you how much I enjoy spending time with your family. I'm in awe of your parents. I can't imagine being a foster parent at their age. Then again, I can hardly recall what it's like to have small children."

"The grandchildren will come soon enough, and you'll get back into the swing of things."

"I'm hoping that's several years down the line for Mel. One of my biggest fears is that she'll decide to marry before she finishes college. I don't want her missing out on her education."

"Women can do both, you know," Angelina said, bending to pick up a tiny sand dollar. She brushed it off, pleased to find it wasn't broken. "Robert and I married in college. When he got his degree, he took a job at a pharmacy in Chapel Hill so I could finish my education. Robbie came along just as I was finishing up. Considering what happened to Robert, I'm glad we didn't wait."

"You've got a point."

"Don't worry, Wes. Melody dates, but she's never been serious enough to bring the guy to the house."

"That's good to know. I know she thinks of you and the Atkinses as her extended family."

"The Atkinses are good people."

"You say that like you're not one yourself."

"I'm an Atkins by the grace of God—the child of their hearts."

"You're adopted?"

"Yes. From what Mom told me, my real parents died when I was five or so."

"Did you have siblings?"

"Yes, but I don't know much about them."

"Do you ever think about finding them?"

"Sometimes, but then I've found it's not good to look back. The past holds a lot of sadness. For now, I've got to concentrate on making a good life for my kids."

"You only have to trust in God to provide. Psalm 118:8 reminds us it's better to trust in the Lord than to put confidence in man."

*Trust in God.* If only he knew how much she wanted to do that; but Angelina was afraid. If something happened to her, what would happen to her children? She didn't want them growing up in foster homes.

"We'd better head back," she said, ignoring his words. "It's late and I need to get the kids into bed."

❄

*What was she thinking?* Wes wondered as they backtracked

to the condo. He'd noticed the way she clammed up when he mentioned trusting in God. Wasn't Angelina a believer? She attended church regularly and unless she was putting on an incredible act, she obviously loved the Lord.

Maybe it was the past making her doubt. Whatever the case, Wes knew from experience that the only way he'd survived the rocky times was by remembering that the Lord loved him. The heart attack had been hard enough—knocking him to his knees—and then Laura's death had laid him flat. For weeks, he'd barely existed until Melody forced him to rejoin the land of the living.

Now he was thankful she had. She'd asked him if he thought this was what her mother expected of him. That had been more than sufficient to push him toward recovery. Throughout her illness, Laura had prayed for God's will to be done in her life. She was ready to go, but determined to fight the cancer to the very end. Tears wet his eyes at the thought of his courageous wife.

Wes pulled the door key from his pocket and unlocked the door, heeding Melody's shushing finger as they stepped inside. The two children were fast asleep on the sofa.

Angelina knelt by Robbie's side, tenderly smoothing back his hair before she shook him gently. "Time to go home, Sweetie." She didn't even try to wake Bee, just lifted the little girl into her arms. Bee sighed and adjusted her head more comfortably against her mother's shoulder. "Thanks for dinner, Wes. You were right about that spaghetti sauce."

"My pleasure. We'll have to do it again soon."

Melody picked up her purse and kissed his cheek.

"I'm going to follow Angelina home, Dad. Talk to you tomorrow."

Wes followed them to the cars, watching as they settled the children in Angelina's SUV. As he watched the taillights disappear around the corner, he admitted he already missed them all. Slowly but surely they had slipped into his heart and mind.

# Chapter 4

A few days later, Wes stopped by Angelina's house to see if Melody wanted to have lunch with him. He was shocked to find four children instead of two.

"Why is he here?" Wes asked when she opened the door with the baby draped over her shoulder. Her hand never stopped its movement as she rubbed and patted. "Mrs. Ruth had a doctor's appointment, and Mr. Edwin wanted to go with her. I volunteered to baby-sit."

"Why do you always take on so much? You don't owe these people anything."

She smiled when the baby rewarded her with a loud burp. "They're my friends, Dad."

Why couldn't she see the truth? "I think they take advantage of you," he retorted somewhat angrily.

"Oh, please, you don't have a clue how cushy this job truly is."

"Cushy?" he repeated doubtfully. "I hardly think caring for two, sometimes four, active children is cushy."

"My friends are slinging burgers and waiting tables until the wee hours of the morning. Compared to that, this job is a breeze."

"So you keep telling me."

"I can see you're dying to talk to Angelina again. Just don't. Okay? Promise me, Dad," she insisted when stubbornness entered his expression.

"But, Melody, you shouldn't be tied down with all these kids."

"I'm exactly where I want to be. Why can't you understand?"

"Because I have no idea why a vibrant, beautiful young woman like yourself isn't out there making friends and enjoying what should be one of the best times of her life."

She turned around and walked into the family room, settling the baby in his car seat. "Maybe you've never understood me then, Dad. I never planned to turn my college years into a constant party. I have my friends from home and friends at church that I go out with occasionally, but I'm not interested in pledging sororities and stuff like that."

Wes had the suspicion he was fighting a lost cause. "I guess I'll head on to the store since you're busy. Can we get together for dinner or lunch soon?"

"Sure thing," she said, her attention diverted when the children ran screaming at the top of their lungs through the room.

❄

"Something wrong, Wes?" Angelina asked minutes later when she glanced up to find him strolling down the aisle toward the pharmacy counter.

"I don't understand my child."

She drew a deep breath. "What parent does?"

"I want to make her life easier."

"Let me guess. You've been arguing about her job again.

What happened this time?"

"She's baby-sitting the foster kids, too."

She chose her words carefully. "I see. I can assure you she's well-paid. Mom doesn't ask her to sit for free, though I will admit that if Melody had her way, she would. She loves babies."

Wes shook his head wearily. "I know. Do you have any idea why?"

Angelina lifted one shoulder and smiled. "No. Why does it bother you so much, Wes?"

"She's young. I'd like to see her out having fun."

"Maybe your idea of fun and hers don't match?"

"I have more fun than she does, and I'm an old man."

Angelina couldn't control her burst of laughter. "You're not old."

"Then why do I feel so old right now?" he challenged.

"Defeated, but you'll live to fight another day," she teased. A customer came to the counter, and Angelina broke away to talk to him. Wes lifted a hand in good-bye and headed out of the store.

As she worked, Angelina found herself thinking of him. Wes was a nice guy. She could appreciate that he didn't like his daughter's choices. Melody and her father were very alike, and she didn't hesitate to tell him to let her live her own life.

The phone rang and she answered, immediately recognizing his voice. "Wes?"

"If I asked you out to dinner, would you go?"

Stunned, she fumbled the pill bottle she held. Why had he gone back to his business and called? Why not ask her in person?

"I know I should have asked you while I was there, but I couldn't get up the nerve."

She caught the receiver against her chin. "To discuss Melody?"

"No," he said quickly.

"You want to consort with the enemy?" she asked, capping the bottle and checking the label one last time.

"I'm beginning to think I'm my own worst enemy."

"I don't understand."

"I'm so eager to have something I never bothered to work for when I should have."

"Huh?"

"Just past regrets. Are we on for tonight? Or do you need more time to make arrangements?"

"I probably should see if Melody is available to keep the kids."

"I'm sure she is," Wes responded matter-of-factly. "How about it?"

"Where did you plan to go?" She hadn't dated in a long time and wasn't certain she had anything in her closet that was date-worthy.

"How about the steak house over on South College? I've been there several times, and the food is great. I'll pick you up around seven."

"I'll check with Melody and let you know."

Angelina rang up the prescription and thanked the customer before reaching for the phone. Melody picked up on the second ring.

"Hear you've got a full house over there."

Melody sighed loudly. "What did he say? He promised."

"He didn't pick a fight," she reassured. "He's worried."

"Well, he can give himself a break. Your mom picked them up a few minutes ago. Said her appointment went fine."

"Thank God. Now, I've got a question for you, and I expect you to tell me nothing less than the truth."

"Is something wrong?"

"Your dad asked me out to dinner tonight. I said yes, but if you have a problem with it, I'll tell him I can't."

"Why would I have a problem? You two share something in common."

"What?"

"Me." Melody laughed at her pun. "Personally, I'd be thankful if you went. Maybe if Daddy got a life of his own, he'd leave mine alone."

"You're sure?"

"Positive. Where's he taking you?"

Angelina shared the restaurant name and time. "I'll run home and change. Are you sure you're not busy tonight?"

"No great plans. Kelly might come over for awhile. Robbie and Bee won't be any trouble."

"Would you like to order Chinese so you don't have to cook?"

"Sounds great."

❄

The butterflies in her stomach must be some gigantic hybrid, Angelina thought as she waited for Wes's arrival. In the bedroom, she'd thought about what she was doing and wondered if it was the right thing. The doubts had been so overwhelming that she'd finally dropped onto the bed and prayed for God's guidance in the matter. She felt a bit more confident after finishing the prayer.

"Angelina, there's some old man here who claims he's your date," Melody called up the stairs.

"Why. . .I'll show you old, young lady." The sounds of muted laughter drifted up the stairs.

She stood and smoothed the lavender knit top. Did she look okay? One last glance in the mirror assured her she was fine. She joined the family in the living room to find Robbie and Bee being teased by Wes.

"Mommy," Bee cried out, running over to wrap her arms about her legs.

"Your mommy can't save you. I'm going to steal all her kisses." Wes laughed.

Her childish screams echoed throughout the room as she ran around behind her mother. Melody stretched out her arms. "Come on, Bee."

"No. Want Mommy."

"She's going out."

"Bee go."

Melody made a sad face. "You have to stay with us. We'll be lonely."

The child looked at her mother and said emphatically, "Wobbie and Meldee go too."

"No, Bee," Angelina said, lifting the child into her arms and delivering the next words with a hug. "Tonight's a grown-up night. Mr. Wes and I are going out, and you're staying home."

"I want to go," she insisted stubbornly.

"Not tonight."

She started to cry.

Angelina forced herself to discipline the child. "Fereby, what did Mommy say?"

"Bee not go."

"That's correct. I want you and Robbie to behave."

Melody took the child from her arms and said, "They're always good for me, aren't you?"

Bee nodded her head before tucking it into Melody's shoulder and sticking her thumb into her mouth. It was a habit the child reverted to now and again, when she felt insecure or didn't get her way. Angelina figured it was the latter tonight.

"We can stay here," Wes said when she glanced back as they started out the door.

"No. She needs to learn."

"Leaving them with others is hard. You're a stronger parent than me. That was the most pitiful expression on Bee's face. I would have given in."

Angelina settled in the car, taking advantage of the moment to study Wes. Was there some hidden meaning in his words? "We can go back."

"No way. You've already told her no," he said, quickly closing the door. He climbed into the driver's seat and asked, "You okay with the place I suggested?"

She nodded and soon they were seated in a booth, enjoying a blooming onion appetizer and iced tea.

"It's been a long time since I went on a date," Angelina said.

"Did you date a lot?"

"There were a couple of guys before Robert, but once we met, I decided he was the one. What about you?"

"Laura and I married right out of college. Then first

thing we knew Mel was on the way. Laura elected to become a stay-at-home mom, and I jumped on the fast track. I was even more driven to succeed after I had a wife and daughter to support. That was the biggest mistake I ever made."

Regret filled his eyes as he continued. "I can't begin to count the nights I came home long after Mel was in bed. I kept telling myself I'd do better, but something always interfered. All too soon she was nearly grown and didn't need to spend time with her daddy."

"That's why I feel guilty about leaving my two," she said. "I spend so much time at work and want to be with them as often as possible."

"You think they're willing to share you?"

She finished wiping her fingers and tucked the napkin in her lap. "Why Mr. Robbins, are you stating your intentions?" she inquired with in an affected drawl.

He chuckled at her playfulness. "And if I were?"

"I might ask what you intend."

"You're a beautiful woman, and I'd like to have you as my friend—and whatever else the Lord intends."

"Well, you leave no doubt."

"Don't you think a man should be straightforward?"

"Yes, I do. And, truthfully, despite our problems over me being Melody's employer, I do think of you as a very good friend."

He touched her hand. "Just a friend?"

"Well, that's important too," Angelina defended.

"Definitely. The best relationships start out that way."

"I find you to be a handsome, personable man with a delightful daughter."

"Are you attracted to me, Angel?"

Angelina felt her face warm at his prompting. "Don't call me that."

"Why not? I like giving people pet names. And don't change the subject."

"I guess so. Otherwise, I probably wouldn't be here."

"Now we're getting somewhere."

Before he could pursue the topic further, the waitress arrived with their salads. After saying grace, they busied themselves sprinkling salt and pepper and pouring salad dressings. "How was your day?" Angelina asked, feeling it best not to pursue their previous discussion.

"Creative. That's one of the problems with a one-man operation. Customers must have radar or something. They have a tendency to arrive just about the time I get started with a new piece. I do lots before I open every day and sometimes after I close."

"You need an assistant."

"I'd hoped Mel might help out."

"Wes. . ."

"You don't need to get defensive."

Angelina rested her fork on the plate and focused her attention on him. "I am not defensive," she insisted.

"You are. From the first time we argued about the situation, I've felt you feel I'm attacking you personally when I make a comment about Mel's job."

"I'm feeling caught in the middle," Angelina exclaimed, lowering her voice when she caught the attention of the other patrons. "You feel I control the situation, but I don't. Melody has told me she wants her job, and until she says differently, I don't plan to find a replacement."

"You're right," Wes agreed. "Let me say that I considered Mel might help out before I knew how things really were here. I thought maybe she'd be interested in working in the family business."

"Does she like stained glass?"

"She thinks it's beautiful but isn't really interested in the creative aspect," he admitted. "Back to the apology. Before I got to know you, I thought it was better for you to fill the bad guy role than me. I felt that if you terminated her employment Melody would do what I wanted. I should know my daughter better than that."

"I can understand your feelings to a certain degree, but if she's happy, why can't you accept this is what she wants?"

"You've got me there. Maybe I'm afraid my workaholic tendency will manifest itself in her. I'd hate to see her make the same mistakes I made."

"I think Melody is one blessed young woman to have a father who cares for her as much as you do, even if you do want me to fill the bad guy role," Angelina added with a huge grin.

"I'll try not to say anything else."

"But if you think she's overloaded, you'll let me know, right?"

"Right," he agreed, squeezing her hand in his. The brown gaze held hers. "We make a good team."

"I'm not on the opposing side, Wes. As a parent I know you want the best for your child, but when they're older and capable of making their own decisions, your ideas of what's best will not always match theirs."

"You're so right. We'd better finish these salads."

❄

Later, Wes said good night and let himself out of the house, double-checking the door to assure it was locked. All in all, their first date had been pretty good. Personally, he hoped it was the first of many. Angelina Collier was quite some woman.

# Chapter 5

"Angel, you've got to come over here right now."

She sighed. The man was hopeless. Maybe he could walk in and out of his business with the flip of an open/closed sign, but she couldn't. People depended on her being there.

"Ah, come on, Angel. Just for a minute. This you've got to see."

"Wes, I've got customers." Actually, she didn't. There had been a lull in business since the lunch hour had passed.

He didn't seem to hear her words. "You know what they say about everyone having a double?" Wes rushed on, not waiting for an answer. "Yours is in my store right now. You've got to see her."

His determination was a trait she'd come to expect. "I don't suppose I'll get any peace if I don't?"

"I could ask her to go over there."

"No. I'll be right there," she said quickly, not wanting to turn her pharmacy into a sideshow.

After telling her cashiers where she'd be, Angelina walked next door. As always, she was in awe of the showroom in the front of his store. Wes had replaced the large expanses of glass on the front of the unit with paned windows and hung various pieces of glass in the windows that he kept sparkling clean. Inside the store, he had more window units and glass walls featuring the various pieces, all carefully lit to enhance their beauty.

Angelina noticed the woman off to the side. Wes hurried over, grabbing her hand and pulling her toward the stranger. "You're not going to believe this."

"Ms. McDaniel, this is Angelina Collier. The woman I told you about."

She turned, a smile touching her lips as she greeted the newcomer.

"Do you see it?" Wes asked impatiently.

They were around the same height but the similarity stopped there. This woman weighed a bit more, and her shoulder-length hair was a light brown and her eyes hazel—far removed from Angelina's blond, green-eyed appearance.

They looked at each other and then at Wes. Angelina offered a little shrug and apologetic smile. "Not really."

Ms. McDaniel shook her head and said, "Me neither."

Wes looked amazed. "I can't believe you don't see the resemblance. When you smile, you both have that little dimple at the corner of your mouth. Bee has it too, Angel."

They gave each other the once-over again.

"I think you missed the mark on this, Wes," Angelina said.

"I agree. I'm Crista McDaniel," she said, holding out her hand, "a consultant from Phoenix. I'm in town for a seminar, and when I saw the glass in the window, I had to stop and take a look. I'm in love with that piece with the balloons."

Angelina's gaze shot to the wall as the woman's words struck a responsive chord. She adored balloons. Back when they first married and their budget was tight, Robert had often given her helium bouquets instead of flowers. She'd even done the children's nursery in clowns and balloons. She knew exactly which picture the woman referred to. "Don't you just love it?"

"Oh yes."

Angelina glanced at Wes and grinned, teasing, "She has good taste. Perhaps that's where we resemble each other."

"You're blind."

"Don't pay him any attention, Ms. McDaniel. Not all of us have his imagination. Are you enjoying your stay?"

"Very much."

She smiled warmly, this time noticing the little dimple Wes spoke of as Crista McDaniel returned the smile. "I've got to get back. It was a pleasure meeting you."

"You too."

❄

Wes watched Angel leave before turning back to his customer. "You really do resemble each other."

"It happens," Crista said. "I've seen strangers with similar mannerisms. I'm going to have to buy that piece."

"You want to take it with you or have it shipped?"

"Oh, shipping would be perfect." She reached into her purse for her wallet and removed a business card. "Here's the address."

As Wes wrote up the sale, they chatted for a few more minutes before she checked her watch and said good-bye.

Later that afternoon, Wes stopped by the pharmacy.

"I can't believe you couldn't see the likeness with Crista McDaniel."

*And I can't believe you did,* Angelina thought. The entire situation had been embarrassing. "Must have been some little something that made you think that."

He shrugged. "See you at church tonight?"

She nodded. "I'm helping with the kids' program."

"Care to join me for dinner before we go?"

"There's no time, Wes. By the time I close up here, run home, and change, we'll probably be late. Besides, Melody has plans to feed Robbie and Bee early tonight, like she usually does on Wednesdays."

"Hey, maybe I should rush on over. What are they having?"

"Beans and franks," she said.

"Maybe another time. See you later. By the way, I invited Ms. McDaniel to church."

That caught Angelina's attention. He was certainly friendly with the young woman. Something stirred inside, and she realized she didn't want Wes to be interested in another woman.

"She coming?" she asked, pushing back the thought as she hoped her feelings weren't evident.

"Thanked me but said as much as she'd love to, she's tied up with work. Reminds me of you with that work thing."

Angelina smiled at that. "Give it a rest. You just need to get your eyes examined."

"I'll have you know my vision is twenty-twenty."

"Oh, that's right," Angelina said. "It's your imagination that's out of control."

"I still say you look like that woman."

"Okay, Wes, whatever you say. Except for the hair and eyes, we're almost identical twins."

"I wouldn't go that far."

"Me neither. You're seeing things that aren't there."

Wes didn't say another word as he turned and walked toward the front of the store, holding up one hand in a silent farewell.

"Bye, Wes. If I see your twin around, I'll call," she teased.

"Do that."

# Chapter 6

I can't be sick."

Those were the last words Wes had heard from Angelina's mouth as the nurses shooed him out to begin preparations for surgery. Now he waited with her mother in the surgery waiting area. The room was designed to be comfortable, but the feelings being in a hospital evoked made Wes want to be anywhere but there. On the other hand, he needed to be there for Angelina.

Wes thought back over the past few weeks. Every day since Angel had come into his life seemed to get better. He loved her intelligence and wit, her sense of humor, and mostly her ability to accept things as they came.

The only negative was when they butted heads over Melody's job, but when she looked tired or seemed overburdened, his first instinct was to confront Angelina. He had to admit that she generally helped work the situation out. She treated Melody more like a daughter than an employee, and Wes knew it was because she cared about them both.

At times, he recognized she was incapable of totally letting go and trusting God. He had been with her during one particularly painful bout and when he tried to approach the need for her to see a doctor, she told him it wasn't necessary. It had only taken one other episode to convince her she didn't have an option. He wished he could make her understand that relying on her own strength limited her. This sickness required God's power to get her through.

"I'm thankful this is a routine surgery," Ruth said.

"Angel's pretty upset that she requires surgery at all."

Ruth Atkins nodded. "She's been having problems with her gallbladder for awhile now. That last attack was bad enough to convince her she couldn't wait any longer. I think maybe that after Robert she was afraid of what the doctors would find."

"But surely she knows. . ."

"The reality of the situation is that she's sick and feels she can't be. No matter what experience tells her, she's afraid. Her dad and I are here for her. We'll do whatever we need to do until she gets back on her feet."

"Mel and I will be, too. I just hope we can convince her to take it easy and heal before going back to work."

"You can have that task," her mother teased.

"I've heard this surgery has a two-week recovery period. I know she's going to be a challenge."

The two of them idly watched a short news broadcast on the waiting room television. "Who has the kids?"

"Edwin has Bee and the baby. Robbie and Jeremy are at day school. Melody plans to bring Robbie and Bee here after Angelina wakes."

"I know Edwin wishes he could be here. Being foster parents must really be difficult."

"We've always had foster kids. I guess it was hard on Angelina. By the time she got used to a group of kids, they'd go away and we'd get more."

"Angelina was the only child you ever adopted?"

She nodded. "Most of the time they're in foster placement because they can't be adopted, but in this case her parents had died, and there was no one to take all the children."

Wes felt saddened by their separation. "It's awful when a family has to be split up. I hope they were all as blessed as Angel."

The older woman blushed slightly at his compliment. "We were the blessed ones. God sent us our own little angel."

Wes chuckled softly. "You think her actions are going to be at odds with her name while she recuperates?"

"You can take that to the bank. Personally, I think God is telling her to trust Him more completely."

"I've told her that. She seems to feel she can't lose control."

"Given the circumstances, can you blame her?"

He understood. Losing her parents at an early age, then going from foster home to foster home until she came to live with the Atkinses certainly didn't help establish stability. Add to that the early loss of her husband and having to raise two children alone.

"Do you know anything about her family?"

"Their name was Richmond. She was in the system for a few months before she came to us. She was a beautiful child—a lot like Bee now."

"They're very alike."

Ruth nodded. "It took time for her to trust that she wasn't going to be sent away. Deep down, I'm not sure she doesn't still feel insecure."

"She's going to get past that soon," Wes promised. He believed in Angelina and knew she was more than capable. She just needed to place her trust in God—much like he'd done when he got sick and then lost Laura.

While they waited, Wes began the task he'd been putting off. Sending Christmas greetings was his way of thanking his customers and offering a special discount coupon generally increased his business over the holidays.

As Wes applied stickers to the pre-printed cards, he didn't care what etiquette said about hand addressing the envelopes. The labels Mel made saved him a ton of work.

Pulling off the next sticker, he noted the Arizona address. Crista McDaniel. Wes repeated the name in his head before recalling the woman. Angel's look-alike. He still couldn't believe they didn't see the similarities. He affixed the label. She was too far away to take advantage of the discount, but she had been a good customer. She deserved a thank-you.

"Did Angel tell you about the woman who came into the store who looks like her?"

Ruth looked up from the embroidery she was doing. "She didn't see a resemblance."

"I wish you'd been there to back me up. Her name is Crista McDaniel. She looks just like Angel when she smiles. Has that same little dimple."

"Well, they do say everyone has a look-alike."

They sat quietly, each lost in their activity until they were called in the private consulting room to meet with the surgeon. As expected, the surgery had gone well, with no complications. Both breathed a sigh of relief.

"No need to worry. It was a textbook case. She'll be in recovery for awhile before they take her to a room," the doctor said. "They'll let you know when you can see her."

Wes stood and shook the man's hand. "Thanks."

When Ruth dabbed at the tears that sprang to her eyes, Wes pulled her into a hug. "It's okay."

"I love her so much. I'm thankful God took care of her."

"Me, too."

Ruth stepped back and looked into Wes's eyes. "You're in love with Angelina?"

"Yes."

"Oh, I'm so glad," Ruth exclaimed, hugging him again. "She needs a good man."

"I'm glad you approve."

"I do. I've come to love you and Melody a great deal. I don't ever want you to leave our lives."

"Well, I don't want to leave. Let's pray it's God's intent for Angelina to agree."

# Chapter 7

Angelina couldn't recall a time when she was more happy to see home. It seemed like she'd been gone for days rather than hours.

Wes hit the remote door opener and backed the SUV into the garage. "You want me to carry you inside?"

She glanced toward the side door. Barely three feet separated the vehicle from the utility room entrance. "You're kidding, right?"

"Well, we don't have a wheelchair."

"I can walk," Angelina insisted, reaching for the door handle.

In one respect, Wes's tender loving care was welcome, but she was afraid to depend on him too much—afraid to let go and need anyone but herself. Right now, she needed to concentrate on getting well and back to work. And that required being strong and doing things for herself. "Only I would require surgery the week before Thanksgiving," she told Wes when he opened the vehicle door.

"Yeah, but think of all those goodies you'll be able to eat now."

"You obviously didn't talk to my doctor. I've got to

restructure my entire diet."

"I know what that's like," he said, taking her arm to assist her.

"I suppose you do," she agreed, grimacing when pain shafted through her midsection. Angelina took a deep breath and said, "It's better if I do it myself."

Wes stepped back, staying within reach. "Take it easy," he said when she stepped onto the bottom step and stopped. "Lean on me."

The short trip took more out of her than she cared to admit, and she was more than a little happy to see the sofa. "Why did you say Mom couldn't come?"

"They think Jeremy might have chicken pox, and she's not sure you ever had them."

Coming to the Atkinses as an older child meant her communicable disease history was sketchy at best.

"She said it's the last thing you need."

"I pray Robbie and Bee don't get them."

"Don't worry. We have a contingency plan if they do," he said, helping her get settled and tucking a pillow underneath her head. He reached for the throw and placed it over her legs.

Wes left the room and returned a few minutes later with her flowers. "Where did you want these?" She indicated the sideboard across the room.

Her gaze fixed on the character balloon her children had picked for her. Angelina thought of how Wes had delighted the children by making it walk. His flower choice had been a dozen peach roses.

"I left your suitcase in the kitchen for now. Is there anything you need?"

She shook her head, and Wes settled in the recliner.

"Aren't you opening the store today?"

"I put up a sign that I'd be closed a day or so."

"Oh, Wes, that's not necessary," she insisted. "How can you make a living closing like that?"

"The Lord provides."

In the back of her mind, Angelina suspected Wes's business was more of a hobby—unlike her own which provided for her family's livelihood. Thank God they had been able to get the store established before Robert got sick. Otherwise, she would have been working for someone else. "I hope everything is okay at the pharmacy."

"It's fine. Don't worry so much."

"Don't worry. I've got two holidays to prepare for, children who need their mother, a house to be cleaned and decorated, in addition to earning a living. I won't even mention my Christmas shopping."

"And somehow most of it will get done, and what's not finished won't matter."

She wished she could look at things in the same way. Striving for perfection was the one thing about herself Angelina sometimes wished she could change. Life would certainly be easier if everything didn't have to be done.

"We can do the shopping right from here," Wes said. "And I've got a store full of glass pieces."

"You'd bankrupt me."

He laughed. "I'll give you the family discount. What if I get my laptop and we do some on-line shopping? It's great. You can go to any of the stores you like and cyber shop."

"You've done it?"

"All the time. Never had any problems."

It wasn't a bad idea. If she could do her shopping while she was recovering, it would free her up to do the other things.

"Mel and I are cooking Thanksgiving dinner. We want to invite your parents and the kids."

"I don't know, Wes. That's a lot of work."

"We did plan to use your kitchen."

"Wes. . ."

"Please let us, Angel," he pleaded. "We want to do this for you."

Right now, celebrating was the farthest thing from her mind. "You don't know what you're getting yourself into."

"It'll be fun. We never had a big family gathering. All our family lived pretty far away and it was just the three of us."

"Okay. But you've got to let us help."

"We'll see. I've been seeing signs about the Flotilla this weekend. Do you ever go?"

"It's been awhile."

"Why don't we go? The kids would love it."

"I might be back at work."

Disappointment flared in his eyes. "Why do you do that to yourself, Angel? You know the doctor wants you home for a couple of weeks."

"I can't afford to sit around for two weeks."

"You can't afford not to. If you don't take care of yourself, you could have complications, and it would take you longer to recuperate."

She knew he was right, but Angelina also knew she had people depending on her—her children, her employees, why even his child depended on her for a job. "I have responsibilities, Wes."

"Do you really trust God to provide for you?"

"Of course I do."

"Do you? Have you let go and accepted that perhaps this inconvenient surgery has a greater purpose? I'm not saying you should sit home forever and do nothing, but you should give God some credit. He's not going to let you or the kids go hungry or homeless."

"But He did, once," she pointed out, unable to swallow the knot of emotion that rose in her throat.

Wes moved quickly to her side. "Angel, I'm sorry. But even though the Lord took, He gave in return."

Filled with remorse, she said, "I know. I feel so guilty when I let the past wear me down."

"It's fear making you feel alone."

"I think about my babies, and I get so afraid. What will they do if something happens to me?"

"I care about you, Angel. I'd never let anything happen to you or the children."

He cared for her. Angelina wasn't surprised by his admission. She knew that—had known for quite some time. Wes had slowly worked his way into their lives and hearts, and even though he frustrated her at times, she cared for him as well.

"I try, Wes. I really do."

"But you've never been able to fully let go and let God?"

"My parents died when I was five, and there was nowhere to go. I got shuffled from foster home to foster home until Mom and Dad chose me as their daughter.

Then I married Robert thinking we'd have at least fifty years together, and he died. No one has ever been permanent in my life."

"God has. He's been right there with you through all the difficult times. It took Him awhile, but He sent you the perfect replacement parents. He sent you a handsome, loving husband, and even when He took him, He left you with two wonderful children."

What he said made a lot of sense, but still Angelina struggled with her doubts. "So is that why you do what you do? Close your store at whim? You trust God to provide?"

"I'm not perfect, Angelina. Years ago when my wife was alive and Mel was small, I lived for the rat race. Giving Mel the things I never had and Laura the things I thought she deserved were my only goals in life. It never occurred to me that I was what my wife and child needed. The heart attack started me thinking. I was home with Laura and Mel for several weeks before they adapted to having me there.

"I was a stranger in my own home, strictly of my own making. I vowed right then and there to change. I prayed to God to help me straighten out the mess I'd made of my life, and when the doctor suggested I take up a hobby, I started working with the glass. I liked it so much I decided to try to make a living doing that."

"I wanted to stay home with my babies," Angelina said softly, regret touching her words. "But Robert got sick. It wasn't his fault. Someone had to make a living."

Wes squeezed her hand. "You've had a difficult life, but you're a better person because of it."

Angelina's attempt at a smile disappeared beneath a huge yawn. "I'm sorry."

"Why don't you catch a nap? Mel and the kids will be home soon. We already warned them to be careful with you. Bee knows she can't jump on Mommy."

"Thanks, Wes. I really do appreciate all the things you've done for me. I'll never be able to repay you or Melody."

He kissed her forehead tenderly. "We don't expect anything in return. We just want to help because we love you."

Her eyes filled with tears.

"Don't cry, Angel. Just let me share your burden. You want to go to your room or nap here on the sofa?"

"Here's fine," she whispered. Wes tucked the chenille throw more closely about her and kissed her forehead again. "Sleep in peace, Angel."

❄

Angelina felt better with each passing day. Frequent calls to the store verified everything was going smoothly. The part-time pharmacist was glad of the extra hours, and though it would cut her profit margin, it was a workable situation.

Tomorrow was Thanksgiving. Wes and Melody had worked in the kitchen the past couple of nights, filling the house with the most wonderful aromas.

When she insisted they give her something to do, Wes gave her a bag of pecans and told her to pick them out. Robbie and Bee ate most of the first ones until she shooed them away, claiming there would be none left.

They would attend Thanksgiving service that night, and the next morning they were helping out at church. They planned to take the kids with them to deliver plates to the homebound.

Angelina had taken Wes's suggestion and found shopping on-line much easier than fighting the crowds in the stores. It looked like Robbie and Bee would get what they had requested for Christmas, and she would definitely consider shopping that way more often.

Wes teased the children with the idea of decorating for Christmas. She wasn't sure what he had in mind, but there was lots of giggling as they made plans. The sounds warmed her heart as she considered her children's enjoyment.

All things considered, she was fairly confident the doctor would release her to return to work when she went for her Monday appointment. She was thankful for God's provision in sending Wes to help out.

When Wes invited her parents for Thanksgiving dinner, they readily accepted. Blessedly, they learned that Jeremy's "chicken pox" was an allergic reaction to something he'd eaten.

Wes launched into planning a meal that made Angelina tired just thinking of preparation time. When her mother came to visit earlier in the week, she suggested that Angelina marry the man. He had to ask first, but her mother's recommendation certainly made her think about what life would be like if Wes were her husband.

Because of the morning plans, they'd decided to have their meal in the late afternoon. After getting everyone back home, Angelina waited as Wes unloaded something from his trunk. She followed him to the patio. He began assembling what appeared to be a cooker.

"What is that?"

"A turkey fryer. I've heard there's nothing better so I

figured we'd give it a shot. It only takes a few minutes a pound to cook and is supposed to be more moist."

"Fried? You're going to fry our turkey? We always cook it in the oven."

"So this year will be a new experience," Wes said, picking up the instruction sheet.

*Not the only one,* Angelina thought. Wes had changed her life. And not all for the bad, she admitted, considering that perhaps moist turkey would be an improvement.

"Can I help?"

"Yes. Go inside and rest for a bit. I think you might have overdone it this morning."

"Don't baby me, Wes. I'm not an invalid."

"I didn't say you were. Please, Angel. Do it for me?" His eyes pleaded with her.

"Oh, okay. Just be careful with that thing."

He winked at her before he went back to reading the instructions.

# Chapter 8

The bells he'd hung on the door jangled as the last customers exited the store. It had been a busy morning, the second day following the holiday weekend. Shoppers, intent on getting a jump on their Christmas shopping, came waving the discount coupons and left with a great deal of the displayed stock, not to mention a number of orders to be completed within the next couple of weeks. He was going to be busy.

Too busy to spend much time with Angel, Wes realized sadly. Unless he hired a temporary clerk to free him up so he could work.

He had really enjoyed the holiday. In fact, it had probably been one of the best Thanksgivings of his life. Dinner had been a huge success. The fried turkey had been little more than a carcass by the time everyone ate their fill. Even the kids asked for seconds. Angelina had admitted it was something she'd like to try again.

Friday had been incredible—the shopping day to end all days. Angelina had kept the kids so Mel could help out.

On Saturday night, they sat in his backyard and watched the boats parade down the waterway, all decked out in their Christmas lights. The creative designs on the boats and the fireworks that followed thrilled the children, and not even the rain that started near the end of the display dampened their high spirits.

He'd stayed busy working on his glass on Saturday with Mel handling the walk-in customers. On Sunday, they attended church together and went out for lunch. Afterward, they took the children to the mall to see the decorations.

Angel had gone for her follow-up appointment yesterday, and the doctor had released her to return to work today. He wondered how she was feeling.

Glancing at his watch, Wes decided he was ready for lunch. Might as well break bread with Angel. He called in an order and, after picking up the food, headed for the drugstore. He went to the back and found her hard at work. "Lunchtime."

"Already?"

"Time flies when you're having fun. You wouldn't believe how busy the store's been this morning."

"And you closed for lunch?"

He grinned at her incredulous tone. "You're not sure about my business sense, are you?" She didn't answer, but Wes knew from her expression that she didn't consider closing for lunch when business was good a smart move. "I'll have you know my customer-appreciation coupons are netting me a small fortune. How are you doing on your first day back?"

"A bit tired but otherwise fine."

"I won't say what I'm thinking."

"Which is just as well since I'm not going to listen to you anyway."

Wes pushed a Styrofoam container into her hand. "Here, eat and build up your stamina."

He noted the look of surprise when she flipped the plate open and revealed a large sandwich.

"I can't eat all this."

"Sure you can. One bite at a time."

"Okay, you win. But only because I'm hungry." She peered into the paper bag that accompanied her lunch plate.

"What are you looking for?"

"Utensils. You expect me to eat with my fingers?"

"You could. It's only a sandwich and fries." Wes extracted the package of utensils from his shirt pocket and handed it to her. "Then again, you might need the fork for your pie."

Angelina grimaced. "You are so hard on my diet."

"Why do you need to diet? You look fine to me."

"So will you love me when I gain ten pounds over the holidays?"

"Just means there's even more of you to love," he teased.

"Go back to work, Wes."

"No can do. I don't like eating alone."

Wes launched into a discussion of where he could find a clerk and what to buy everyone for Christmas. Before he realized it, the lunch hour had passed. "I'd better get back to the store. I'm going to be pretty busy the next few days. I've got several orders for pieces."

"Thanks for lunch. I'll see if I can return the favor one night this week." She leaned to kiss his cheek. "Thanks for everything. I can't tell you how much I appreciate the way you take care of me."

"Anytime, Angel."

Back at the store, he used the lull in customers to do a bit of restocking. The phone rang just as he came out of the storeroom with a box of sun catchers. Taking care to place them safely on the countertop, he picked up the phone. "Wes's Glass."

"Hello, is Mr. Robbins available?"

"Speaking."

"This is Crista McDaniel from Arizona. I've enjoyed my balloon piece so much that I've decided to order some pieces as gifts."

"I appreciate you thinking of me."

"Sending that Christmas card with a discount coupon is good advertising."

Wes grabbed an order pad and began writing as she listed the various pieces she'd chosen from his Web site. After totaling, adding tax and shipping, he quoted her a price. She gave him a credit card number. Wes grinned at the blessing. So much for thinking sending a card out of town was a waste. Ms. McDaniel had definitely proven him wrong.

"Thank you very much. By the way, I'm sorry about that episode when you were here before. Angel thought you might have been embarrassed."

She chuckled. "Not at all. In fact, it would have been nice to find another of my long-lost sisters."

"Another?" he asked.

"Yes. I found my oldest sister recently. It was very exciting to learn I had siblings. I was young when my parents died."

"Angel was young, too. Tell me, how did you and your sister find each other? I'd love to help Angel locate her family. From what her mother told me, the family name was Richmond."

"Is Angel her real name?"

Wes caught the surprise in her voice. "Actually it's Angelina."

He jerked the phone back from his ear at the woman's excited scream.

"I can't believe it! Eden will never believe this!"

"Eden?" Wes repeated, wondering whom she referred to. One minute they were having a calm discussion, and then she started shouting.

"My sister. Mr. Robbins, based on what you just told me, I think you might have found our sister for us."

"What?" Wes demanded, finding the situation incredible. "I mean Angelina has no idea where she lived or even her siblings' names. All I know is her name was Angelina Richmond before she was adopted by the Atkinses."

"And my sister was Angelina Richmond!" Crista exclaimed happily. "It's hard to be positive without checking, but her name certainly gives me cause to pursue the matter further," Crista explained. "Then there's this resemblance you see."

Wes heard tapping on a keyboard, and then she spoke again. "Eden has one, too."

"Has what?"

"A dimple. Do you have a pen handy?" She gave him a Web site address. "That's my site for business, but I have a personal link to Eden's page. We posted all the information she could recall about our family and her search there and

240

on the adoption boards. She was eight. This is incredible," she said. "I call to place an order and find a sister."

"You need to verify that," Wes warned, afraid she was getting carried away too soon. He didn't want to raise Angel's hopes only to find out it was a mistake.

"I'm going to call Eden. If she agrees, we'll need Angelina's number so we can call her. She has a birthday coming up on the seventh, doesn't she?"

"Yes. How did you know?"

"Eden remembered the date. It's here on the site."

Things were snowballing, Wes realized as the coincidences continued to pile up. "*If* she's your sister," Wes cautioned once more.

"It does seem too easy. A fluke that I'd come to North Carolina, meet a complete stranger, and later find she's my sister."

"How can we verify this?" he asked.

"I'll start checking here on my end. Perhaps you could see if her adoptive parents have any information that would help."

"I'll ask. What if I call you back with anything I learn?"

"Sounds wonderful."

Wes hung up the phone a couple of minutes later with a substantial order and quite possibly the names of Angel's sisters and their phone numbers. She was going to be mighty surprised if Crista McDaniel really was her sister. He grinned at the thought of being proved correct in his idea that they resembled each other.

Wes reached for the phone. "Hello, Ruth. Wes here. You sitting down? You're probably going to be as surprised as I was."

# Chapter 9

There was a festive air about the house as the holiday preparations advanced. Angelina found herself looking forward to going home in the afternoons, eager to see what Wes and the kids had been doing. He closed his shop around five o'clock while she stayed open until six, and that gave them plenty of time to get started on whatever mischief they could manage.

When she mentioned getting her artificial tree out of the attic, Wes insisted she had to have a live tree. Her arguments that they were fire hazards prompted him to find a tree farm. Wes had taken her SUV and gone tree shopping, obtaining not only a freshly cut tree for her but also trees for her parents and himself.

Angelina wasn't certain why he needed a tree. He spent more time at her house than his own, but she really didn't mind. In fact, a day when she didn't see Wes made her feel depressed. She accepted she cared deeply for him, even though she wasn't sure what he intended with their relationship.

He was always a complete gentleman and often indicated that he loved her. It was a comfortable relationship.

Often they just sat and held hands while they talked. A few weeks back, Wes had started kissing her good night, and as much as she looked forward to his kisses, she was beginning to hate telling him good night. Was she ready for their relationship to move forward?

Her thirty-first birthday was in a few days, and Angelina knew she didn't want to grow old alone. When her children grew up and left home, she wanted a companion. She wanted to be in love again. For that matter, she was fairly certain she was in love.

Unlocking the door, Angelina called out. She followed Wes's voice to the family room to find him adjusting the tree in a stand. The room was fragrant with the scent of the magnificent tree.

"Where's everyone?"

"Up in the attic looking for lights."

"They're in the storage chest. Maybe I should—"

"Go change. I'll tell them where to look."

Angelina was anxious to help. "I'll be right back to help get the stuff down. There are boxes and boxes of decorations."

"So you do like Christmas?"

Angelina paused and looked back at him. "Of course. It's my favorite time of year."

Wes grinned broadly. "Mine, too."

"I already knew that," she said, heading for the stairs.

❄

He needed to marry that woman soon, Wes decided as he watched her dash up the stairs. Angel was everything he admired in a woman. When Laura died, he never thought he'd meet someone else, but he had and all thanks to his daughter. Mel had led him to this new family. He just prayed she would be as happy about his decision as he was. His other prayer was that Angel would say yes.

He and Mel were going to visit her grandparents over the weekend since he had plans to spend the holiday with Angel and the kids. Wes envisioned the type of life they would have. He looked forward to having Angelina as his wife, and he wanted to help raise her children. He also had plans to make her upcoming birthday one to be remembered. And when they were married, he could help out with the kids, and Mel would have more free time. Life would be wonderful.

He'd already been to the jeweler's several times in hopes of finding the perfect ring. Thus far he'd been unable to find anything he felt was right for her. He'd look again this weekend. Maybe he'd find something in New York.

"Come along, Mr. Robbins. We have an attic full of decorations to unpack. You're not going to believe what I've got up here."

Wes didn't realize how long he'd stood daydreaming until she spoke. "I can hardly wait."

❄

With Melody out of town, Angelina took Saturday off to be with the children. Ordinarily, she'd be up to her eyeballs in trying to get the house decorated, but thanks to Wes, the task was completed. It felt like a major burden had been lifted from her shoulders, and she was freed to spend time doing her holiday baking.

Bee loved the tree, and they were constantly warning her to be careful and taking ornaments from her inquisitive fingers. Her favorite was a little wooden train that had belonged to her father when he was a boy.

The child also loved the Nativity set. It was one of the things she and Robert had splurged on for their home, deciding that a nice set would last a lifetime. At first, Angelina was fearful that Bee would break the expensive pieces, but she seemed to know just how to handle them, and Angelina resisted putting them out of reach.

Both kids bounced on her bed early, reminding her that they were going to bake cookies. She pulled the pillow over her face, and they tugged it away. "Can I get dressed first?"

"Hurry, Mommy," Bee insisted.

Angelina noted the child had already dressed herself, choosing colors that suited her fancy but didn't match. Her shirt was on backward, the seams on the outside and tag under her chin. She shrugged. No sense in making her change. The clothes would be covered by the time they finished.

They spent a wonderful day baking several different variations of the cookies. Angelina leaned against the counter, sipping cocoa as her children decorated cookies. All the scene required for completion were Wes and Melody. She missed them.

"You guys want to go see Santa this afternoon?" she asked, thinking it best to get out before she allowed the melancholy feelings tugging at her heart to take control. She had some shopping to finish, and she'd promised Wes she'd run by the store and make sure his temp help was doing okay.

"Yeah," Robbie cried.

Bee shook her head. The child hadn't decided she liked the jolly one all that much.

"Let's finish up here and change clothes."

"But we have clothes," Bee said, tugging out the cookie-dough-stained shirt.

"Fereby Collier, you look like a gigantic sugar cookie," she teased, advancing slowly. "In fact, I think I'll eat you up."

"No, Mommy," the child screamed, jumping to her feet and darting about the table.

Angelina grabbed her and squeezed Bee in a hug.

"Do me, Mommy," Robbie insisted.

She hugged her oldest and set him back to his feet, whispering a word of thanks for her two precious gifts. "Let's get going."

❄

Wes called late Sunday night to let her know he was back.

"Melody's grandparents needed her to stay on a day or so. Hope that doesn't cause a problem for you."

*Only about what to do with my children,* Angelina thought. What were they thinking? Of course, Wes probably encouraged Melody to take the extra time. "I'll have to see if Mom can watch Bee tomorrow. I wish she'd given me some advance notice."

"Mel deserves a break."

"I didn't say she didn't," Angelina snapped, a bit put out by his defensiveness in light of the situation. "But last I heard employees cleared stuff like time off with their bosses."

"She's not your servant."

"I never said she was."

"This is exactly what I meant. Melody hardly has a moment to call her own between classes and this job."

They'd been down this road many times before. Every time she thought it was leveling off, something spurred another argument.

"I'll handle it, Wes."

"You don't have to get so upset."

Angelina was furious. She required people she could depend on in her life. "You wouldn't understand. Good night."

His cavalier attitude irked Angelina to no end. She supposed he'd never been subjected to the aggravation of child care. She didn't think she was being unreasonable to expect Melody to be there to do her job or to make prior arrangements.

Angelina called her mother and thankfully she could take Bee the next morning. Otherwise it would mean she'd have to pay a substitute pharmacist for another day. She went to bed early and fell into a deep, dream-filled sleep. The ringing phone woke her.

"You're right. I'm sorry."

"Wes?" she asked groggily.

"I should have realized that you'd be in a bind. I can take Bee to the store with me in the morning if that would help."

Visions of a bull in a china shop filled her head at the thought of turning her three year old loose around all that glass.

"It's okay. She's staying with my parents."

He released a deep sigh. "I'm really sorry. I was thinking of Mel."

"I know, Wes."

"Next time we'll make prior arrangements."

"It would be appreciated."

"Mel wanted to call. Her grandparents have some estate matters they needed her help with. I told her I'd explain. She's going to be upset with me, too."

"Not if we don't tell her."

His tone perked up considerably. "Now I remember why I love you so much. Did you miss me?"

"Yes." Angelina pulled her pillow up and leaned against the headboard. "We made cookies yesterday."

"I love cookies."

"I'll bring some to work tomorrow. How did your weekend go?"

She listened to him talk about the time with his wife's parents.

"I told them about you. They'd like to meet you and the kids."

He'd told his former in-laws about the new woman in his life. This sounded pretty serious. Still it seemed highly unlikely that she'd ever meet them.

"Melody said to tell you she's sorry and she'll definitely be here for your birthday."

Was he suggesting Melody wouldn't be back until Friday? Angelina kept her thoughts to herself. She'd talk to her mother tomorrow.

"I'll let you get back to sleep. See you tomorrow."

After hanging up, Angelina found herself unable to drift off to sleep again. Obviously Wes was pretty serious if he'd talked to his former in-laws about her. But the creeping doubt arose in her heart as she considered his attitude about the situation with Melody's job. Would he ever stop being so defensive of his daughter?

"What do I do, Lord?" she asked as the turmoil in her spirit grew. "Is this what You intend for me?"

She waited in the silence of the night for an answer and finally drifted to sleep.

# Chapter 10

Overwhelming déjà vu struck that night when Angelina paused in the doorway of the family room. Never before did she recall seeing so many balloons in one room, and yet it reminded her of something.

"Happy birthday, Mommy!" Robbie and Bee shouted, running forward to grab her hands and tug her into the room.

"Are you surprised?" Robbie asked.

Angelina nodded.

"More surprise," Bee announced.

"Bee, not yet," Wes said, swinging the little girl up in his arms and leaned to kiss Angelina's cheek.

She looked from children to adults, wondering what else was planned.

"First things first," Wes said. "We're going to your favorite restaurant for dinner. Then we'll come back here for dessert and presents."

"Yeah, presents," Bee said, throwing her arms into the air.

"For Mommy, Bee," Melody said.

"Mommy?" she repeated, looking perplexed. "Me want present, too."

"When you're four," Melody promised.

"Four?" The child worked her fingers, managing to come up with three.

"You can help Mommy open hers," Angelina promised.

"We thought about having a big party but decided to limit the celebration to family."

Angelina was glad. She had never cared for big parties. More often than not, because of the number of foster children, the Atkins family celebrated with a cake after dinner.

After giving her a few minutes to freshen up and change, they loaded into the SUV and headed for the restaurant. Like every Friday night, the line of waiting patrons extended along the front of the building.

"Better get our name on the list," Angelina suggested. "Wait here."

Wes disappeared inside and soon returned to guide them to the small room he'd reserved for their celebration. Her parents and the foster kids were already seated, and their cries of "Surprise!" resounded about the room as Wes pulled out the seat of honor for her.

Angelina felt like a queen surveying her domain as she viewed the loved ones gathered around the table to celebrate her birth. Who needed blood relatives when they had love like this? Life couldn't get any better.

After dinner, they took the party back to her house to eat their fill of her favorites, chocolate cake and custard ice cream. Torn between helping unwrap gifts and collecting a balloon bouquet, Bee darted about the room. Soon Robbie and Jeremy joined in her quest to collect all the ribbon streamers their little hands could hold. As the children danced and giggled, Angelina was again struck with a sense of familiarity that refused to go away. All too soon the baby began to whine.

"We'd better be heading home, Ruth. Time to get these children into bed," her dad said.

"It's early," Angelina protested, disappointed that the evening was drawing to a close. "Don't go yet."

Her dad kissed her cheek. "We'll see you Sunday for lunch. Your mom's making all your favorites."

"Don't go to all that trouble."

"No trouble," her mother insisted as she placed the knit cap on the baby's head.

Angelina helped gather their things and thanked her parents for their gift, hugging them good-bye. She stood in the doorway watching them settle the children in the car, stifling a fit of giggles when her dad attempted to fit Jeremy's balloons in the trunk.

"Wish I had a camera," she told Wes as yet another balloon made its escape and danced into the sky. Jeremy's dismayed cries filled the air.

"I'll get Bee and Robbie ready for bed," Melody announced, taking their hands and leading them up the stairs.

Back in the family room, Angelina plopped down on the sofa beside Wes. "I'm exhausted."

He wrapped an arm about her shoulder, giving her a reviving squeeze. "But did you have a good birthday?"

"Wonderful. I couldn't ask for better."

"I'm glad. And thankful to be part of this momentous occasion."

She frowned and tapped him lightly on the arm. "I wouldn't go that far."

"I say the second anniversary of your twenty-ninth birthday deserves to be celebrated."

Angelina grimaced at him.

Wes reached for her hand, holding it tightly in his. From the seriousness of his expression, she knew he had something on his mind.

"I suppose you know me well enough by now to know I'm not the most romantic man in the world," he began slowly. "I wish I knew how to make this more special for you, but I'm just going to come out with it. Angel, we've known each other for almost six months, and I know that's not very long, but sometimes it doesn't take forever to know how you feel about someone. I love you, and I'd like to ask you to do me the honor of becoming my wife." He reached into his pocket for the ring box and flipped it open, showing her the beautiful solitaire he'd picked out.

Angelina didn't know what to say.

"Marry me," Wes implored. "I'll do better than I did with Laura and Mel. I promise. I intend to help with the children. I figure Mel can concentrate on her education if I'm helping out here."

Fear welled up inside Angelina as she considered his words. "Would you marry me to free Melody from her job?"

The moment the words left her mouth, she recognized Wes couldn't have been more shocked if she'd struck him.

"That's ridiculous, Angel."

She pulled away. "I don't think I'm being ridiculous. You told me not so very long ago that you planned to convince Melody to give up this job. This way you still come out the good guy."

"If you don't want to marry me, you don't have to make excuses," he declared impatiently.

What was she doing? She loved Wes and Melody. Why was she jeopardizing their future happiness? She pushed her hair behind her ears. "I just want to be, sure, Wes. I need to know you'll be there for me."

"I'm asking to spend the rest of my life with you. There's no way I can be sure how long that will be, but I can promise no one will ever love you more than I do. Say yes, Angel."

"I don't know. I need to think."

Wes lifted her hands in his. "Don't look back, Angel. Look forward to what we can have. Let go of the fears and doubts. Trust God. He's taken mighty fine care of you over the years."

The phone rang, and she wondered who was calling this time of night. She prayed nothing had happened to her parents.

"Angelina, phone," Melody called.

"Who is it?" she asked, irritated by the interruption.

There was a rumbling of voices. "It's a Ms. McDaniel. She's calling to wish you a happy birthday."

Lines of confusion scored Angelina's forehead as she got to her feet. "I don't know any McDaniels."

Wes shot to his feet. "Angel, wait. We need to talk."

"After I take this call."

"Angel—"

"Not now, Wes," she said. "I'll take it in the kitchen, Melody. Hello, this is Angelina."

"Hi, this is Crista McDaniel. We met at your friend's store. He thought we looked alike."

Angelina recalled the episode. But how had this woman known it was her birthday? She never shared that information with complete strangers.

"I contacted Wes recently, and he told me today was your birthday," Crista explained.

Why on earth would Wes tell her that? Was it her birthday, too, or—and why was she calling Wes?

"Did he tell you I was going to call?"

She glanced around and found him standing nearby, a mixture of emotions, mostly regret, playing across his face. What was going on here? "No."

Crista giggled nervously. "Then I suppose I should explain before you think I've lost my mind. Oh, by the way, happy birthday! I hope it's been a good one?"

"Yes," Angelina responded vaguely, growing more curious by the moment.

Perhaps she was one of the foster kids, Angelina thought, struggling to recall some of their names. Never a McDaniel that she could remember, but then some had stayed only briefly.

"Wes told me you were adopted," Crista began.

Angelina felt stunned by the amount of personal information Wes had taken upon himself to share with this stranger. Nervousness centered in the pit of her stomach.

"I'm adopted, too. It was pretty exciting to learn I have two sisters and a brother."

"I'm sure." Angelina thought of how she'd react to such news. But why was this woman telling her this?

"That's why I'm calling. I think you're my sister."

"Your sister?" Angelina repeated incredulously.

"Our parents were John and Anna Richmond, and we lived in Covington, Kentucky. We're the youngest of their four children. I'm your baby sister."

Angelina had few memories of her childhood prior to the time she arrived at the Atkins's home. The past had been painful—filled with loss. Somewhere along the way her parents had explained she was the child of their heart, and that had been enough for her. "I don't know."

"Your mother verified their names. We also have an older sister named Eden and a brother named Tim."

Angelina sank into a nearby chair and demanded, "Are you sure?"

"I'm fairly confident. When Wes mentioned you were adopted at a young age and said your name was Angelina, I knew that was my sister's name. It's not an ordinary name," Crista pointed out. "I think our mother was a bit of a romantic. Then he said you were a Richmond, and that cinched it for me. You have the same birthday our older sister said you had. Then there's this similarity in our appearance Wes sees."

It was an overwhelming abundance of coincidences, Angelina thought.

"I talked to Eden, and she agrees that it's likely you're the one. Wes and I have been in contact a couple of times. He verified some facts, and when we became more certain, he suggested I surprise you for your birthday."

"But how? Who put you in contact with Wes?"

"It had to be God," Crista explained. "It's too miraculous. I'd hoped to find you one day but never dreamed I'd stumble across you in my travels. Some people might call it luck, but I think it's a blessing from above. I know you need some time to absorb all this, but Eden and I both are anxious to meet and talk with you as soon as you're ready. Wes has a site address where you can look at Eden's research facts. Eden has photos of us there. Be sure to look for the dimple."

"Dimple?" Angelina lifted a finger to her cheek, thinking she must sound like a moron.

"Yes, we all share the dimple."

"This is a shock. Where do you live?"

"I know. It was for me, too. Eden lives in Indiana. I'm in Phoenix."

Overwhelmed, Angelina asked, "Crista, is it possible you can give me a number so I can call you back later?"

"I hope this hasn't upset you?"

"No, not at all. It's just a lot to take in at once." Wes's proposal had already put her mind into overload. And now this stranger was claiming blood ties. "I promise to look into it and get back to you as soon as I have all the facts."

"That would be wonderful. Wes tells me you have two children."

"Yes. A boy and a girl, four and three."

"This is so incredible," Crista said. "I'm a sister and an aunt. I see my Christmas list growing by leaps and bounds."

"Oh no, you don't have—"

"Sure I do. You can tell me more about them next time we talk."

Numbly, Angelina said good-bye and allowed Wes to take the phone from her hand.

He replaced the receiver and dropped to his knees before her. "I'm sorry. I thought you'd be excited to find them."

Angelina's thoughts drifted back to the times as a child when she'd daydreamed about having brothers and sisters who didn't come and go like the foster kids. "I never expected to meet up with one of them in your shop."

Wes's expression softened. "Would you like for me to bring up the site on the computer?"

The future looked vague and shadowy, too confusing for her to grasp. "Just give me the address. I'll find it."

"Angel?"

"You need to go home, Wes."

"But, Angel—"

"No 'buts.' I have to think. I promised Ms. McDaniel I'd look into this and get back to her."

"But what about our discussion?"

Angelina was keenly aware of his scrutiny. Wes didn't understand her withdrawal and she couldn't explain. Not yet. She needed time to consider the ways this would change her life. "I'll be in touch when I'm ready to talk."

"I'm sorry everything went wrong. I love you, Angel. Believe that, please."

His pleas stayed with her long after Wes had gone. The first thing she did was pull up the site. As she read the facts, Angelina found herself hoping it was true. She reached for the phone, "Hello, Mom."

"Angelina, I hope you're calling with good news."

Wes had been busy. "Just questions. Wes says he's talked to you about this woman who claims to be my sister."

"Yes, we've checked what facts we know."

"Do you think it's a scam?"

"No. I honestly feel the woman is your sister."

"This is unbelievable."

"You owe it to yourself to be sure. Meet them. Learn about your family."

Angelina had never loved her mother more. What a wealth of emotions she must be experiencing to encourage her child to form a relationship with her siblings. "In the back of my mind I've always wondered what it would be like. Now I'm afraid."

"No one can ever have too much love, Angelina."

"I suppose."

"Now, what about Wes? Did you say yes?"

"I think Wes should have asked me before telling everyone else."

"You refused? But I thought you really loved him."

"I do. But I'm not sure about his motives."

"Motives? He loves you and wants to share your life. He's a decent, Christian man. What else can you want?"

"I suppose a bit of certainty wouldn't hurt."

"Haven't you heard nothing's certain but death and taxes?"

"And I've had my share of both."

Her mother's sigh reached over the distance through the phone. "I've always given you credit for being a smart girl, but if you let this one get away, I'm going to think I was wrong."

"And you don't think it's smart to be sure?"

"Angelina, I would never suggest you go against your heart. But I do suggest you trust your instincts."

It was all too much. How could she follow her heart

when her doubts were so great? And now her confidence seemed too weak to support a sensible decision. "Why does everyone preach trust to me?"

"Because we can see you fighting God in a battle you can't win. Jeremiah 29:11 says, ' "For I know the plans I have for you," ' declares the Lord, ' "plans to prosper you and not to harm you, plans to give you hope and a future." ' God knows that future, Angelina."

"So God's already made the plan, and I just blindly follow?"

"No. You open your eyes wide and pray mightily that you make the right choice. God gave us freedom of choice, but that doesn't mean the wrong ones don't have consequences."

"But what about Wes's promise to free Melody from her job?" Angelina argued. "He actually suggested he could help with the kids and she could concentrate on her studies."

"Oh, Angelina, you've been a parent long enough to understand how protective parents can be."

"Well, yes," she admitted reluctantly, "but Melody doesn't want him interfering in her life."

"And I'm sure she's adult enough to tell him. Didn't you ever question Robert's motives?"

"Maybe."

"No maybe about it. Every couple does from time to time. The key to the situation is communication. Discuss the matter freely and try to understand what Wes is telling you. Honey, don't reject the opportunity to be happy. Pray about it."

"I will. Night, Mom. And thanks for everything."

"I love you, Angelina. I thank God every day for sending you to us."

"Even when you doubt my intelligence?" she teased.

"Even then."

# Chapter 11

Angelina was awake early the following morning, preparing breakfast in hopes of wearing away some of the nervous energy that consumed her. She fed the children and sent them upstairs to finish dressing. When Melody came down, she slid a plate of pancakes on the table in front of her.

"Did you have a good birthday?" she asked as she drizzled syrup over the stack of pancakes.

Considering the jumble of emotions she was feeling right now, Angelina didn't know the answer. She'd tossed and turned until she'd been forced to get up in the middle of the night and remake her bed.

Finally, she'd opened her Bible to the verse her mother had quoted and prayed. She'd long since learned prayers weren't always answered immediately, sometimes never, and often in a way far different than you wanted. Now she only wanted peace.

Angelina set a glass of orange juice on the table. "How much do you know about what happened last night?"

"Dad said he was going to propose."

Angelina nodded. Exactly what she thought. Wes

had been a busy man. No wonder everyone disappeared so quickly last night. "Did he mention his other surprise? Finding my sister?"

Melody's head popped up. "No. I didn't realize you had one."

"Two, actually, and a brother. She called last night. Seems your dad thought it would be a perfect birthday surprise."

Melody's eyes grew wide with amazement. "He's a bit misguided at times, but you have to admire his originality. Not every man can find long-lost relatives for a woman's birthday gift."

Angelina laughed, releasing a flood tide of emotions, and it felt good. "That's true."

"How does it make you feel?"

"Excited. Frightened. Confused. What if they don't like me?"

"They have to like you, Angelina. You're their sister."

She had a point there. They were strangers with a common bond. The relationship with them started now as adults, not with the children of the past.

"That must seem like a blessing from above," Melody commented.

*Blessing from above.* The words triggered remembrance of the same words Crista had spoken last night. When had she stopped expecting blessings from above? Had she even thanked God for Wes?

"Can I ask you something personal, Melody?"

"Sure."

"How do you deal with your father's determination?"

"I listen to him and respect his viewpoint, but I tell

him what I'm feeling, too."

"So you don't feel railroaded by him?"

"I feel loved," the young woman admitted with a warm smile. "Everything he does is because he cares about me, and even if it irritates me at times, I understand why."

Angelina nervously folded and refolded a napkin. "You know if I marry your dad, he plans to help with the children so you'll have more free time for school? You'd be out of work."

"I wouldn't feel right charging my stepmom, anyway. And having a man around would be good for Robbie and Bee."

"Will it hurt you to see him doing things with them he didn't do with you?"

"I'm sure Dad will do everything in his power to make it up to me," Melody pointed out. "Actually, I'll be glad to get some of the attention focused elsewhere. I'm sure you can distract him until I'm an old married woman giving you both grandchildren."

"You make it sound so simple."

"It is. Just trust God to show you the way." The young woman glanced at her watch. "Look at the time. I'll drop Robbie and Bee off."

❄

Angelina sat at the table long after Melody left, thinking about what she'd said. Just trust God. *Trust me, Angelina.* She looked around the room. No one there but her. And God, she realized. Wes was right. God was with her now and always, providing exactly what she needed.

"I do, dear Father," she whispered. "I know I haven't always given You control of my life, but I'm putting it in

Your hands now. Thank You for these wonderful people You've filled my life with—Mom and Dad, Robert, Robbie and Bee, Melody, Wes, and now my sisters and brother.

"I believe You sent Wes to love me and led me to a trusting relationship with You. I know I've set limitations for myself by trying to be the one in control. Please help me break free of the bondage. Thank You for caring, and please continue to guide and direct my path as You would have me go. I am nothing without Your love."

Peace like she'd never felt radiated throughout Angelina. She'd finally released herself from the bonds she'd imposed over the years. She walked over to the wall phone and dialed Wes's number.

"Wes's Glass."

"Hi, it's Angelina."

"Angel? I didn't expect. . . Are you okay? You said you'd call when you were ready. . . . Does this mean. . . ?"

"Take a breath, Wes. Is it okay if I stop by the store this morning? I need some help planning our future."

"Is that a yes?"

"What do you think?"

"Praise God," he cried jubilantly. "I love you, Angel."

"I love you, too."

For the first time in a long time, Angelina looked forward to the future, knowing that looking back would never hurt as badly when she was loved by such a man.

## TERRY FOWLER

Terry makes her home in North Carolina where she works for the city of Wilmington. The second oldest of five children, she shares a home with her best friend who is also her sister. Besides writing, her interests include genealogical research through the Internet and serving her small church in various activities. She is the author of two **Heartsong Presents** titles.

# To Keep Me Warm

by Gail Gaymer Martin

*Two are better than one. . .*
*If one falls down, his friend can help him up.*
*But pity the man who falls and has no one to help him up!*
*Also, if two lie down together, they will keep warm.*
*But how can one keep warm alone? . . .*
*A cord of three strands is not quickly broken.*
ECCLESIASTES 4:9–12

# Chapter 1

In the church fellowship hall, Tim Richmond leaned against a wall, peering at men and women talking comfortably in friendly clusters while he squirmed. He wished he'd never let his friend convince him to come along. He eyed Jack across the room, looking relaxed and in control. Not Tim. He clung to the wall like ivy. Poison ivy, at that. No one had spoken to him.

"Excuse me," a woman said, brushing past.

He watched her dash across the floor to greet a friend, he assumed.

A singles' group. . .even a church singles' group gave Tim as much pleasure as the thought of poking his eye with a stick. He scanned the red hearts with Cupid's arrows decorating the hall and pushed himself closer to the plaster. Valentine's Day was meant for couples. . .not one, lone, miserable man who still didn't feel at all single. With four years of marriage and a wonderful son, two years widowed seemed like a moment in time.

Refocusing on the crowd, Tim peered at his friend, Jack. A few years older than Tim, Jack had been widowed for four years. Would two more years make that much difference? Tim couldn't imagine it.

Shifting his gaze, he spotted a vaguely familiar face, a woman engaged in conversation with another female. He narrowed his focus, groping through his mind to identify from where he knew her.

She turned toward him, her attention locked with his. A puzzled expression stumbled across her face before switching to recognition and a pleasant smile. After speaking a moment to her companion, she rose and headed straight for Tim.

Pulling his back straight, he heaved his disheartened shoulders upward, hoping to present a semi-pleasant look.

She approached him, hand extended. "Mr. Richmond? You're Timmy's father, right?"

"Yes," he said, embarrassed that he was still in the dark.

"Central Orthopedic," she said. "I'm a nurse at the clinic, Julie Gardner."

The image of her bright smile as she talked with his six-year-old son, Timmy, took shape in his thoughts. "I knew you looked familiar but couldn't place you," he admitted.

"I should have worn my uniform." She flashed an infectious smile.

He sent one back, admiring the wavy ash brown hair brushing against her shoulders. "I suppose that would've helped." Though he tried to joke, he felt tongue-tied.

"What are you doing here?" she asked.

His shoulders drooped for a moment as he asked himself the same question. Nabbing his fading confidence, he straightened his back again. "I was dragged here by a friend for moral support."

A burst of laughter filled the air, and sensing she was laughing at him, he cringed for a fleeting moment until she continued.

"You, too?" she said, amusement bubbling in her words. "I didn't want to do this either." She motioned toward the woman she'd been speaking with earlier. "I'm with a friend." Her gesture faltered. "Was with a friend. I see she's occupied."

When she turned back to face Tim, he had the horrible desire to run out the door. Not that he didn't enjoy Julie's company. . .he did, but he felt awkward, like a man cheating on his wife. He'd never had such feelings—but tonight the emotions bounded through him.

"Care to sit?" she asked, pointing to an unoccupied table.

Angry at his unbidden feelings, Tim found his common sense. "Sure, thanks."

She led the way, and he followed like a sheep, instead of the shepherd. Where was his masculine charm? Buried in memories, he guessed. When they reached the table, he found his manners. "Would you like something to drink?"

"Yes, thanks. A cola, if you don't mind."

He nodded, then escaped, needing time to get himself under control. Why did he feel so inept? This wasn't a date. He was talking to a woman he'd seen numerous times at his son's orthopedic clinic.

Tim's heart twisted thinking of his son bound in braces from Blount's disease. He prayed the supports would help the boy's problem, but the doctor hadn't been hopeful. Surgery, he'd said, would probably be the only permanent solution. Surgery? Tim's heart was weighted with the possibility.

When Timmy was a toddler, Tim recalled his wife and him laughing at Timmy's bowed legs. Yet, concerned, Jan had asked the pediatrician about the problem. He dismissed it as natural. After Jan's death, Timmy's abnormality became more pronounced. Tim pursued the problem and learned about this uncommon deformity.

Tim pulled his thoughts back to his task and ordered two colas, then headed toward Timmy's nurse. If he kept her in perspective, he could handle the evening. She knew his son and the child's disease. They had something in common.

"Here you go," Tim said, sliding the glass onto the table. He settled into the chair across from her, his mind scrambling for something to talk about.

"Thanks." She lifted the glass and took a delicate sip.

Tim's gaze latched onto her full, shapely mouth. Generous mouth. Not large, but eager to smile or articulate with her soothing, mellow voice.

"You're quiet," she said.

Discomfort riffled up his neck. "I'm new at this. I don't have much time for socializing."

She nodded and lifted her glass for another sip, but her eyes searched his as if trying to read his thoughts.

"Your son?" she asked. "I'm sure he takes time."

"Yes, I'm. . .a, uh, widower," he said, finding it difficult to say the word. "My wife died two years ago."

"I'm sorry," she said, a look of sincerity spreading across her face.

"Thanks." He dragged his finger across his glass,

wiping away the condensation. "So I'm, uh, a single parent."

Her face washed with a mixture of responses, and he wondered.

"I'm sure being an only parent is difficult," she said, seeming distracted. "It's often the woman who's left with little ones. . .not men. Divorce and unmarried girls getting pregnant. . . Today's morals are terrible."

"Yes, I guess they are," he said, confused by her comment. "Single or widowed, raising a child alone isn't easy."

She drew her attention back to him. "I'm sorry," she said. "I don't know what got into me. We should talk about something more pleasant."

"It might not be pleasant, but it's real," he said.

Curious, Tim searched her face for understanding. He'd heard an inference in her voice, but it had faded as quickly as it happened.

"I do as much as I can for my son, but he needs more than I can give him sometimes. Then, I don't want to spoil him. It's a tough road to walk."

She gave his arm a reassuring pat. "Timmy's a great kid," she said. "Shame about his problem. . .but surgery will. . ." Her voice trailed off and she flinched. "I don't suppose surgery is what you want, but from my experience, it's proven wonderful in most every case."

"I've heard," Tim said, not eager to discuss the topic.

"There I go again," she said, apparently sensing his discomfort.

He drew his fingers through his hair. "Are you. . .eh, widowed?"

Her head shake answered before she did. "No. Just

plain old single. Never married. I'm too old now."

Surprising himself, a laugh burst from his throat. "You! You're not too old for much of anything."

She grinned. "I feel that way though."

"You shouldn't. You're young."

"Thirty-three," she said.

"I'm thirty-two."

A scowl flashed across her face. "You're a young widower. What happened?"

"Blood clot," he answered. "Jan had surgery. . .a pulmonary embolism took her. . .so fast."

Julie's face paled. "Mr. Richmond. . .I'm sorry. I suggested cheering up our conversation, and now I've pulled it back down again."

"Please. . .I'm Tim," he said, understanding how conversation often tugs at the heart. He despised talking about feelings. "It's not your fault. Happens all the time. I guess that's why I'm not very sociable."

"Sure you are," she said, renewed color brightening her face. "You're always friendly at the office, and sometimes I've watched you with Timmy. I know you're a good father."

"I try." He thought of so many times he'd fallen on his knees begging God to give him strength and patience.

"God is good," she said.

His head jerked upward. Had he mentioned his prayer aloud?

"Are you a religious man, Mr.—Tim? I'm guessing you are."

"Without God, life leaves little to cling to," he said, wishing he hadn't after he saw her expression.

She wanted him to explain, he was sure, but he didn't. Too much background information would be needed. Too much personal pain would be explored. "How long have you been at the clinic?" he asked.

"Two years," she said. "I worked at Beaumont Hospital but decided I'd prefer straight days. I got very tired of the shift changes."

"I can imagine," he said, inwardly breathing a relieved sigh that he'd changed the subject. He knew about shift changes. So often, he'd wished a college degree had been an option. So little money and moral support had led him to take a quick job—not a career like Julie.

Her gaze shifted toward her friend. "Oops, I see Teri's alone over there. I'd better get back." She gestured toward the woman sitting across the room. "Would you like to join us?"

His chest tightened. He would, but he knew it was foolish. "No, but thanks. I was smart enough to drive here myself, and since Jack's pleasantly occupied, I think I'll just slip away. I have a sitter with Timmy."

"Aah," she said, rising. "Well, it was nice to see you. . . Tim. I imagine Timmy has another appointment at the clinic."

"Always," he said, rising. "Thanks for coming over to say 'hi.' "

She extended her hand. "You don't have to thank me. It was fun."

He grasped her small palm against his, giving it a firm shake, and she flashed a smile before she walked away.

Her soft curls bounced as she crossed the floor, leaving

him feeling extra lonely. Though he'd seen her at the clinic often, his attention was always focused on Timmy. He'd never noticed how pretty she was. He was a head taller, he guessed. He liked her figure, not too curvy or thin. Just right. Firm and cozy-looking.

He ran his fingers through his hair, amazed at his wayward thoughts. Single, he was—but not like people who were really alone. He had Timmy and memories. Some mornings he woke, and the empty bed sent shivers of longing through him.

Having a wife to share his life had been a blessing. He'd asked God often what he'd done to deserve the deep ache that he felt from Jan's loss. Then he remembered that the Lord didn't promise a life without sorrow or pain. He only promised forgiveness and salvation.

Tim knew those gifts were his. Still, he wondered if life held anything else in store. A child who walked without pain and braces. That would be a blessing. And a wife? That picture, he'd never envisioned. But today, Julie had rekindled old yearnings.

Perhaps one day God would have another earthly mate for him. Someone like Julie perhaps, but not Julie. She was worthy of far more than Tim could offer. She deserves a man with a career. A man with a suit and white shirt. Not a factory rat like him.

# Chapter 2

"I can't find Mr. Meier's chart," Julie said, plowing through the stack of manila folders on the office counter.

"Dr. Hubbard took it," her coworker said.

"Thanks, Casey. I thought I'd lost it." She sent her friend a smile, thinking that she'd really "lost it" lately, and pulled the next appointments from the stack. *Timothy Richmond, Jr.* Julie's pulse lurched as she eyed the child's file. But instead of the boy, his father's amiable face rose in her thoughts.

Though she'd given up on men, she'd been riddled with unwanted feelings since meeting Tim Richmond at the singles' group. When she made the invitation, she'd hoped he'd join her and Teri, but he said "no" and vanished shortly after she'd walked away.

It was not his good looks but his gentleness that interested her. He was a good man—a father devoted to his child.

Thinking of them, she inched to the receptionist window and peeked into the waiting room. Her heart skipped when she saw him. Always, he seemed so sophisticated with his distinguished appearance—a large man, not plump, but impressive in size and manner.

Whenever he came into the office, he was softspoken with an air of reserve, almost as if he were larger than life. She'd admired him from Timmy's first office visit.

As she watched through the window, Tim held a storybook while Timmy leaned against his arm, all ears, his tender brown eyes enchanted by the colorful picture book. A lopsided grin turned at the corner of Timmy's mouth. She'd seen that same look on his father's lips, on rare occasions, as if he were hiding a sense of playful mischief.

Before she could duck from the small window, Tim's gaze lifted. A look of recognition washed over his face, and she felt a deep blush shoot up her neck and warm her cheeks. Now she had to go into the waiting room to say hello or he'd think she was unfriendly. . .or disinterested.

Disinterested? Well, yes, she was—at least, she wanted to be. But the truth niggled at her, and she found herself drawn to the man ever since they'd run into each other.

She recalled him saying something that gnawed at her: *Without God, life leaves little to cling to.* Though the thought saddened her, she understood what he meant. Things on earth could be fleeting: success, wealth, friendship, hope, even life—like his wife. The only thing humans could count on was God.

Strong in her faith, Julie wondered about Tim. He spoke of God, but did he really follow God's ways? A bad experience in her past made her leery of men. More than that, she didn't trust men—and that's why being single was how she'd stay. Men's morals seemed different from women's. Women prized their chastity. Men seemed to prize the conquest. She'd had enough of being pursued and then dropped when she didn't give in to a man's demands. And how could she tell from one man to the next? Tim? Did he share her morals? She'd probably never know.

She peered through the window, and Tim's attention lifted from Timmy's book. Catching his gaze, she gave him a nod and headed out of the office area to the waiting room door.

Steeling herself, she headed for the boy. "Hi, Timmy, how are you today?"

"Fine," he said, grinning at her. "Daddy's reading me a story."

"I see that." She allowed her focus to shift to Tim. "And how are you doing?"

"Fine, thanks," he said, his hands fidgeting with the storybook cover.

"I noticed you made a quick escape a few weeks ago." She swallowed, hearing her words. Time had marched along while she wondered when she'd see him again.

"I was miserable that night. I hope I wasn't rude."

She shook her head. "Rude? Not at all. I enjoyed talking with you."

"So did I," he said.

"Thanks." His response caught her unprepared. Had he really enjoyed her company, or was he only being polite? She glanced over her shoulder at the receptionist window. Doctor Brady gazed out at her. "Guess I'd better get back to work." She leaned closer and lowered her voice. "My boss is watching."

She spun on her heel and darted through the doorway. The doctor had vanished, and Julie picked up the stack of folders and tried to focus on her work, but her mind lingered in the waiting room.

By the time she returned to the receptionist's window, Tim and his son were gone. Curious, she wove her way through the examining room corridors. She grinned when she found their room.

From inside, she heard a child's sweet voice singing a Sunday school song. She waited until he finished, then knocked and peeked inside.

"No doctor yet?" she asked.

Tim shifted toward her and shook his head. "We've only been waiting a couple of minutes."

"I'm sure he'll be in soon." She paused, feeling like a ninny, trying to conjure up appropriate conversation. "I heard you singing, Timmy. You have a nice voice."

"Thank you," he said, tucking his head into his father's arm.

"I sing, too," Julie said.

The boy lifted his face, his eyebrows arched high. "You do?"

"Yes, with my church choir. We're having our Easter concert in two weeks. I practice very hard."

"I sing in Sunday school," Timmy said.

"You sing all the time," his dad said with a warm grin before turning to Julie. "So. . .you sing with your choir. That's nice."

"Do you?" she asked.

He chuckled. "No, I'm not much of a singer—but I'm a pretty good audience."

With her pulse gaining speed, Julie garnered courage. "We need all the support we can get. I'd love you to come and be a pretty good audience. It's Sunday at seven P.M."

"I don't know. . . ," he said with a look of discomfort. "Where is your church?"

"First Community on Fifth and Washington in Royal Oak."

He only nodded while she filled with disappointment.

Outside the door, Julie heard the doctor's voice. Saying a quick good-bye, she exited, feeling defeated.

❋

Pulling himself from under the sink, Tim thumped his head against the cabinet. He rubbed the spot a moment, felt a lump forming, and controlled his mouth from uttering a curse. Swearing was something he'd learned to avoid when he'd become a true believer.

His divorced neighbor, Penny, who lived in the adjoining townhouse, often asked him to help with tasks she couldn't handle. . .like plumbing. Tim never refused and did the task without grumbling. Often, she'd pitched in for him by watching Timmy or bringing in his paper and mail when he was traveling.

Conveniently, her son, Buddy, and Timmy were play-mates. And the bonus was Sammy, their young spaniel. Timmy adored the dog. Having Sammy nearby saved Tim the need to buy his son a puppy. Before Sammy, his son had begged daily for a dog of his own. Tim prayed his scheme continued to work.

As the thought faded, Sammy bounded into the kitchen and nosed beneath the sink. Tim scooted the dog away, closed the cabinet door, and tried the disposal one more time. "Penny," Tim called through the doorway, "looks like it's working now."

She hurried into the kitchen, a full-figured woman with a flirtatious demeanor. "You always come to my rescue, Tim," she said, giving him a poke. "What can I do in return? I'd be happy to keep Timmy for an evening."

"Thanks, but. . ." Before he finished his refusal, Julie's concert invitation for that evening replayed in his mind. The offer sounded tempting. Tim had done nothing alone in weeks, and Julie would certainly be surprised to see him.

"Maybe you could watch him tonight, if you don't mind," Tim said. "I've been invited to a concert, and if you'll sit with Timmy, I'd like to go."

"Concert? You mean at the Silver Dome? A rock—"

"No," Tim said, grinning, "a church concert. For Easter."

"I should have guessed," she said. "You've never looked like a rocker to me." She let loose a giggle. "I'd be happy to keep Timmy for you."

"I shouldn't be too late, Penny. I'll send him over after dinner."

He gathered his tools, then headed home, wondering why he was tempting himself. Julie was a great woman, but he didn't want to lead her on. . . . He didn't want to lead himself on either. Every time she entered his thoughts—which was more often than he wanted—he knew he was heading for trouble.

❄

Tim slid into the pew near the back of the old church. Surveying the large stained glass windows, he wondered what they might look like with the sun penetrating the colorful glass and washing the room with varied hues.

When the organ silenced, the choir filed in through a side door and formed rows across the front. When Julie stepped into the sanctuary, Tim filled with pleasure at seeing her again. She looked sweet and angelic in her ivory robe and a red stole accented by a gold cross. Her hair fell in soft curls and brushed her shoulders as she moved into place.

The organ struck a chord, and the choir's powerful music filled the vaulted ceiling. Somber, then joyful, the music of Christ's death and resurrection washed over him with waves of emotion. When the concert ended, Tim rose, wrapped in a sense of renewal, and headed into the reception area, sure that Julie hadn't noticed him among the audience.

But before moving too far, a hand grasped his jacket sleeve, and when he turned, Julie's glowing face smiled at him. "Thank you for coming," she said.

"My pleasure. The choir was excellent."

"Really?" Her eyes searched his.

"Really." He tucked his nervous hands into his jacket pockets. "I didn't think you'd noticed me."

"I saw you right away," she chuckled, "but I have to keep my eye on the director."

Tim nodded.

Her arms hung against the front of her choir robe, her fingers woven into a tight knot. "I didn't expect you to be here." Her stifled voice brushed against his ear. "But I'm glad you are."

"Me, too," he said, not wanting to say he hadn't planned to, but providence—or God—moved him to come.

"I have to get out of this robe," she said, a strained look on her face, "but. . .would you like to, uh, drop by the house for some coffee and dessert?"

Tim's shoulders stiffened.

Julie unwound her fingers and lifted one to her neck, playing with the satin collar. "That is, if you have time."

Tim shuffled his feet, eyeing the pretty woman waiting for his answer. He had no reason to say no. . .except his good sense. "I'd like to, but just for a few minutes," he said. "A neighbor lady has Timmy, and I don't want to keep him out too late on a school night."

"Oh, no, I understand." She stepped backward. "Okay, then, I'll get my coat and be with you in a second."

As she darted away, Tim longed to disappear. Why had he agreed to have coffee with Timmy's nurse? Coffee at her house? He felt like a man standing on the edge of a sandy cliff and feeling the ground shift beneath his feet. One wrong move and he'd be lost. No. . .his heart would be lost.

She returned in a moment, and they stepped outside into the brisk air. Julie pulled her coat up around her neck, and Tim walked stiffly beside her. Finding her car, she gave him directions, and he followed.

In a few minutes, Julie turned down a wide street lined with large, well-kept homes—homes he could never afford. Noticing her turn signal, Tim faltered, wanting to drive off.

Julie had pulled into the driveway of a large brick colonial with an attached garage. The door lifted as she edged forward and pulled inside.

A rush of panic filled Tim. He lived in a rented town-house, one unit joining the next, small rooms, noise seeping through the nicked walls. A classy woman like Julie should be entertaining a man who had. . .

Relief spread through him as he considered a probable error. Looking at the well-kept house with dark shutters and French pane windows, he realized the house glowed with lamplight. Certainly someone was already inside. Could this be her parents' home?

With the thought, he gained confidence and released a fettered sigh of relief. He turned off the motor and stepped into the chilling air.

With a pleasant smile, Julie waited for him at the front walk.

"Your parents have a nice house," he said.

"Yes, they do." She took his arm and steered him up the brick steps. "But they live a few miles away. This house is mine."

# Chapter 3

Tim's stomach tumbled to his feet, then slammed into his throat. *Stupid.* A nurse probably made a great salary. She had a career. Why would he con himself into believing this was her parents' home? He should have excused himself at the church and said he had to get home to Timmy.

Too late. When she pushed open the door, he forced himself forward and stepped into a small foyer, featuring an open staircase and a well-shined table holding a vase of flowers—real flowers sending a subtle, sweet aroma into the air.

Swinging open a closet door, Julie extended her arm. "Let me hang up your jacket."

Clinging to it for a fleeting moment, Tim chided his foolishness and unzipped the garment. "I'll just toss it on the stairs," he said, draping it on the steps and sensing that if he left it there, the situation was less permanent.

She shrugged, closed the closet door, and headed through a doorway.

Tim followed and found himself in a cozy kitchen.

"I'll put on the coffee," she said. "Would you be more

comfortable in the living room?"

"No, I'll just watch," he said, afraid if he were alone he'd bolt.

She went about the business of filling the coffeemaker and slicing pieces of orange-colored cake with creamy white frosting. The pungent scent rose from the brew and wrapped Tim in familiar comfort.

Finished, Julie filled his mug with the right amount of coffee and cream. Each carrying their cup and plate, he followed her to the living room.

Sinking into a plush chair, he let his gaze sweep the brick fireplace, the broad mantle adorned with porcelain birds and candlesticks on each side of an antique clock.

"That old clock was my grandfather's," she said, apparently noticing his wandering gaze.

"Your place is attractive, Julie—and homey."

"I like a house to be comfortable."

"You succeeded," he said, pulling his focus to her. He preferred to look anywhere but at Julie. When he did, his pulse galloped inside his veins, leaving him bewildered.

Then, reality smacked him, and his mouth opened, allowing the truth to tumble out. "I'd be embarrassed to show you where I live."

Her head bolted upward. "Why?"

"I rent a townhouse. . .you know, units all connected, each one looks like the next, the size of matchboxes."

She shook her head. "You shouldn't feel uncomfortable about that. You have a son to support as well as yourself. Look at me. I'm single. No one to spend my money on but me."

Her face glowed with sincerity, and Tim felt his stiff

shoulders ease backward into the chair. "Yes, but—"

"No 'buts,' " she said. "You're such a good father. I bet you lavish Timmy with everything you can."

Guilt poked at him, and he lifted a fork of delicious carrot cake and savored the bite rather than respond. She was correct. He did lavish Timmy with what he could. But he wished he didn't. "You see right through me," Tim said finally. "I suppose I try to make up for his loss of a mother. . .and I refuse to allow him to have a childhood like I had."

Her face twisted with concern. "You had a difficult life?"

Sipping the warm brew as a stall, Tim wanted to kick himself. Why had he told her that?

"I was raised by my aunt," he continued, sensing he owed her an explanation, "on a farm in Michigan. Times were hard. My uncle died shortly after I moved in, so I was the only 'man' in the family. At six years old, that was a responsibility. She had only one daughter. No boys to help out. We all pitched in."

"Sounds difficult. . .and sad." She leaned forward on the armrest and gazed at him. "What happened to your parents?"

Tim blew out a stream of pent-up air. Why had he opened his mouth? She didn't want to hear his tale of woe. . .his *vague* tale of woe. God had blessed him with a failed memory. Only indistinct pictures of people from his past poked at his thoughts, and then only on rare occasions. His mother, bound to her bed, was a gentle image. Tim barely recalled his father, a big man, but apparently a defeated one. And sisters. Somewhere in the world he had sisters.

"I shouldn't have asked," Julie said, her face etched with discomfort. "Please forgive me."

Realizing he'd been lost in thought, Tim pushed the hazy memories aside. "No, it's natural to ask. My memories are faint. I was so young when my aunt came to get me, I don't recall much."

Her puzzled expression triggered the need to tell her more. Tim delved into his mind to organize his blurred recollections. "My mother died. I don't really remember it, except the fear and loneliness. I recall the others crying. Sisters. I had three. My aunt didn't want to talk about it much. I mostly think of Eden. She was the oldest."

"Have you ever tried to find them?" Julie asked.

His heart heavy, Tim shook his head. "My memories are so vague, and my aunt was no help. My cousin's as bad. I'm not sure where to look. My father's dead now, but he'd vanished from the picture after my mother died. When my aunt came for me, I was living with a neighbor, I think."

"I can understand why being a good father is extra important to you."

*Extra important.* That was it. Vital. Necessary. Driving. His son would never know the pain of abandonment and degradation that he'd felt as a child.

Drawing his focus back to Julie, he studied her concerned face. Why didn't she have a husband and children? Her turn, he decided. He took the last bite of delicious cake, then set down the plate.

"Enough about me. Tell me about you, Julie. Why aren't you married with children of your own?"

She grinned as if accepting the inevitable. "I have a career. That's all I figured I could handle. When I worked at the hospital, I was on different shifts, sometimes doubling back. Socializing seemed nearly impossible, and. . .I don't know, I guess I figured all the rituals of dating and courting were more than I could handle."

"You make it sound like a task instead of pleasure. Where's your sense of romance?" Tim squirmed at asking such a personal question. Jan had always called him a romantic. He had loved to surprise her with trinkets and flowers for no reason at all, except that he loved her.

Julie remained silent. Then, she said one word. "Romance?" She paused again. "I've never wanted it."

"What?" Tim said before he could stop himself. "I thought all women reveled in romance. . .candlelight dinners, floral bouquets, sappy cards decorated. . ." His mind flew back to a few weeks earlier at the singles' activity. ". . .with hearts and Cupids."

Julie blushed. "Sure, that kind of romance is fun. I suppose most woman would cherish that."

What kind of romance did she mean? He searched her face. Then, her blush answered his question. Intimacy. Did she think that dating meant being intimate? He'd never be like that with a woman. Not until marriage, naturally. Or did she mean she *never* wanted intimacy? He didn't know her well enough to ask.

"I went with a man for awhile a few years ago," Julie said. "We met at the hospital. Different shifts. Different values. Different—" She stopped. "You know what I mean."

Different *morals.* Is that what she meant? He nodded.

"I suppose sometimes relationships are more work than they're worth." *Like this one*, he thought, though the idea washed an empty sadness over his heart. Julie would make a good wife—for someone.

Tim glanced at his wristwatch. "Listen, I'd better get going. My neighbor will think I'm lost." He stood.

"Timmy needs his sleep for school," she added and rose, following him toward the doorway.

"Thanks for the carrot cake and coffee. The cake tasted homemade."

"It is," she said, giving him a grin. "Really homemade, except I have a secret ingredient."

Playfully, he lifted an eyebrow. "Nothing alcoholic, I hope."

"Heaven forbid, no. I use baby food carrots. No grating."

He grinned at her excitement. "And I didn't even need a bib."

She shifted forward as if she were going to touch his cheek, but she let her hand drop.

"I'll see you around, I suppose," Tim said, wanting to see her but knowing how ridiculous his wish was.

"Well, at the clinic, for sure," she said.

A flash of disappointment shot through him and from her expression, she seemed to have noticed.

"How about the singles' group? They're having a St. Patrick's Day party," she said.

"Do I have to dye my hair green?" he asked, being silly, but unable to answer her question.

"I won't if you won't," she said.

His heart nudged his vocal chords. "Okay, I'll see you then. No green hair."

"It'll be fun," she said.

He sensed she was correct. When he opened the outside door, the chilling air didn't penetrate the warmth that covered him.

❄

Julie took an occasional sip of her foamy, green ice cream punch and eyed the doorway. Tim had said he'd come, but for some reason, she sensed his hesitation. Maybe she'd pushed herself on him. Yet, why would she? He was a nice man with a difficult past, and she longed to help him heal. Her nursing persona, she was sure.

The yearning to aid people in distress, to solve others' problems, to soothe people's hurts seemed part of her nature. It was also what got her in trouble.

She cringed thinking of Jeff, her old steady. He'd pressed her so often to give herself to him fully. She could hear his plaintive voice in her head. "If you love me, you'll trust me not to hurt you. We're getting married someday anyway. What difference will it make?"

She wanted to please him, wanted to make him happy, wanted to meet his need. But she couldn't. And the more he pressed, the more resentment and frustration she felt. She could never trust a man again. What would she do if Tim was like that? If he pleaded with her? Told her how much he needed her? Told her she could make him feel less tense?

Sadness washed over her, and she closed her eyes with a new realization. She'd be better off if Tim didn't come at all. Then she'd never have to face dealing with those issues again. Loneliness prickled at the back of her neck.

Opening her eyes, she saw Tim come through the

doorway. He waved, and her heart lifted with an unexpected joy, then sank to her toes. But watching him smile as he approached her, she set aside her guilty fear and gave him a wave in return.

"Hi," he said, slipping off his jacket and hanging it on the chair back. "My neighbor was late getting home. She's watching Timmy for me."

"I thought you were standing me up," she said, giving her voice a lighthearted lift to cover the real feelings she'd had.

"Me? Never." He gave her a wry smile.

"Neighbor? You must have really great neighbors."

"One, anyway," he said. "It's the same woman who watched Timmy for the concert. She's alone, too, so we help each other out. Besides, Timmy and her son are best friends. . .and Sammy."

*Sammy?* Concern, as well as curiosity, riffled through her. "Who's Sammy?" But her mind tangled with his single woman comment. What was Tim's relationship with her?

"Sammy's their dog." He chuckled. "Timmy wants a puppy, but I encourage him to play with Sammy and save myself the grief."

"Smart man," she said, longing to ask him more about the neighbor lady.

The conversation drifted to Timmy, the orthopedic clinic, Julie's choir, and finally, food was served. They nibbled on appetizers with green cream cheese and hot dogs with green catsup. Laughing, they lifted their voice with an Irish sing-along. When the others wrapped their arms around each other, shoulder to shoulder, and swayed to the music, Tim drew her to his side, rocking to the lilting tune. Warmth traveled through her.

Too soon, the evening ended, and Julie longed to invite Tim to her house. Still, she'd been the pursuer, and this time she hoped he might suggest an activity together.

In the parking lot, he stood beside her car while she unlocked the door and slid in. "I hate to have you drive alone. I should've been a gentleman and offered you a ride."

"That's okay," she said, knowing in her heart she'd have loved a ride.

Hesitating, he teetered, hands in his pockets, then finally spoke. "If you'd like to follow me home, I can offer you some coffee."

Surprised, Julie stumbled over her thoughts, trying to weigh her decision. Instead, she listened to her heart. "Sure, if it's not too much trouble."

He gave her directions, then closed her door. She sat a moment before backing out of her space. She longed to know more about him—to know where he worked and to see the house that had tugged out an apology. Yet being alone in his house made her nervous. Did he have an ulterior motive for inviting her? Maybe he had a platonic interest only—just a friendship, nothing more.

But if she faced the truth, she liked Tim more than she cared to admit. He needed to know where she stood in terms of her faith and her morals.

# Chapter 4

Tim opened the door, snapped on the light, and invited Julie inside. His stomach knotted, and he feared looking at her face, knowing that she'd find his place inadequate compared to hers. Inexpensive furniture, small, and crowded.

"Cozy kitchen," she said as soon as she stepped through the doorway. "Very nice for a small family."

Small. Cozy. The words themselves sounded fine. . . and truthful, but what was she really thinking? As he guided her to the living room, he couldn't help but recall her solid antiques in contrast to his glass and brass tables.

Julie paused in the doorway. "I like it," she said. She stepped into the room and moved to the glass etagere, eyeing the two plants that Tim had managed to keep alive. "Good choice. Big, overstuffed furniture would dominate the room, but you've managed to make it masculine, yet homey." She touched the plant and gestured to a colorful toss pillow that gave life to his plain, brown sofa. "I can't believe you said you'd be embarrassed to show me your home."

*Home.* He liked the sound of the word as it left her

lips. And no matter how he twisted her sentences, they sounded sincere and positive. "Thanks," Tim said, finally.

She sank into the streamlined sofa, nestling against a pillow, and grinned at him.

"I'll put on the coffee," he said, then turned and hurried from the room to catch his breath. He filled the pot, then picked up the telephone to call Penny. To his relief, she volunteered to run Timmy home.

He rotated his shoulders to relax them before pulling out the mugs and finding some store-bought cookies to serve. He wished he had something more impressive.

A rap sounded on the door, and Timmy entered, sleepy-eyed but curious. "Thanks, Penny," Tim said as she gave a wave and darted back home.

After giving his son a hug, Tim sent him on his way to say hello to Julie while he brought in the coffee. He could hear Timmy's shy, yet curious, tone as he greeted Julie in the living room.

Tim carried in the tray, offering Julie a mug, then led his son up the stairs to bed. When he returned, Julie had slipped out of her shoes and curled her legs beneath her on the sofa with the mug clasped in her fingers.

"Good coffee," she said. "Is it special?"

He grinned. "Hazelnut." He lifted his own cup and slipped into an adjacent chair. "Have a cookie," he said, clamping his teeth together so he wouldn't apologize for the packaged dessert.

"They're my favorite, but I'm too full from all that 'green' food," she said with a smile. "Coffee's great."

She surveyed the room again. "Did your wife decorate, or did you?" she asked.

"We'd moved in just before Jan got ill so most of the choices were mine. What I could afford at the time."

"You've done a nice job, Tim. Never be embarrassed to show your home. It's very attractive." She took another sip of the brew, her gaze riveted to Tim's. "You've never mentioned what you do for a living."

Tim sank deeper into the cushion. Enjoying her company more than he wanted, he'd always feared the day she would ask, figuring she'd be turned off by a factory worker.

Garnering courage, he answered. "I work at Sterling Stamping. In the press room."

"The big three," she said. "Great benefits, I hear. That's important, especially with Timmy."

Studying her face, Tim realized that she didn't bat an eye hearing his confession. "It's not a career, but it pays the bills."

"Nothing wrong with that." Her animated voice touched his ear. "Not everyone has the same opportunities. Have you been there long?"

The question tugged at his old hurts and sorrows. "I joined the army right out of high school. Basic training at Fort Knox, then the Presidio in San Francisco, and finally San Antonio."

"Nice experience," she said. "You had opportunities to see the country."

He laughed. "Right, that and a lot of rain and mud during bivouac."

"I suppose." Her look grew tender. "What made you join the service?" she asked.

"College was out of the question. I'm grateful to Aunt

Selma for raising me, but she didn't have much, especially after my uncle died, so I was a burden."

Julie's expression melted to sadness. Leaning forward, she rested her hand against his forearm. "Never a burden, Tim."

He wanted to say that she didn't know the situation, but he held back his bitterness. His aunt, he supposed, had done the best she could. "It was difficult. I've always wished I could pay her back somehow. . .but now she's dead, too."

Her hand lingered on his arm while they sat in silence as if neither knew what to say.

"Will you be at the April singles'?" she asked, finally. "I heard they're planning some kind of a scavenger hunt or something. It should be fun."

"Sure—that is if Timmy's okay then."

"Right. His surgery's getting close, isn't it?" She looked toward the staircase in thought. "I can imagine you're getting nervous."

"Anxious, but hopeful. I pray a lot and trust that the Lord will bless Timmy."

"Timmy *and* you," Julie said. "God will bless you both."

The warmth from her hand spread up his arm, but a shiver of concern wrapped around his heart despite his faith. He'd never felt totally fulfilled—totally in God's favor—but he asked the Lord to give Timmy a good life. A life with laughter, joy—and health.

❄

Julie stared at the manila file folder with Timmy's name marked on the tab. She knew he was in the waiting room for a checkup following his surgery.

Disappointment had filled her at the April singles' event. Tim hadn't come. Prickled with fear, she'd worried that something had gone wrong with Timmy's surgery. Still, too uncomfortable to call Tim and ask, she'd looked through Timmy's file, feeling like a spy, finding no complications with his osteotomy. The surgeon had used compression plates, she noted, and the procedure had gone well.

Filled with frustration, Julie wondered why Tim hadn't called. He had to know that she cared about Timmy. . .and about him. Her invitation to the singles' group seemed bold enough.

Hit by uncertainty, she ran her finger over Timmy's name on the file tab. Maybe the neighbor woman meant more to Tim than Julie wanted to face. Wisdom told her to back off.

She drew in a calming breath and stepped to the waiting-room door. "Timmy Richmond," she called, giving the boy a smile.

He sent back a shy grin and rose on crutches, his leg in a cast. Tim followed beside him, concentrating on the child, not her.

"Hi," he said, without looking at her as he held the door for Timmy.

"I'm glad to see things went well," she said, motioning him down the hall. "Room five."

He went ahead of her, and at the door, she slipped the file into the holder mounted outside the door. "The doctor will be with you shortly," she said, grasping the knob and stepping into the hallway as she began closing the door.

"Julie?"

She hesitated, hearing Tim call her name.

Drawing in a ragged breath, she pushed the door open. "Yes?"

His gaze caught hers. "I'm sorry I didn't call to tell you about Timmy. Life has been hectic."

"I imagine."

"To confuse things, I've been on overtime. That's so hard with Timmy home now that school's out. . .and the surgery. I've had to depend on my cousin, Nancy. . .and Penny."

*But not me,* Julie thought, then chastised herself. Why would he depend on her? She worked all day at the clinic. And they were new. . .friends.

"I've been on afternoons at the plant," he continued. "It's a hardship shift change, just temporary while Timmy needs extra care."

"Afternoons?" Understanding filtered into her mind. He left for work before she arrived home.

"On top of that, I've had to work the past two weekends. It's been a challenge."

"I'm sorry, Tim. I was concerned. . . ." She glanced down at Timmy, looking at her with wide eyes. "I hoped everything had gone well." She prayed her comment didn't frighten the child. "How are you doing, Timmy?" she asked, crouching beside him.

"Okay," he said. "Pretty soon, I'll walk good."

"I know. I'm so happy for you."

"But not for my birthday," he said, furrows growing in his smooth brow.

"Birthday? When's that?"

He glanced at his father who held up two fingers. "In two weeks. I'm having a birthday party."

"July twelfth," Tim added.

"You are? What fun. I love parties, don't you?"

He nodded his head. "Will you come? We'll have cake and ice cream."

She rose filled with discomfort and embarrassed that she'd mentioned she liked parties. "I, uh. . ."

"Can she come, Daddy?" Timmy asked, turning to his father.

"Well. . .sure. Why not? That is if she'd like to come."

Struggling to keep her face from announcing her humiliation, she faltered. "I'd love to." She caught Tim's gaze.

He nodded his approval. "It's a week from Saturday. Around six. We'll order pizza."

Timmy slid his tongue over his lips. "Pizza! Yummy!"

Tim grinned, and Julie backed toward the door overwhelmed with confusion. No doubt Timmy wanted her, but did Tim? She asked God for guidance, longing to do the right thing.

❄

"Here we are," Tim said, trepidation inching through him as he turned off the motor and gazed at the singles' crowd gathering for the Fourth of July picnic.

"I'm so pleased you asked me to come with you," Penny said, sliding from the car.

Tim swallowed, wanting to explain that it wasn't a date. He feared he'd made a grave error. Trying to be kind, he'd inadvertently misled her. One thing had led to another. He'd mowed Penny's lawn, she invited him to dinner, and at the end of the meal, he opened his mouth. "How would you like to go to the Fourth of July picnic with the singles' group next weekend? I know it's difficult going places alone."

He'd thought the invitation was clear, but her response nailed him to the spot. "Oh, Tim, I'd love to go with you. My size scares off most men."

Obviously she considered it a date, but that was as far from Tim's mind as mountain climbing. His hesitation wasn't her size at all. She'd been a good friend and neighbor, and an attractive one, but that's all he felt for her. Of late, Julie filled his thoughts.

He'd longed to see her at the picnic, but now with Penny at his side, he feared Julie wouldn't understand. The past week at the orthopedic clinic when she'd called Timmy's name, Tim's pulse had reared on its hind legs like a stallion until he noticed the hurt expression on her face.

Neglecting her. . .not calling had been foolish. Rude was more accurate. She'd shown friendship to both him and Timmy, but things had gotten in the way. He was at work when she was home, and he didn't feel right calling her at the clinic. Weekends he spent running errands, grocery shopping, and trying to spend time with Timmy. Though he missed her smile and easy good humor, too much seemed to be in the way for. . .friendship.

*Friendship?* No. . .he longed for more than that.

Penny bounded from the car, grabbed a canvas bag, and latched onto his arm. "Let's go," she said with a little nudge to his ribs with her elbow.

"Let me get the cooler," he said, loosening her grip and heading for the trunk. He hoisted the heavy container from the back, grateful that he needed two hands to carry it, and headed toward a picnic table.

Penny scurried along beside him. Reaching the table, she pulled a plastic cloth from the bag and spread it over the surface while Tim plopped the cooler at the base of the table and lifted the lid.

"How about a soda?" he asked.

"Sure," she said, accepting the drink he offered. From the canvas carryall, she brought out a large bag of chips and tore the wrapper.

Groping for courage, Tim scanned the area and held his breath. No Julie. Jack waved to him from two tables over where he sat with a young woman he'd dated a few times. Tim was pleased for him and wished God's blessing on their growing friendship.

Sitting at their table was another man. Tim beckoned to Penny and led the way. "Hi," he said as they neared.

Jack raised a questioning eye, and Tim gave him a "don't ask" look, hoping he could explain his predicament.

"Jack, Cheryl," he said, "this is my neighbor, Penny."

Each greeted her before Jack introduced Ray.

"You're new with the singles?" Ray asked, looking from Penny to Tim as if wondering about their relationship.

Tim took advantage of the situation. "Penny's been such a great neighbor, I invited her to come along and meet all of you."

Penny gave Tim a puzzled look.

Ray focused on Tim. "Then you're not—"

"Oh, no," Tim said, "we're only friends."

He felt Penny stiffen beside him, but Ray's face brightened, and he patted the empty bench. "Why don't you bring your food over here?" Ray asked. "We could all sit together."

Jack nodded in agreement, and with gratitude, Tim turned toward his gear as he overheard Ray invite Penny to be his horseshoe partner after lunch.

Fearing he'd hurt Penny's feelings, Tim felt relieved when Ray showed her attention. God had worked out his predicament. Sorry that he'd bungled, Tim's guilt lightened with Ray's apparent interest in Penny. As Tim neared his cooler, he spotted Julie across the lawn. She looked like sunshine in yellow shorts and a matching top as the light's rays played on her wavy brown hair. He grasped his resolve and headed for her.

❄

Pivoting away, Julie held her breath. She'd seen Tim arrive with a woman, and her heart had dropped to her shoes. He looked so handsome, tall and powerful, his muscles bulging from carrying the heavy cooler. But she'd been right. Apparently Penny meant more to Tim than Julie had hoped. She could handle it though. She had to.

"Julie." Tim's voice sailed on the breeze.

She pushed an amiable smile to her face and turned toward him. "Hi, Tim."

"I hoped you'd be here. I wanted to remind you of the birthday party next week."

Unbidden, her gaze drifted toward the blond woman seated at the distant table. "Oh. . .Tim, I'm, uh, sorry. I don't think that I can—"

"That you can come?" His gaze searched hers. "But Timmy'll be so disappointed. He's talked about nothing else since we invited you."

Guilt filled her. Not one real reason stood in her way of attending the party—except the blond and pure, sinful jealousy. In the span of a breath, she asked God to forgive her foolishness and drew up her shoulders, fortifying her courage. "I don't want to disappoint Timmy." She meant that with all her heart.

"Then I hope you can come. He'll be so disappointed if you don't. To be honest, so will I."

Her heart faltered for a moment. She searched his face, wondering why he would say such a thing. But for Timmy, she reconsidered. "I'll, uh, maybe I can work something out."

"Please do." His eyes searched hers. "Are you. . .with someone?"

She nodded.

"Oh." Surprising her, a forlorn look spread across his face.

She could tell from his expression that he thought she meant a man. "I'm with Amy and Barb. We rode together."

"I thought. . ." He grinned and a flush crept above his collar. "If you're alone, would you like to join us?" He motioned to the table across the way.

"But you're with a date, Tim." Her earlier jealousy spiraled to aggravation. Why was he playing games with her?

"No. No, that's Penny, my neighbor. I invited her to come, hoping she might meet someone."

Panic riddled his face. She stifled a laugh—at his expression *and* her own sense of relief. "I should eat with the ladies, I think. We're sharing a picnic basket."

A look of disappointment crossed his face. "I don't know what's wrong with me, Julie. I should have asked you to the picnic. I'm very backward when it comes to—"

"Don't apologize, Tim. We can visit after lunch."

His expression relaxed. "How about horseshoes?"

"What?"

"They're playing horseshoes after lunch. And don't worry, Penny's playing with Ray." He gestured toward the group at the other table. "I'd like you to be my partner."

*His partner?* She'd longed to be his partner, but one of a different kind. "Sure. Why not?"

She gave an inward chuckle. When he realized how badly she played horseshoes, he'd know "why not," but for now, it would be her surprise.

# Chapter 5

Tim stood in the kitchen, wondering what was keeping Julie. He'd spoken to her on the telephone, and she'd indicated she was coming to Timmy's party.

In the living room, he heard his cousin, Nancy, talking to Jack. She didn't seem pleased when he told her about Julie. Always in her "downing" way, she reminded him that he was a blue-collar worker and Julie was a professional. "That kind of thing only leads to hurt," she'd said. "A woman like that doesn't need you one iota."

Nancy was right. He had nothing to give Julie. Money, home, car, lifestyle—she had him beat in every area. She was worth far more than he could ever dream of giving her. So why did he tempt himself? He shook his head in disapproval. He'd tried to leave it in God's hands, but had he?

Outside, balloons bounced past the window, then a knock sounded on the door. Tim's chest tightened. Penny or Julie? His heart told him that Julie had brought the balloons.

When he opened the door, he found Julie standing on

the porch holding a gift, surrounded by a colorful floating bouquet. Mesmerized by the display, Tim faltered,
drawn back in time. So far back, his mind swirled to
another place and time, to a scene out of proportion—a
vague memory filled with soaring colorful balloons.

"Are you okay?" Julie asked, a frown edging out her
smile.

He laughed. "Sure. I was mentally clicking my heels
and saying, 'No place like home.'" He pushed the door
open, allowing her to manipulate her lavish gift into the
room.

She chuckled. "I could have flown to Kansas if the
wind had caught me."

"I think you overdid it, but you'll thrill Timmy." He
closed the door. "Timmy," he called.

In a heartbeat, Timmy came through the doorway
and reeled when he spied the gift.

"Balloons," he said, clapping his hands and scurrying
as quickly as he could toward Julie. "Yippee!"

"What do you say?" Tim asked.

"Thanks, Julie." He held the package in his arms and
clasped the balloons that bobbed above his head with one
hand.

A sense of déjà vu spilled over Tim as Timmy returned
to the living room. He heard Jack and his young daughter,
Patti, oohing over the bright gift, but Tim remained
smothered in undisclosed sensations.

Nancy's voice sailed into the kitchen. "Must be someone with money who could afford that."

Tim caught Julie's glance and motioned her into the
living room. Nancy's focus was glued to Julie.

"You've met Jack," he said to Julie. "This is his daughter, Patti."

Patti said hello, her gaze darting from Julie to the balloon bouquet.

"And my cousin, Nancy Johnson," Tim said. "We grew up together."

"My mother raised Tim. . .out of the goodness of her heart," Nancy muttered, interrupting the introductions.

Tim froze at the comment, so inappropriate to the time and place.

"Yes, I've heard," Julie said, her voice calm and gentle. "That was wonderful of your family."

"A hardship for all of us," Nancy added. "We only had a small farm and—"

"I'll order the pizza," Tim said, halting the conversation. "Penny and Buddy should be here any minute."

"And Sammy?" Timmy asked.

Tim stifled a grin. "Sammy wasn't invited, Son, but you can show him your balloons later."

"Okay," Timmy said, his enthusiasm undaunted.

❄

Her hands knotted in irritation, Julie watched Tim leave the room. How dare this woman humiliate him like that! Cousin or not, she had no reason to drag out the past in front of Tim's company.

Deciding to stay as far away as possible from her, Julie headed toward the sofa, but Nancy patted the empty chair beside her.

"Sit here," she commanded. "We can get better acquainted."

That was far from Julie's hope, but not wanting to add

to the uncomfortable moment, she followed the woman's direction. Before Julie could take a deep breath, Nancy began her inquisition.

"You work at the clinic, huh? A nurse, Tim said."

"That's right," Julie responded, turning her focus to the others. "How've you been, Jack?" Julie kept her eyes directed at him and Patti.

Jack grinned. "Great. And you?"

"Why a clinic?" Nancy prodded. "More money?"

Julie swiveled her head. "No. Less, in fact, but I prefer the hours."

"You must be well-off then," Nancy said.

Julie avoided her comment and steered the conversation to Patti and Timmy. From there the talk became safe, until sounds from the kitchen attuned everyone to the new guests who were arriving.

A young boy dashed into the room, ogling the balloons. Then the large blond from the picnic, Penny, stood in the doorway.

"Wow! Those are dandy. Nearly fill up the room," Penny said.

Nancy swung toward Julie. "I'm sure your living room is much larger than this one. You see, Tim and Penny have some things in common that you—"

"Small living rooms are *very* common in townhouses," Tim shot from the kitchen doorway.

Nancy bit her bottom lip.

"What can I do to help?" Julie asked, giving Penny her chair and stepping toward Tim. As she did, the doorbell rang, and the pizza delivery man saved the day.

Doling out pizza and salad kept Julie busy and Nancy's

mouth occupied. By the time they'd disposed of the paper plates, Timmy was eager to open his gifts; then the candles were lit and a round of "Happy Birthday" filled the air.

After dessert, the guests rose and left one by one, but Julie remained behind to help with the cleanup. Rinsing flatware at the sink, she overheard Tim at the door with Nancy.

"Any reason why I should remember a room full of balloons?" he asked.

Nancy sniffed. "Wishful thinking, I'd guess. Don't all kids like balloons?"

"I suppose," Tim said, his voice filled with disappointment.

"You take care," she said, "and I'd keep my eye on Penny. She's a good lady. Suits you well, and she's a woman who really needs you."

Her voice faded, and Tim hesitated a moment before closing the door.

Julie paused, letting the warm water slide over her hands, taking away the chill of the encounter.

"Sorry," Tim said, his voice hushed. "She's like that, and I can't do much about it. But she's the only blood relative I know, and despite her negative attitude, I'd hate to lose her."

Julie wiped her hands and stepped forward, grasping his shoulders. "Look, Tim, you're not responsible for other people's behavior. Nancy's like a mother who hates to lose control of her grown child."

"I know," he said, his eyes looking deeply into hers. "You're a fine woman, Julie. You never balk at anything and always see something nice in the worst situation."

"Don't give me too much credit. I grumble just like anyone." She lowered her hands. "But I sit in a closet so no one hears me."

His face broke into a smile, and a soft chuckle spilled from his chest. "Listen, Timmy wants you to meet Sammy—and show the dog his balloons. Why don't you take him outside and let me finish up here."

He lifted his hand and brushed her cheek, an inscrutable look in his eyes. His touch tingled down her shoulder and reached her heart, sending it skipping for a moment.

"Okay," she said, catching her breath, "if you don't mind."

She called Timmy, and again in a temporary leg brace, he hobbled into the room, tangled in the balloon strings. She laughed and unwound him from the cords, then headed outside with one last lingering look at Tim who watched them from the sink.

Timmy headed across the grass and reached the chain link fence. "Sammy," he called.

A floppy-eared spaniel gave a rousing yip and bounded to the fence. "Isn't he great?" Timmy said, grinning up at Julie.

"He sure is." The dog's shining cinnamon coat glistened in the summer sun, and he darted back and forth along the fence, occasionally scooting back on his front paws to bark at the bevy of color tangled in Timmy's hand.

"I'll give him a balloon," Timmy said, struggling to unwind one of the strings.

Before Julie could dart forward, one escaped, sailing upward on the wind. Timmy shielded his eyes from the sun and watched it. "My balloon's flying away?"

"Sure is," Julie said, watching it lift higher and higher above the houses, moving toward the clouds.

"Is it going to heaven?" Timmy asked. "Like my mom?"

Julie's chest tightened, and she wrapped her arm around the child's shoulders, unable to speak for a moment.

He tilted his earnest face to hers. "Maybe my mom will find it in heaven and know it's from me."

How could she tell him no? How could she say it would fall to earth when the helium escaped? The image of the child's smiling mother finding the balloon filled her mind. "Maybe, Timmy," she said, struggling to keep her voice steady.

Sammy's bark distracted him, and soon they were heading inside minus one balloon, but enriched by a lovely thought and a shared moment.

❄

After tucking Timmy into bed, Tim lumbered down the stairs, caught in a mixture of feelings. Julie had been a positive in his day; Nancy, a negative.

Julie sat curled up on the sofa, sipping a soda, her head leaning against the cushion—like she belonged there. But, Tim feared, she didn't. As much as he disliked Nancy's comments, she'd been right. Unlike Penny, Julie didn't need him. Tim knew he should pry Julie from his thoughts and let God lead him to a woman he could support, a woman who'd be content with his meager living.

Instead of listening to his head, Tim's heart guided him to action. He grasped his soda can and settled beside Julie on the sofa. A sweet, tantalizing fragrance drifted from her—one he'd enjoyed before—reminding him of flowers in the rain.

"Thanks for all your help," he said.

"I enjoyed myself. And so did Timmy." She placed her palm against his arm. "You have a great son. You must be so proud of him. He was well-behaved all evening."

"Unlike my cousin," Tim said, his voice sounding bitter in his ears.

" 'Sticks and stones can break my bones. . . .' Remember that, Tim. Nancy's words can't hurt you one bit, unless you let them. And you shouldn't."

He drew in a deep breath filled with her lovely aroma and slipped his arm across the sofa back, his fingers brushing the silky texture of her blouse.

In silence, she turned to him, their gazes locked as if in understanding.

Yearning swept over Tim. He lowered his gaze to her lovely, soft mouth, her warm breath so near it caressed his neck. Unable to hold himself back, he leaned forward, gently catching her sweet lips beneath his. She didn't resist as he expected, but yielded, leaning into his touch, and released a shuddered sigh that prickled on his arms.

Drawing back, he caught her chin with his thumb and finger, awash in her alluring, heavy-lidded gaze. "You're so good to me, and I give you nothing in return."

"You don't?" she said, her voice a murmur. "I beg to differ."

He didn't understand and accepted her words as kindness. What had he ever done for her? He'd never taken her to dinner or to a concert. If nothing more, he needed to repay her for the joy she'd given him and Timmy. God would lead him. All he had to do was follow.

# Chapter 6

Julie stared at the greeting card and shook her head. Tim had outdone himself the past weeks. Telephone calls, dinner dates, greeting cards, and now flowers. Admiring the floral bouquet sitting on the living room gateleg table, she drew in the sweet scent of carnations nestled among lilies and baby's breath.

Letting her gaze drift back to the card, she reread the words, telling her how special she was to him and Timmy—no words of love, but sentiments that touched her heart. The message thrilled her, yet unsettled her.

Tim seemed to run like a faucet—hot and cold. But unlike a spigot, she had no control over which came out. She sensed he was afraid, but of what, she had no idea. In conversation Julie had tried to touch on his past, but since she'd met Nancy, he'd simply shrug and remind her of his cousin's attitude.

If his life had been peppered with words and actions dragging him down, his lack of confidence and feelings of being unworthy were understandable. He'd shown them in so many ways. Now she wondered what she could do to help him understand that he was worthy, both as a man and as a child of God.

The flowers had spurred a dinner invitation, and Tim and his son were due to arrive within the hour for a home-cooked meal. With most of her food preparation complete, Julie walked into the living room and picked up her worn leather Bible, the pages dog-eared from use. What could God's Word tell Tim that he didn't already know?

Her memory guided her to Ecclesiastes, and she studied the verses until her focus faltered in chapter four, verse nine: "Two are better than one, because they have a good return for their work: If one falls down, his friend can help him up. But pity the man who falls and has no one to help him up! Also, if two lie down together, they will keep warm. But how can one keep warm alone? Though one may be overpowered, two can defend themselves. A cord of three strands is not quickly broken."

Sensing God had led her to the verse, Julie bowed her head and prayed that Tim would be guided by the Lord's message. She closed the cover and set the Bible in its familiar spot on the side table. Then she rose and returned to the kitchen. When the doorbell rang, her pulse surged and she hurried to the screen door.

"Hi," Tim said, holding a paper bag in his arms.

Timmy stood beside him, carrying a box of building blocks.

"Come in," she said, trying to monitor her anxiety. "Thanks again for the flowers." She gestured toward the gateleg table. "They're beautiful."

"Are those from us, Daddy?" Timmy asked.

"They sure are," Julie said, giving him a hug. Her focus settled on the package in Tim's arms. "What's in the sack?"

"Homemade bread."

"From where?" she asked.

"From me," Tim answered.

"You?" She saw the pride on his face and believed him. "You bake bread?"

He nodded and handed her the package.

What other wonders didn't she know about this man? She opened the sack and pulled out the large loaf, admiring the golden crust and the yeasty scent. "Looks wonderful. How many more secret talents do you have?"

Tim chuckled. "I hope it goes with dinner."

"Perfectly. I made a couple of salads and thought I'd let you grill steaks. I have hot dogs if Timmy prefers."

"Yummy, hot dogs," Timmy said.

Julie laughed and led them into the kitchen where she set the plate of steaks in Tim's hands and guided them outside to the readied barbecue.

While Tim grilled the steaks, Julie brought out the pasta and lettuce salads, thick slices of the bread, and a pitcher of lemonade, setting them on the umbrella table.

Soon they were forking into the meal and slivering off tender pieces of steak while Timmy chomped on his hot dog, better to him than filet mignon.

"Dessert now or later?" Julie asked.

"Later, if you don't mind," Tim said.

Julie agreed, and after cleaning off the table, they sat on lawn chairs on the small patio surrounded by burnished asters, gold and white mums, and multihued snapdragons. Timmy had made friends with the neighbor child, and the two boys played together on the grass.

"I've been curious," Julie said, hoping she wouldn't

ruin the lovely day, "about the balloons. I heard you ask Nancy the night of Timmy's birthday. What's that all about. . .if you don't mind my asking?"

"I don't mind at all, but I can't answer your question." He shifted in the chair and wound his fingers together, resting his elbows on his knees. "The day you arrived with the balloons, I had a strange sense of déjà vu. I asked Nancy because I thought after I came to the farm—maybe for a birthday or something—they'd given me a ton of balloons like that; but she didn't remember."

"You were six," Julie said. "Was it before. . .before you lived with them?"

She noticed his shoulders tense and was sorry she'd asked.

"I've blocked much of that time from my memory. Fear. Frustration. Anger. I don't know why or what caused it, but a horrible sense of abandonment comes over me when I try to think back. Bad feelings."

Touching his shoulder, Julie massaged his taut muscles. "Maybe you'll know someday, Tim. God can answer those prayers, too. Little miracles."

"Maybe," he said, sending her a tender smile.

The tenseness faded from his shoulder, and he leaned back against the chair and looked into the sky. "Nice to enjoy the end of summer this way, sitting outside."

"It is. Winter comes too soon."

Tim nodded. "Lots of things come too soon."

Frustrated with herself, Julie studied his face, wondering if he was thinking of his wife's death or his mother's. "Life plays tricks on us sometimes, I suppose, but I like to think there's a reason and a season for everything, like God tells us."

"I believe that. But I wish we understood things better." He turned toward her and slid his palm over her hand resting on the chair arm. "Like you and me, Julie—I wish I understood us. You know I care for you. You're the first woman to unsettle my thoughts since I first met Jan. But I'm afraid that I care for you. . .too much."

A twinge of fear spiraled through her. "Too much?" She struggled to keep the concern from settling on her face. "How could that be?"

He wove his hands through hers, then lifted them to his lips and kissed her fingers, his eyes focused across the lawn to where the children played. "As much as I dislike Nancy's negativity, she has a point. I have nothing to offer you, Julie." He shifted his gaze to hers. "You don't need me."

"Need you? Do you mean money? Financial security?"

He lowered his head and nodded.

"You're right, Tim. I don't need your money. I don't need material things. God's blessed me with a good education and a career. I give thanks daily for that." Her body shook with emotion. "But there's so much that I do need."

He sat in heavy silence, a hush so loud she could almost hear the gears in his mind grinding over her words, looking for their meaning.

"But. . .I can't just take from a relationship, Julie," he said finally. "I have to give, too."

Tears filled her eyes, sensing the deep ache so evident on his face and in his voice. She couldn't teach him about love and relationships. Only God could do that. She breathed deeply, letting the cleansing air renew her. "Tim, you spend your life giving to others—doing for others. Don't neglect yourself along the way. God doesn't want that. When you have a quiet moment, read Ecclesiastes, chapter four. Read it and study it. Then you'll understand."

"Ecclesiastes," he repeated, his eyes focused heavenward. "I will."

"Good." She squeezed the large hand wrapped so tightly around hers. "Now, how about some strawberry shortcake with real whipped cream?"

"See, like I told you," he said, "you always know the way to a man's heart."

She smiled as she rose, sending a prayer to heaven that not only she but God's guidance would enter Tim's heart and give him understanding.

❄

The aroma of bacon and fried eggs filled the air as Tim stepped into the diner after the Sunday church service. Timmy followed behind him along with Jack and his daughter, Patti.

"I want pancakes," Timmy said as he slid into the booth.

"Me, too," Patti said, looking up at her father for approval. "And sausage."

Jack chuckled, reached behind the metal napkin holder for the menus, and passed them out.

As they studied the fare, a waitress came by; when their orders were placed and coffee and milk arrived, they leaned back to wait for breakfast.

"So, how are things going?" Jack asked, a teasing edge to his voice.

"Great," Tim said, letting him dangle.

"Seeing Julie?" Jack asked, then lifted his cup and took a swig of the hot brew.

"Now and then," Tim said.

"We see Julie lots," Timmy volunteered. "She likes me."

A lopsided grin tilted on Tim's mouth. "Son, some things are best left private."

Jack burst into laughter while Timmy eyed him curiously.

"Timmy, why don't you and Patti go watch the goldfish for awhile. I'll call you when the food comes."

"Angelfish, too," Patti said.

"Angels, too," Tim agreed.

The men shifted, letting the children head for the large aquarium filled with colorful species.

Jack leaned on his elbows, pinning Tim with his look. "What are you avoiding, Tim? It's been over two years since Jan's been gone. She'd want you to find someone, and Julie seems perfect."

"She is perfect. She's more than perfect. But I have so little to offer anyone, especially a woman like Julie. And I don't know, Jack, I'm not sure I need anyone. It's hard to explain."

"Doesn't make sense to me," Jack said, falling back against the bench. "She likes you. . .a lot, I'd say."

"And I like her. . .a lot. But I'm not sure I have enough love to spread around. Timmy fills my life, and Jan's memory is still there. What's left for Julie?"

"Be honest, Tim. Your 'like' for Julie has already grown into love. It's obvious."

Tim shook his head, knowing that Jack was right.

"And stop worrying about spreading love," Jack said.

"You don't have to. Love grows like ivy. Ever see how it takes over a building?"

Tim smiled, thinking of the ivy that had crept to the top of Julie's fireplace chimney. In the midst of that thought, the children returned, and he rose. Jack stood, too, while Timmy and Patti settled into the booth.

"You can try to prune ivy back," Jack continued, "but before you know it, it's spread over everything, wrapped around every nook and cranny. Love's just like that."

"I suppose you're right," Tim said. "I loved Jan and seemed to find plenty for Timmy."

Timmy tilted his head. "I love you, Daddy. And I love Sammy."

Tim laughed as a puzzled expression settled on Jack's face. "Who's Sammy?" he asked.

"The neighbor's dog."

"You're in good company, my friend," Jack said.

Before Tim could respond, the waitress appeared carrying their breakfast plates on a large tray. As she set the plates on the table, Tim's mind drifted to more "good company." Julie. Her face rose in his thoughts and, with it, came her suggestion: "Read Ecclesiastes, chapter four. Then you'll understand."

The two families joined hands for the table blessing, and as Jack lifted his voice in prayer, Tim sent up another petition. *Please, Lord, help me find the answer in Your Word.*

# Chapter 7

Closing the Bible, Tim placed it in his lap and peered at the black leather cover. He'd never read the book so much as he had in past weeks. The verse from Ecclesiastes had lived in his thoughts since the first day he'd read it. Julie's suggestion had been a good one. The verses held great meaning for him.

He rose and set the Bible on the kitchen table, then wandered to the window and gazed outside. Autumn leaves drifted from the trees, swirled on the brisk wind, and settled into piles along buildings and fences.

Since Jan's death, winter's icy promise had settled on him like a heavy cloud. This year, Tim felt different. No matter how keen the wind or how high the snow, a new warmth radiated through him.

The need to talk with Julie urged him forward. He grasped the wall phone and punched in the numbers. When he heard her voice, a feeling of comfort blanketed his restless thoughts.

"Time to talk?" he asked. "I'd like to see you."

"I'm running out for a few groceries," she said. "I can stop by for awhile."

As always, Julie was there to fill his needs, to wash away his sadness, and to make him smile. A hush drifted over him. Timmy had gone to Buddy's after dinner, Sammy being the special attraction. One day, he'd have to give the boy his dream.

With the sun sitting heavy on the horizon, Julie tapped on the door, and instead of staying inside, Tim suggested they walk. He needed the fresh air to clear his mind and help him say what needed to be said.

"Sounds good," Julie said. "Grab your coat, and I'll run next door and tell Timmy. I saw him in the backyard."

By the time Tim met her on the sidewalk, she'd talked with his son and Penny. He slipped his hand into hers, a feeling he had grown to love, and they set out toward the nearby park.

Julie talked about her day at work, then finally asked, "So, what's up? You said you wanted to talk."

Tim gave her hand a squeeze, pleased that she didn't sound concerned. "I've been reading the Bible."

She tilted her head and smiled. "Was I right?"

He sent her back a reassuring grin. "I think I know what you mean."

"I'm glad. I'd be a fool to say financial security wasn't important, but many things are as important—much more important than luxuries."

He lifted her chilled fingers and nestled them against his cheek. "I know."

They'd reached the park, and Julie broke away and ran toward the swings. She settled on a wooden seat and pushed her legs back, sending herself aloft. Pumping with her whole body, she gained momentum.

Tim pressed into a seat, laughing at the tight fit, then gave up and hurried behind Julie to give her a push. She flew away with his helpful boost, and he jumped to reach the seat as she sailed backward.

"It's too cold up here," she called her voice fading as the swing hurled forward.

He stepped back, letting the swing slow at its own pace. When Julie braced her feet against the ground and came to a full stop, she bounded up from the seat and wrapped her arms around his body.

"Hug me," she said. "I'm freezing."

With joy, Tim wrapped his arms around her, nestling her against his jacket, feeling her body heat permeate the cloth and warm his heart.

"This is what love is," Julie said. "I pick you up when you fall, I hold you when you hurt, I defend you when you're attacked, and I wrap my arms around you to keep you warm."

Tim lifted her chin upward and looked in her eyes. "I thought *I* was keeping *you* warm."

"We're keeping each other warm," she said.

He drew back and slipped an arm around her shoulder, and they headed away from the trees into the brighter sunlight. When they found a bench, Tim drew her down, his arm around her shoulders, and looked into the blue autumn sky.

"What would I have done without you, Julie? I've spent my life feeling I had nothing to give anyone. When I met Jan, she'd just lost her job. I was working and felt on top of the world. She needed me, and I needed to do for her."

He paused, fearing she might not understand. "Don't think that I didn't love Jan. I did. But my love was founded on something different than my feelings for you."

"You don't need to explain, Tim. Love begins in many ways. The result can be the same when God shares in it." She squeezed his arm. "The threefold cord, remember?"

She rested her cheek against his shoulder, the sunlight shining on her upturned face. "Tell me about your parents," she said.

His pulse skipped, then settled. "Most of what I know is what I've been told. My mother was sickly. My dad. . .I don't know. . .I guess he couldn't handle four kids and our mother's death. He lost his job from spending so much time caring for our mother. At least that's what Aunt Selma said."

"That's terrible," Julie said. "How could a company do that?"

"I don't know. We lived in a small town in Kentucky. Supposedly, he went out of town looking for a new job and left us with neighbors. A pastor, I think. He never came back."

With a look of concern, Julie lifted her head, her eyes searching his and a question on her lips that, he guessed, she hesitated asking.

"Cowardice? Maybe. I don't know," Tim said. "He died or. . ." The old memories put a stranglehold on his heart. He swallowed back the emotion that erupted into this throat.

"Sometimes I've hated my father," Tim confessed. "I'm ashamed, but I can't think of anything else. I've prayed so often that one day I'll have the answer. One day

I'll understand and can forgive him."

With misted eyes, Julie leaned up and kissed his cheek. "Telling me this, you've explained so much. I've watched you with Timmy, your love and protection so strong and steadfast—almost as if you're driven. At first I thought it was because of his legs. But it's more than that. I understand now."

"I wanted to be the father for Timmy that I never had. I'll never hurt him. . .God willing. A boy needs a father."

"Children need a father," Julie said, "but you always had a Father, Tim. Your heavenly Father. I know that's different in a way, but Jesus has always been at your side, guarding you and guiding just like an earthly father."

"And God never turned His back and walked away," Tim said, awash in the pure and wonderful reality. He tilted his head toward the sky, expelling air from his lungs and drinking in the rich splash of color washing the horizon in the autumn sunset.

God was as sure as the setting sun. As sure as the love that wrapped around his heart.

❄

With the telephone's ring, Julie rose and grabbed the receiver; she heard Tim's frustrated voice on the other end.

"You're a woman," he said.

"Thanks for noticing."

"That's not exactly what I meant," he said with a chuckle. "Timmy's in the Sunday school program, and he's balking because of his braces."

"What can I do, Tim?"

"There's more," he said.

"More?"

"He needs a costume. I'll get him to be in the play, but I can't sew. The woman in charge gave me a pattern and said I'd have to make the costume."

"You want to borrow my sewing machine?" Julie smiled at the receiver.

"Do you have one?"

"Yes, but I hate to sew."

"Oh," he said, his voice fading with disappointment.

"But I love doing things for you," she added quickly.

"Does the positive negate the negative?" he asked.

His question made her laugh. "I'll be over later."

"I'll cook dinner," he offered.

Julie hung up and reviewed the changes in their relationship since their walk and talk in the park. One of those little miracles she'd mentioned to him.

She found her measuring tape, tossed it into her purse, and headed for her car. *Two are better than one,* she thought, awed by God's wisdom.

In a matter of minutes, she pulled into the townhouse parking lot and walked toward Tim's door. As she passed Penny's, Julie noticed Ray from the singles' group ringing the doorbell. She grinned to herself, hoping God had sent Penny someone special at last.

Julie stepped onto the small porch, and Tim opened the door before she knocked. The scent of food and his smile lured her inside.

"Looks like Penny has a steady," she said.

"Right; I'm relieved. Since the mix-up she's been a little distant with me. Though I have to admit, she's continued to be the best neighbor. I felt bad about it until

Ray started coming by. Now Penny and I talk like nothing happened."

"That's good," Julie said.

He drew her to him, his eyes bright. "Not as good as this," he said, kissing her tenderly before taking her hand and leading her into the living room.

"You're a lifesaver," he said, handing her an envelope detailed with the drawing of a shepherd and an angel on the front.

"Okay, which is he?" she asked

"Which do you think?"

"I think he's an angel," she said, grinning, "but probably a shepherd in the program."

"Right on both counts," Tim said, standing beside her. "So what do you think? Can you make it?"

She arched a brow playfully as she tugged the costume pattern from the package. "Let me look. . .if you don't mind."

While she struggled to unfold the pattern pieces, he pulled her down beside him on the sofa.

"You're not making this easy," she said, but thinking how truly easy it was to love him. They'd never said the words to each other, and she longed to hear them.

Gazing at the simple shepherd's robe, Julie shifted her head and caught a glimpse of Timmy hiding on the stair. "Hey, Mr. Shepherd, come here."

"I'm no shepherd," he said, peeking around the corner.

"Why not?" she asked.

He climbed down the last two steps and stuck out his leg. "Braces."

"So?" She widened her eyes, waiting for an answer.

"Shepherds don't wear them."

"They do if they've had surgery." She beckoned to him. "Anyway, look. The robe goes all the way to the ground. Not even the sheep will notice."

That made him giggle, and he came toward her, allowing her to measure his height and the length of his arms. She jotted down the measurements, then folded up the pattern. "I think you'll be one of the handsomest shepherds in the whole field watching their flocks by night."

"Be happy," Tim said. "They could have made you an angel with wings and a halo."

"Girls are angels," Timmy said, giggling.

"Don't tell Gabriel," Tim whispered in Julie's ear, sending a chill down her arm.

A savory aroma drifted into the room from the kitchen, and Tim hurried away, calling them moments later to a dinner of meat loaf with baked potatoes and a salad.

"By the way," Julie said as the meal ended, "I'd like both of you to come for Thanksgiving dinner. You can meet my family."

"That sounds dangerous," Tim said. "What if they don't approve?"

"They will," she said, remembering a time when his words would've had a sincere ring to them rather than humor.

Timmy asked to be excused, and when he ran off to play, Julie rose and carried the dishes to the sink. When she turned back for the others, Tim captured her in his arms.

"I have something to tell you," he said, his expression serious.

Her heart plummeted to the ground and didn't bounce

back until he drew her closer, his eyes searching hers.

"What?" she asked, her voice breathless.

"I love you, Julie."

The words she longed to hear hung on the air as beautiful and glorious as the sunset they'd shared that day in the park.

"I love you, too," she said, certain that God was smiling down on them.

# Chapter 8

"Away in the manger, no crib for a bed." Tim's heart swelled hearing the children's sweet voices filling the church with the words of the familiar carol. With her eyes focused on the shepherds, some kneeling and some standing over the manager scene, Julie sat beside Tim smiling as brightly as he was. The angels—all girls—stood on a platform behind them, their wings and halos glistening with gold foil.

On his other side sat Nancy, who, to his surprise, had called to invite herself to Timmy's Sunday school program. Though she'd not mellowed totally, her recent conversations had been more accepting of Julie and his relationship with her. Tim figured she had to accept the inevitable.

Another treat had occurred when Nancy asked for Timmy to spend the night. She wanted to take him to an animated Christmas display at a mall near her house and let him select his Christmas gift.

After the children recessed from the sanctuary, Tim led the others to the Sunday school classrooms. Timmy waited for them, his face beaming with pride. "I remembered my lines," he said.

"You were great," Julie agreed, kissing his cheek.

Tim's heart warmed at the natural way Julie showed love to his son. After offering his congratulations, Tim located Timmy's coat and they headed outside.

Scattered snowflakes drifted from the sky, and Timmy rushed ahead with Nancy, waving his hand with excitement at the anticipation of seeing the display and selecting his gift.

"He was the best shepherd of the bunch," Julie said.

"He was." Delight shivered through Tim, watching the woman he loved sound like his son's mother. She'd make a wonderful parent for Timmy and. . . His thoughts swelled, imagining marriage and the birth of another child.

Tim opened the car door and Julie slid inside. He joined her, and a cool blast from the heater hit their legs until they pulled into traffic and the heat kicked in, warming their feet.

Enveloped in the Christmas spirit, Tim anticipated their evening, helping Julie put up her tree and hang the ornaments as he'd promised.

With the snow falling heavier, Tim parked in the driveway and, arm in arm, escorted Julie to the front door. Inside, she snapped on a Christmas CD and headed for the kitchen with the promise of hot chocolate.

Tim wrestled the tree from the garage, and he guided it into the stand while Julie directed him. When the last bolt had been tightened and the tree still remained straight, he relaxed his shoulders and sank into the sofa.

"Your turn," he said.

"Oh, no, you don't. I need help with the lights."

Lights, garland, then boxes of bulbs were opened, and

they took turns hanging them on the limbs, then standing back to admire the beauty.

"This bulb's special," Julie said, showing him a pink bulb, decorated with sparkling silver lines and a gauzy angel attached to one side. "My aunt gave me this when I was a teenager. She died a few years ago."

With great tenderness, she lifted the nostalgic piece, placing it in a convenient opening in the branches. "I always think of her at Christmas."

He heard the love in her voice and longed to own that kind of family memory. "I'd guess many of the bulbs have meaning," Tim said, containing the familiar yearning.

"Yes, this one," she pointed toward an ornament, "was a gift from a friend who bought it in Europe. And my mom and dad gave me this one when I had my first Christmas tree." She lifted a golden angel to the tree. "This was a gift from my godmother."

"I envy you, Julie. I know it's a sin, but I wish I had wonderful memories like you."

Her hand drifted from the angel and touched his cheek. "Don't envy me, Tim. Our memories can begin now—ones we'll cherish."

He captured her hand beneath his, then lifted it to his lips and kissed her soft, warm skin. "You've given me a million wonderful moments, times I'll never forget."

She nestled against his chest while his heart pounded wildly against his breastbone. *Cherish.* Not just memories, but Julie herself. He'd cherish her and love her forever.

When she tilted her head back to look into his eyes, he lowered his lips, and she tiptoed to meet him. He'd never known such tenderness.

"Let's sit," she said, drawing him to the sofa. She nestled at his side while carols filled the air and happiness filled his heart.

"I hadn't thought much about my family until I met you," he said. "And since then, I've had the strangest desire to find them—my sisters."

"Why don't you?" she asked, bolting upright. "It's possible now with television and the Internet."

"I wouldn't know where to begin," he said, his mind reeling from his admission.

"At the beginning," she said. "Ask Nancy for help. She's a lot older than you and she's changed. . .a little. Who knows what she might remember if you bug her enough."

He laughed. "And she deserves it. She's bugged me enough for a lifetime."

Like tinkling bells, Julie's laugh rang in his ear. She gave him hope for so many things. He only prayed he could give her as much happiness in return.

❄

Julie watched Tim's anxious face, looking as eager as his son waiting to open his Christmas gifts.

"Ready for your surprise?" Tim asked the child.

Timmy stood beside the tree, studying the packages piled beneath, his face glowing with anticipation. "Which one?"

Julie chuckled. "None of those. Your dad hid it."

"Where?" Timmy said, circling the room, his gaze darting from one place to another.

"At Penny's," Tim said finally. "It's too hard to wrap."

"A bike?" Timmy asked.

"You wait here," Tim said, "and when you hear me coming, close your eyes." He turned to Julie. "Make sure he does." Tim gave her a wink.

"Okay," she said, her heart swelling with the excitement of the surprise. She delighted in watching the boy as he jiggled beside the tree. Though still in braces, his legs grew stronger each day. She'd grown to love him as if he were her own.

"What is it?" Timmy asked, giving her a pleading look.

"Only a minute more," she said, keeping her eye focused on the door. When she saw Tim through the glass, she reminded Timmy of the instructions. "Okay, close your eyes."

The child pinched his eyes shut, his face puckered like fingers too long in water, and Julie motioned to Tim that it was safe to enter. He pushed open the door, his arms weighted by the squirming bundle of canine energy. Beside the tree, he set the puppy at Timmy's feet. "Open your eyes," he said.

Timmy's focus latched onto his father's, but a yip from below drew his attention downward. A mixture of laughter and cheers bubbled from the boy's throat. "A puppy!" Timmy slid into the chair and the floppy, golden-hued terrier jumped into the child's lap.

His face covered with doggy kisses, Timmy giggled and squirmed while his father beamed and Julie brushed tears from her eyes.

"You'll have to think of a name," Julie said.

"Animals tend to name themselves," Tim said, chuckling at the puppy's antics.

Julie bent down and retrieved a colorfully wrapped

present. "Open your gift," Julie said, shoving the box into Tim's hands.

"Why me?" he asked, a childlike grin glowing on his face as he peered at the package.

"You'll see," she said.

He pulled off the paper and uncovered a flash camera. "Perfect timing." He eyed the gadgets and checked the indicator for film.

"It's ready," Julie said, motioning for him to photograph Timmy with the puppy.

When the camera flashed, the puppy bolted from Timmy's lap, darted across the carpet, and squatted. Before they could nab him, the deed was done.

"Puddles," Tim said through his laughter. "I said he'd name himself." He dashed to the kitchen and brought back a stream of paper toweling.

"Puddles," Timmy repeated, running toward the puppy. "No. No. You have to go outside."

Tim knelt and mopped up the mess. "Here's the leash," Tim said as he pulled the leather strap from his pocket. "You can take him out for a minute."

Timmy snapped on the leash, and the dog bounded ahead of him toward the doorway. Tim raced after them with the boy's jacket.

When he closed the door, Tim returned and captured Julie's hand in his. "Now it's your turn."

"Okay," she said, curious about the box that sat beneath the tree.

Tim lifted the package and placed it on her lap.

Too big for what she'd hoped, she studied it, eager to learn what was inside. Peeling back the tissue, she eyed a long gold cord. She picked up the end and studied it, trying not to look disappointed. "What is it?"

Tim sat beside her and slid his arm around her back. "A three-strand cord."

Puzzled, she looked again, plucking at the fibers as if trying to understand. "Three strands?"

"Have you forgotten already? 'Two are better than one; if two lie together, they will keep warm: but how can one keep warm alone? A cord of three strands is not quickly broken.'"

"Ecclesiastes," she said, still bewildered.

"I'm the one God meant to keep you warm," he said drawing the cord from the box. When the end rose from the tissue, a ring glistened at the bottom.

Julie caught the glistening diamond in her trembling hand. The solitaire flashed fire in the soft light.

"I have little to give you, Julie, except my heart, but it's filled with love and gratitude."

"Love is all I need, Tim."

"Will you marry me. . .and soon?" he asked.

Shyness gone, Julie reached up and captured Tim's face in her hands, her lips caressing his. Catching her breath, she drew back and looked into his eyes. "Yes, I'll marry you as soon as you want. You're all I've ever wanted. You and your wonderful son."

"And one day, maybe another son or a daughter," Tim said. "Like the Bible says, 'Two are better than one.'"

# Chapter 9

*Eleven Months Later*

"Sit down, Julie, you're doing too much," Tim said.

"I always bake Christmas cookies after Thanksgiving and freeze them. It's my tradition." She brushed the flour from her hands and leaned her back against the kitchen counter.

"But you've never made cookies while expecting a baby," he said, delighting at the tiny protrusion that protected their unborn child.

"In olden times, women only stopped work long enough to give birth. I'm no more special."

He stepped to her side and clasped her shoulders. "You are to me. I've been thinking these past months how many years I spent yearning for my family, not stopping to think that I already have one." His gaze moved over her belly while his thoughts drifted to his son recently freed from his braces. "The best in the world."

"That's different," she said, swiping his nose with her floured finger. "Now leave me be. I need to finish this so

I can start dinner. Timmy'll be home from school soon."

Tim chuckled and brushed at his face in case she'd left a telltale smudge. "Different, maybe, but I don't have that feeling of being lost. Now I feel whole and complete, and I—"

He halted at the telephone's ring.

"Stir the dough," Julie said, scooting past him, "and I'll get the phone."

Tim picked up the wooden spoon and tugged it through the thick, buttery dough. Hearing Julie's voice lift in excitement, he paused and listened.

"Tim." She beckoned to him. "It's for you."

Her face looked mottled, and fear rose in his heart. His son? Had something happened at school?

"Hello," he said, trying to remain calm.

"Timmy?"

*Timmy.* No one called him that. . .but a haunting voice rose from the depths of his memory.

"Is this Timmy Richmond?" The woman's voice faltered.

"Yes," he said, struggling with his wavering hope.

"This is Eden. Your sister."

"Eden." His voice was a whisper. "Eden," he repeated more loudly. "Is it really you?"

Soft sobs quivered from the line. "Yes, it's me. You're the last one, Timmy. I've found everyone. You, Crista, and Angelina."

"Crista and Angelina," he repeated, feeling the names on his lips, stunned by her news.

"All of you," she said, her voice tinged with emotion.

"How? Where? What?" Words tumbled from his

mouth. He longed for a lifetime of information.

"Let's wait," she said. "We're getting together at my place in Indiana, the weekend before Christmas. Can you come?"

"You mean my family?" His thoughts tumbled over each other.

"We thought just the four of us for now. Next time, we'll bring our families. It's been twenty-four years. We have so much catching up to do."

"We do," he said, drawing in a calming breath.

"You can come?" she asked.

"Nothing could stop me, Eden. I've waited a lifetime."

# Chapter 10

## The Reunion

Tim pressed his back against the easy chair and focused once more on his three sisters. The hours had been precious: The greeting, the sharing, the love, and their first meeting were only a beginning. They'd already made plans for a summer reunion—the whole family together, at last.

Eden's husband, Josh, had kindly taken the children on a mini-vacation for the weekend, leaving the four siblings alone to share the two days without distraction.

Studying his sisters, Tim realized Angelina and Crista resembled each other. Their smiles and the dimples. They looked like their mother from what his faded memory allowed him to recall.

He was large and darker, like his father. He recalled his aunt Selma saying the same. The idea triggered a prayer. *Lord, never let me be like our father.* Knowing the love he had for his own son, Tim wondered how a parent could leave his children behind and vanish from their lives.

"Okay," Tim said, "you've told me how you girls got together, but what about me? How did you find me?"

Eden laughed. "Once I was determined, nothing would stop me. I'd tried locating the family we'd stayed with—"

"The pastor?" Tim asked.

"Yes, but they weren't home when we got there."

Angelina chuckled. "What did you expect?"

"Miracles," Crista said. "Like right now. I can't believe we're all sitting here together."

"It *is* a miracle," Eden agreed. "Anyway, I didn't give up. I decided to take a weekend trip and drive to Covington. I figured I'd recognize the house and maybe that would lead to something."

"Did you find it? Did you recognize it right away?" Crista asked, her excitement so evident she appeared ready to catapult from the sofa.

"I have no memories at all of our house," Angelina said.

"Maybe it's for the best." Tim remembered his own feelings of loneliness and abandonment.

Eden arched an eyebrow. "But we have a few memories, Tim. Angelina and Crista have nothing."

Shame washed over him. "You're right, Eden."

Crista reached over and touched his arm. "It's okay, Tim. When you can't remember, you don't have the good times or the *bad* times."

"I just felt something was missing in my life, and I never knew what it was," Angelina said.

Tim wished he'd kept his mouth closed. "I felt the same way. Like I was cheated." He pushed away the negative feelings that had seeped from his old hurt. "Go ahead, Eden, tell us what happened."

"I found the pastor's house," she continued, "but as I said, they weren't there."

"And?" burst from the three siblings. They laughed at their simultaneous reaction.

"So what did you do?" Angelina asked.

"I'd about given up when a woman walked by with her dog; she told us the pastor was out of town. Something about her was so familiar."

A lengthy pause filled the room.

"Well?" three impatient voices said in unison. Another burst of laughter bubbled through the air.

"She'd been a playmate of mine when we stayed with Pastor Brittan's family. She lived across the street and invited us in; it turns out Molly had written to Aunt Selma Johnson, Daddy's sister, in Michigan asking about me. She still had a letter from Aunt Selma and her address! Except when I went there, an elderly woman named Gabby Summers lived there."

"But how did that help?" Angelina asked.

"She was a longtime friend of Aunt Selma's. Apparently she'd bought the house when our aunt and uncle moved to a nearby farm in Remus, Michigan. I thought all along that Aunt Selma was a spinster. Obviously I was wrong. Memories came to Mrs. Summers in bits and pieces. Months passed before she called me. Once I had the right information, that's all I needed to know. I was able to check your school records in Remus, learned you joined the military and settled in the Detroit area."

Tim fell back against the chair. "Are you sure you're not a detective?"

Crista chuckled. "I think my Brad is the detective.

He's the one who found Eden." She pressed her hands together. "I can't wait for you all to meet him. He's perfect for me, although I didn't know that at first. And he loves hot air balloons like I do."

"Remember the stained glass balloon you bought from Wes, Crista?" Angelina asked. "I like them, too. I always feel a little nostalgic when I see any kind of balloon, but I have no idea—"

"What?" Tim and Eden blurted at the same time.

"Balloons," Angelina repeated, her eyes wide, studying them.

The four sat in silence looking at each other.

Tim was awed by the information. So many years he'd felt a strange twinge when he saw a bunch of balloons, like the day Julie brought them to Timmy's party.

"Awhile back, I asked my cousin—" Tim gave a soft chuckle. "I should say *our* cousin, Nancy, if balloons would have some special meaning for me. They always give me a feeling of déjà vu. Nancy said it was natural for kids to love them." He shrugged. "So I let it drop."

"Balloons," Eden said, closing her eyes. "A room full of balloons."

"Yes," Tim said, "all the way to the ceiling."

"Mother's birthday." Eden's voice was a whisper. "I remember." She opened her eyes, her face glowing. "It was Mother's birthday."

"I sort of remember something. . .vaguely," Tim said. "It was in a bedroom."

"Her bedroom," Eden said. "She'd been so ill and. . .I remember it clearly now, looking at all of you. All these years, I've had something in my distant memory nudge at me, and you've all helped to bring it out."

"Tell us," Crista said, sitting on the edge of her seat. "I can't wait another minute."

"We wanted to celebrate Mom's birthday, and she was so sick. Dad suggested we have a cake, but Mom was too sick to eat. . . . We wanted something special."

"Who suggested balloons?" Angelina asked.

"It was my idea, I think. But Dad was willing. I can almost see him going through his pocket pulling out dollar bills and counting them."

"We didn't have much. I remember that," Tim said.

"We were poor. Dad had been let go because he missed so much work caring for Mom. I think that's it."

"You're right, Eden," Tim said. "I faintly remember Aunt Selma muttering about how terrible the company was to fire Dad under the circumstances. I don't think I knew what 'fired' meant back then."

"So our father brought home some balloons?" Crista asked.

"A roomful, Crista. I remember he let us help fill them from a tank." Eden's voice had become a whisper.

"Helium," Tim said as the story settled into his awareness. "Then you mean. . ." His throat tightened, the reality so unbelievable. "You mean that he rented a tank and did all this to give Mom. . ." His voice choked with emotion, and he stopped to gain control.

"To give her a birthday surprise," Angelina said, tears rolling down her cheeks.

Tim swallowed. "I've been angry at him all these years. Angry because he didn't love us enough to keep us together, and now—"

"And now, we learn how much he really loved all of us," Angelina said. "When he didn't have a job, he sacrificed to give Mom a special birthday." Her eyes were rimmed with tears.

"Her last birthday," Eden said.

Tim lowered his head to hide the moisture in his eyes, but when he looked up again, he needn't have been embarrassed. His sisters were wiping away their tears.

"Dad was looking for work, I think," Eden said. "The family I lived with told me when I was older that they'd heard he had slipped on ice crossing a street and was hit by a car."

"I thought maybe he committed. . ." Tim's voice faded, feeling ashamed that he'd thought his father would take his own life.

"Don't blame yourself for wondering," Eden said. "We were only little kids. How would we know?"

Angelina shook her head. "We didn't understand things when they happened. All we knew was that we'd lost the security that we'd known."

"Cheer up," Crista said. "God brought us together now so we could learn the truth and find forgiveness."

"Forgiveness," Tim repeated, his mind boggled with the past and present—pieces of the puzzle telling the true story.

"And love," Angelina added. "God has given me so much love. He's been there for me every step of the way, putting special people in my life, and now. . .He's sent the three of you."

"God's given us all so much," Eden said. She rose and stretched her hands out at her sides. "How about joining in a prayer of thanksgiving."

"For finding each other," Crista said.

"And for forgiveness," Tim said, grasping Eden's hand and reaching for Angelina's.

"And love," Angelina said.

Standing in a circle, Tim gazed at his three sisters, hearing them sniffle and seeing tears of joy in their eyes. He didn't care if his own droplets rolled down his cheeks and dripped from his chin. He was in good company.

He listened to Eden's strong, confident voice and knew that someday he would travel heavenward like one of the helium balloons. One day he'd stand at Jesus' feet with his whole family—including his mother, father, and three precious sisters: Eden, Angelina, and Crista.

He felt Eden squeeze his hand and knew, without a doubt, that God was smiling down on them.

## GAIL GAYMER MARTIN

Gail loves nothing more than to write, talk, and sing—especially if it's about her Lord. Beginning her career as a freelance writer, she has hundreds of articles and stories in religious periodicals, many anthology devotionals, and numerous church resource books, but since 1998, she has been blessed as a multi-published romance author with nearly ten contracted novels. "If God blessed me with a 'bestseller,' I'd continue writing worship materials. It's a direct way I can share my faith with worshiping Christians." Gail has two **Heartsong Presents** novels and two novellas published with Barbour fiction. She is also a contributing editor and columnist for *The Christian Communicator*.

Besides being active in her home church, Gail is an adjunct English instructor for Davenport University, Warren campus, and maintains her professional counselor license in the state of Michigan. She is involved in a number of professional organizations and especially enjoys public speaking and presenting workshops to help new writers. Gail loves traveling, as well as singing with the Detroit Lutheran Singers. She lives in Lathrup Village with her husband Bob Martin who proofreads all her work. "I praise God for Bob and my gift of writing."

# A Letter to Our Readers

Dear Readers:

In order that we might better contribute to your reading enjoyment, we would appreciate you taking a few minutes to respond to the following questions. When completed, please return to: Fiction Editor, Barbour Publishing, Inc., P.O. Box 719, Uhrichsville, OH 44683.

1. Did you enjoy reading *Home for Christmas?*
   ❑ Very much. I would like to see more books like this.
   ❑ Moderately. I would have enjoyed it more if _____
   _____
   _____

2. What influenced your decision to purchase this book?
   (Check those that apply.)
   ❑ Cover          ❑ Back cover copy          ❑ Title          ❑ Price
   ❑ Friends        ❑ Publicity                ❑ Other

3. Which story was your favorite?
   ❑ *Heart Full of Love*          ❑ *Don't Look Back*
   ❑ *Ride the Clouds*             ❑ *To Keep Me Warm*

4. Please check your age range:
   ❑ Under 18        ❑ 18–24          ❑ 25–34
   ❑ 35–45           ❑ 46–55          ❑ Over 55

5. How many hours per week do you read? _____

Name _____

Occupation _____

Address _____

City _____ State _____ ZIP _____

E-mail _____